THE MARBURG
MUTATION
A Unit 1 Novel

Allen Kent

AllenPearce Publishers © ©
Previously published by Amazon Press

Library of Congress Cataloging-in-Publication Data
Allen Kent
The Marburg Mutation
Kent, Allen
ISBN: 978-0-9964036-4-1
Cover Design: Jillian Farnsworth

AllenPearce
PUBLISHERS

Allen Kent © 2016

To my grandchildren,
all of whom inspire me with their talents.

The Marburg Mutation

1

A few minutes before 3:00 a.m., the man residents of Ålesund, Norway, referred to as *den Serbisk*, the Serbian, slipped quietly from bed. He had showered and shaved the evening before and dressed quietly in the half-light of the Norwegian summer night that filtered through the open windows of the Hotel Brosundet. Below his window, the silent harbor mirrored the Ålesund fishing fleet like a tarnished silver mirror. In an hour, men would begin outfitting the boats. Gulls would wheel and squawk over the departing fleet. He needed to be gone by then, headed to the airport. But on the way, there was cleanup work to be done.

Before leaving the room, he paused to admire the figure of the woman who remained sound asleep on her side, the sheet covering her to the waist. He allowed his eyes to linger for another moment on breasts that were so beautifully accented by the white patches of her bikini line. She had been among the best of his Ålesund conquests. He had her number and would call her again when he returned to the city.

The Serb took the elevator to the main floor, assured the night clerk that the room should be left on his card and that the lady would check out before eleven, then retrieved his rental from the small harborside lot. Five minutes later, he descended into the tunnel that crossed beneath the fjord to Ellingsøya Island. Upon exiting, he turned right past the sleeping village of Hoffland and drove east along the coastal road until a gravel lane turned away from the water's edge up into the pines. The lane skirted the side of a steep, rocky hill, then looped back toward its crest. Near the top, he braked in front of an ornate wrought-iron gate.

Leaning from the window, the Serb entered a six-digit code into an electronic pad that stood on a black post beside the gate. The barrier swung silently inward. He eased the vehicle forward through the wall of heavy gray stone. The inner drive was paved and curved left through trees that circled a small lake to the front of a dark two-story country manor of the same smoky-gray rock.

As he stepped from the car in front of steps that led to an arched portico, the wide beam of a flashlight circled him from the far edge of the house. A hoarse voice demanded in Norwegian, "Who is there?"

"It is just me, Geir," the Serb said in English to the caretaker. "I need to pick up a few things before flying back to Frankfurt. I will be about an hour and will close the gate when I leave. My flight is at eight."

The ancient caretaker grunted an acknowledgement and turned back toward a cottage that was no more than a dark impression among the trees beyond the drive. The Serb unlocked and entered the house, closing and latching the door behind him. Down the central hallway, a door opened beneath a staircase onto steep steps that descended into a musty half -basement. By the light of a single dim bulb, he made his way through a scatter of old outdoor furniture and lawn statuary to a row of rough wooden shelves. Pulling a stool from beside the stairway, he climbed carefully onto it, pushing upward on what appeared to be a section of ceiling beam. The shelves in front of him slid forward and to the side, revealing an aged steel door with a wheel-combination lock and lever handle. He lowered himself heavily from the stool and knelt before the door, twirling four numbers into the lock. As he forced the handle downward, the man rose to his feet and pushed against the steel slab.

The metal plate swung inward into a brightly lit stainless-steel prepping station with two showerheads to his left suspended over a circular drain. To his right, an open closet held three white hazmat suits and, on a shelf above, contamination masks and goggles. The Serb stripped to his underwear and donned the largest of the suits.

2

He carefully taped wrists and ankles, then pulled on a mask and goggles. When certain he was properly protected, he pushed through a second metal door into a long, narrow observation room. A tightly sealed full-wall window separated him from another stainless-paneled cell beyond.

This third room was a twelve-foot-square, furnished with a plain metal table, wall-mounted bench, steel toilet, and sink. An assortment of fruit browned on the table in a wooden bowl. A partially eaten loaf of bread and block of white cheese sat on heavy paper plates. The emaciated body of a woman faced him on a thin mattress that covered a low cot attached to the back wall, her corpse seeping thin red liquid from weeping blisters that covered most of her exposed skin. Dried blood covered her chocolate face, staining it even darker where fluid oozed from her eyes and nose. She wore only a pair of tight red shorts. What had been a white tank top lay beside her on the floor. Little of the white remained, a few unspoiled islands in a sea of reddish brown. The floor beside the cot was splattered with dark, bloody vomit.

The Serb stood at the window for five minutes, considering what he was seeing. Three weeks earlier, when he'd brought her to the house from Oslo, the woman had been quite beautiful in her own way. Large dark eyes; full, inviting lips; skin as smooth as polished ebony. She had been a willing and aggressive lover, believing that if she pleased him, he would return her to the street near the park where he had approached her for sex. But then he had given her one of the latest experimental antiviral drugs and kept her in the chamber for two weeks to allow antibodies to develop. After the injection had been given time to work, the most recent strain of the virus had been released through the ventilation system into the cell. As the Serb had anticipated, the antiviral treatment hadn't stopped or slowed progression of the disease. The woman had died within a week. She was his fourth test subject. None had survived. The Serb had two more drugs to test, but neither was considered as effective as those that had failed.

With gloved hands, the Serb snapped open the latch on a metal cabinet on the wall of the observation room. He flipped two switches into the On position and twisted a flow knob above each. They bore the label *Verbrennungsanlage.* He watched dispassionately as the temperature in the furnace rose on a large central dial to 900 degrees Celsius. It was considerate of the woman, he thought, to choose to die on the cot. Wrestling the body back onto the bed would have been messy and potentially dangerous.

Another switch released a panel in the rear wall of the steel chamber. The cot tilted on extended legs into the wall, sliding the mattress and the ravaged body down a chute into the waiting flames. Had the night been cold, some mother soothing a restless child or an insomniac gazing from a Hoffland window might have seen the shimmer of hot air rise from the manor's central chimney. But there was no smoke. As the body joined the gas injectors in fueling the furnace, a catalytic converter ignited remaining visible gases, sending a clear stream of hot vapor into the night sky.

The Serb flipped the switch downward, and the metal cot returned to horizontal. Overhead jets deluged the cell with disinfectant, soaking its contents from floor to ceiling. The pink fluid swirled across the floor into stainless troughs that edged the room, collecting and draining through a wide silver grate in a back corner. A detergent spray followed, then blasts of superheated steam. Once the sterilizing process was complete, the Serb stepped into the room, lifted the food and its containers from the table, and dumped them with the woman's stained top into a smaller wall chute that emptied into the incinerator. He scanned the sterile interior thoroughly for anything that might hint at its recent use, then returned to the dressing area. He showered, first in the suit, then again after removing it, and hung it in a smaller ultraviolet decontamination chamber beside the closet.

4

Forty-five minutes after entering the house, the man exited the hidden rooms. If his flight was not delayed, he should reach Frankfurt before noon. By evening, a message to potential clients would give them an update. While the final two tests were being completed, he planned to provide a demonstration of the virus's astonishing kill rate and begin to narrow his buyer pool. Within the month, the product should be ready for delivery, and *den Serbisk* would be a very wealthy man.

2

Janet McIntire sat erect in a high-backed brown-leather chair on one side of a polished mahogany conference table and tried to control her voice as she responded to the question. It had come from Special Agent in Charge Jason Weathers of the FBI's Springfield, Illinois, regional office, her immediate boss. Two chairs to his left across the table sat Genaro Serna, the Bureau's deputy director and the man who had called the meeting.

"No, sir," Janet repeated, looking directly at Weathers. "I am not at liberty to reveal the source. I've promised the person absolute confidentiality, and I won't violate that."

"But if your source is right," Weathers said, "someone is offering to the highest bidder sale of a weaponized biological agent—and one that sounds extremely dangerous. Without knowing the source, our ability to investigate is seriously hampered."

"Without the source, we wouldn't know the bio-threat existed and that the offer had been made," Janet countered. The two men exchanged a quick glance—so quick and involuntary that she wondered if her tip hadn't been the first time the Bureau had heard about the sale offer. "I can tell you this much," she added, watching the pair more closely. "The offer reached certain circles in the organized-crime community in the US. Not only are they not interested, they'd like to see the seller chased down and the threat eliminated."

"How noble!" Serna muttered. Janet chose to ignore the comment, keeping her eyes on Weathers. But Serna had decided to take control of the conversation.

"Did this tip come from your friend Michael Bond?"

Janet knew that her Scotch-Irish ancestry and accompanying

6

difficulty managing her temper were bringing added color to her face, fusing the smattering of freckles. She turned to lock the deputy director in her emerald gaze. "Is this meeting about the information I reported on the potential bio-threat, or about Michael Bond?" she asked, struggling to keep the flush the only change in her demeanor.

"You know there's been concern about Bond since the Curren kidnapping case was wrapped up in Quincy. You claimed to have thoroughly checked out his background and found nothing suspicious. But our own investigation suggests that some clients in his purported role as financial adviser are members of the D'Anotto crime family."

"My investigation uncovered and disclosed those transactions," she said. "Michael provides counsel on the purchase of bonds—particularly municipal bonds. He made recommendations to the D'Anotto family. They made purchases. Michael was paid. Aside from the fact that it was the D'Anottos, it was all very much aboveboard. There was nothing unusual or illegal about the transactions. But I take it you elected to have someone duplicate my investigation."

"You've dated Bond since the Curren case . . ."

Janet felt the flush tickle the follicles of her coppery hair. "Yes. Several times," she confessed.

"And you must be aware that the man has a reputation for showing up at places where a convenient suicide or two serve to bring closure to some unresolved problem—such as in the case of the Curren kidnapping."

"I'm aware of those allegations. And tell me, what did your investigation find concerning his involvement?"

Serna's face folded into an accusing frown. "You seem to be getting a little defensive about this, Special Agent McIntire."

Her green eyes darkening a shade. "First of all, sir, this seems to have turned into something of an interrogation when I was told we were meeting to discuss my report. Second, I'm confused as to why we're suddenly so concerned about Michael Bond when the report had to do with the prospect of a bioterrorism agent being sold on the world market."

"To be frank," Deputy Director Serna said, "it's not Bond we're concerned about as much as we're concerned about all of these coincidental connections. You mentioned that the organized-crime community was aware of the bio-threat. Bond is linked to the D'Anottos. You are linked to Bond. That's an uncomfortable chain of relationships for one of our senior agents in Illinois."

The two sat in silence, each examining the other's face to see what it might reveal. Weathers watched expectantly from the sideline.

"Do you have any indication of improper conduct or poor professional judgment on my part?" Janet finally challenged.

"Other than dating a man with a questionable history? No."

"A history you have chosen to *view* as questionable," she corrected.

Serna gave an assenting nod. "He's a party of interest."

"A party of interest in what? The Curren case has been closed for several months."

"In your anonymous tip about the bio-threat."

"At the risk of appearing insubordinate," Janet ventured, "it seems to me that you are more concerned about Michael being the source than about the credibility of the threat."

Serna sniffed. "We are taking the threat very seriously, Agent McIntire. But it does trouble us that he might be the source."

"That he might know about it? I've already made it clear that the organized-crime community knows about it. It's not what I would call a tightly guarded secret."

"That's enough, McIntire," Weathers said sharply. "Remember who you're addressing."

Janet kept her gaze on Serna. "Am I being placed on disciplinary notice? Being suspended?"

"No. But we have a new assignment for you."

"You're moving me from Quincy?"

Serna straightened in his chair. "We have a specific need for your unique heritage and appearance. We've been approached by Britain's MI5 to help with what appears to be renewed activity by a group calling itself the Real Irish Republican Army, working mainly out of Dublin. MI5 is looking for a woman with an Irish background to infiltrate the group. We think you'd be just the person for the assignment."

"British security doesn't have any of their own agents with an Irish background? Perhaps someone who sounds Irish?"

"None who aren't well known in old IRA circles. They need a fresh face."

"So, you want to loan me to the Brits for a while. When would this happen?"

"Immediately. I'd like you to be in Washington by the end of the week to be briefed on Monday."

Janet sat silently for several minutes, wondering if this might be the time to announce a change of career but deciding caution was the better part of wisdom.

"Do I have any choice in this, sir?"

"Not really. You're perfect for the assignment. No one else in the agency fits the profile as well as you do."

"And it gets me out of town," Janet said, knowing she was again bordering on insubordination.

Serna seemed unfazed by her tone, responding with a thin smile. "That, too, Special Agent McIntire."

"And this information about the bio-agent. I believe it to be very credible. Is anything being done about that?"

"We're following up, and that's no longer a concern of yours." The deputy director turned purposefully toward Weathers. "We've discussed a replacement for Janet. Anything else from you?"

Weathers shook his head.

"Then that will be all, McIntire. We'll see you in Washington on Monday."

Janet sat again for a moment in silence, looking curiously from one superior to the other, then stood, smoothed her navy suit against her trim figure, and left the conference room. She walked to a turn in the hallway until out of sight of the meeting room's door, then stopped to decompress and regroup, head tilted back and eyes trapped shut.

What the hell was that all about? Did they know somehow that the information had come to her from Michael? They couldn't know. The couple had last met at Big Cedar Lodge near Branson, Missouri, when she'd had an open three-day weekend. She was certain no one had followed her there—or knew where she was going. Michael had been just as careful and was a man who paid close attention to such details.

Serna was right about Michael's profession and about why he had showed up in Quincy during the Curren kidnapping investigation. When they first met during one of her predawn jogs, he had presented himself as a financial adviser who liked to run in the mornings. But by the time the case was over, she knew he had been hired by Andrea Curren's father to hunt down the girl's abductors and eliminate them—and he had stayed one step ahead of her and the FBI team during the entire investigation. Though Serna and Weathers would never understand it, she had learned that he was a hired killer of conscience. He got rid of terrible people who did unthinkable things to decent people. She had developed a certain appreciation for his talents and personal code and a much deeper admiration for him as a man—something Serna clearly wasn't thrilled about.

But the thing that troubled her most about the last hour was that she was positive her superiors already knew about the bio-threat and the impending sale. It hadn't come out in any classified briefing documents or as a coded alert to offices across the country. She was certain of that. And their concern about Michael's involvement seemed intent on making certain no one was about to interfere with this ungodly transaction. Did they want the sale to go through for some reason? To catch the perpetrator at the point of sale? To see who the other potential buyers were? Or had she been meeting with some of those prospective bidders?

Janet slowly released the tension from her body and turned toward the elevator, playing the possibilities through as she walked. She may have just stuck her freckled Irish nose into the middle of some major sting, in which case she needed to make a quick exit and warn Michael to do the same. Or, remote as the possibility may be, she might have been meeting with players in a transaction that was so messy, even the crime world didn't want to touch it—the purchase of what was being advertised as a maximum-kill bio-agent.

3

The sale offer for a biological agent, described as a highly lethal airborne virus with an 80 to 90 percent kill rate, had come to the attention of the Bureau two days before the Washington office received the tip from Special Agent Janet McIntire. The notice had not come directly from the person or persons offering the sale but from the office of the director of central intelligence. It had been accompanied by a very specific request, supported by the NSA, to leave the sale offer alone.

We will be assuming complete operational responsibility for following up on this threat, the highly classified message read. *As you learn about it from other sources, assure them that it is being addressed at the highest level. Do not become involved in any way.*

At CIA headquarters in Langley, Virginia, the two men the director *had* involved were Don Hendren and Jay Bedford. Neither was a field operative. Each had more than a decade of experience in threat analysis: Hendren as a specialist in Middle Eastern radical groups, Bedford as a bio-threat analyst. The pair met with the director in his office overlooking the Potomac and were surprised to find the man alone. Without formality, he seated the men across from him at a small conference table and slid a brief typed memo in front of each, sitting silently while they read.

We have developed an aerosol strain of a highly lethal virus that our testing indicates will spread quickly and will result in a kill rate of 80 to 90%. Four vials of the virus and instructions for how to further cultivate it will be placed on the market in one month's time. There will be three rounds of open bidding, one day apart, with the winning bidder receiving the product in return for cash payment to a numbered account. An encryption key is attached to this message. If interested in bidding, send an encrypted response to the address included with the key. You will then be instructed how to obtain your own private key through our certifying authority and receive further instructions. It has taken us decades to develop this strain. It will take you as long, though we suspect some of you are trying. Once the vials are sold, we will discontinue our work. The buyer will own a weapon that can be used to control the actions of virtually any other nation on Earth.

Hendren slid the message back across the table. "How did this reach you, sir?" he asked.

The director smiled thinly. "It actually came in on my public-access e-mail. These people don't seem to be too tech savvy."

"They know about encryption keys," Bedford noted.

"Someone's helping them with that part of their communication," the director guessed. "But they apparently didn't want this technical adviser involved in contacting their bid list. Those who choose to reply will use their keys. From then on, communication will be pretty much in the dark."

Bedford returned his copy of the memo. "Do you see this offer as credible?" he asked.

The director nodded. "We do know that it went to an extensive list of international terrorist and security organizations. Everyone you might expect."

"And I gather you want us to locate this vendor," Hendren said. "Isn't that more an NSA responsibility? It won't be easy—and may not even be possible—once the encoded communication begins"

The director nodded. "Both we and the NSA will be trying to track and identify the source. But I want more than that. We need to acquire the product."

Bedford pulled his copy back in front of him and read it through again. "You want us to acquire this virus? Not just locate and destroy it?"

"I have no confidence the buyer will be the only one with this strain, if it exists. We need to know everything we can about it, and get our people working on an antidote."

Hendren's brow furrowed. "If this is for real, the bidding is going to go high. This is just the kind of thing our terrorist enemies would love to add to their arsenals."

"Exactly," the director acknowledged. "As the bidding time gets closer, we'll meet and discuss what we want to offer. But you basically have carte blanche. I have people working on locating the source. Your job is to win the bid. One way or another, we need to end up with the product."

Hendren also retrieved his copy. "Did the message also go to the Bureau and NSA? We could be treading all over each other's toes."

"It came only to us, but I've shared it with both. The directors met early this morning and agreed that it would be ours. NSA is working on cyber tracking, but otherwise, they'll keep their people out."

Hendren lifted the sheet of paper. "May I keep this? We'll need that key code and address. Who else has this internally?"

"Just you two. And keep it that way. Make a note of the information you need, and leave the copies here. Now, let's win that bid."

4

For all but four weeks of the past fifty years, Anita Diaz had lived in an unobtrusive, ranch-style house clad in pale-yellow asbestos siding, a few country miles outside of Ashburn, Virginia. During that half century, she had never received guests and had never ventured more than an hour from the house. In all of that time she had never heard her last name mentioned and had simply gone by *Nita*.

Nita had been born the daughter of an American-educated Cuban who was the Caribbean island's only native-born expert in radar technology at a time when men of every profession were struggling to stay in the shadows of an increasingly polarizing revolution. Roberto Diaz was a man whose obsessive fascination with the neophyte world of integrated circuits made him of particular interest to both sides of the Cuban struggle, a fascination that was passed along to his gifted daughter. By the time Fidel Castro firmly gained control of the government and Anita was assigned to a Russian-administered technical academy in Havana, she had surpassed her father's understanding of the fledgling science and what were popularly being called computers. As a quiet, slightly overweight seventeen-year-old with a mind that both mesmerized and terrified her faculty, the intense teen with the pleasant, round face and severe, square-cut brown hair dazzled them with her imagination, insights, and ferocious independence. The men of the academy hand-fed the girl every article and technical brief they could harvest from official and underground sources funneled into the country from the United States, Germany, and Great Britain. They then passed along to their superiors as their own work the inventive ideas percolated in the young woman's fertile brain.

At night, Anita's independence led her from the academy to a ragtag group of anti-Castro liberationists, transmitting coded radio messages to agents of the US government in Miami and in training camps in Guatemala. There, other men took advantage of her intellect as they planned an invasion by expatriate Cuban freedom fighters that would be launched against the island's south coast at a place called *Bahía de Cochinos*, the Bay of Pigs.

On April 17, 1961, as a forewarned Cuban defense force pummeled the beach head at *Bahía de Cochinos*, first stalling, then crushing the invasion, Anita Diaz and two other members of the Cuban underground joined the CIA's principal Havana operative in a dash to the western coastal city of Matanzas. There, a six-passenger Cessna 210, unnoticed in the panic that was rushing most of the country's military assets to the southern shore, flew the fugitives west to Guatemala. A month later, Nita was taken to the house near Ashburn and introduced to a second casualty of war and of the CIA's failures. He was an older man, a former station chief named Bud Liljigren. Along with the plain yellow house, he had become the totality of Nita's life.

At age seventeen, Bud Liljigren had made his own escape—slipping away in the dead of night from a farmhouse in the west Kansas prairie town of Lindsborg. His mother would find a brief note on the kitchen's checkered tablecloth explaining that the defenders of freedom in Britain needed her son much more than did the wheat farmers of west Kansas. He had gone to join the RAF.

Under the command of Squadron Leader J. W. Donaldson, Bud had been trained to fly Gloster Gladiators in northern Europe, the last double-wing aircraft to see action in World War II. In the spring of 1940, the 263rd Squadron had been sent to provide air cover for a British attempt to recapture the Norwegian coastal city of Trondheim from the Germans. Bud's squadron had staged off a frozen lake inland near Dombås, where overnight temperatures plummeted below zero. The following morning, a patrolling

Messerschmitt found nineteen pilots desperately attempting to crank over their sluggish Glosters on the thick sheet of ice. Within an hour, the sky teemed with Luftwaffe attack aircraft. Only six Gladiators made it off the lake. Bud had been one of them. Low on fuel and out of ammunition, he made a desperate attempt to reach the sea to the west. His aircraft made it as far as Valldal at the tip of a coastal fjord before the engine starved, flattening the prop against the wind like a Kansas barn side and dropping the Gladiator onto the ice pack in a broken pile of scrap. Bud awoke in a fisherman's cottage in the village of Ålesund along the Norwegian Sea. His back had been broken in two places, leaving his body lifeless below the waist. To everyone beyond Ålesund, Bud Liljigren was considered lost in action.

Then in the spring of 1942, a new voice began to broadcast from the Norwegian coast. Code named Northern Lights, the voice relayed vital German ship and troop movements to allied warships hidden at the edge of the horizon. The information was always good—so good that stopping it became a full-time obsession of the Gestapo. On an April night in 1943 with an icy wind whipping the sea into frothy foam, two members of the Norwegian underground lifted Northern Lights from his bed at midnight as German agents pounded at the front door of the fisherman's home. His rescuers carried Bud from the rear of the cottage to the harbor where they ferried him across a strait to Godoya Island at the mouth of the fjord. After a day in hiding, he was secreted in the bottom of a fishing trawler for two days at sea, then transferred to an American destroyer. Three weeks later, Northern Lights made port at Norfolk, Virginia.

For almost two decades, Bud Liljigren had managed the CIA's Baltic desk. Then, during a late afternoon in June, he was unceremoniously "fired" by the director. The next day, he was in the yellow asbestos-sided house being introduced to Anita Diaz.

"The Agency's being forced to operate too close to the surface," the director told the pair while walking them through the empty shell of the Ashburn home. "I'm tasking the two of you with developing our first deep-cover unit that, for lack of a better name, I'm calling Unit One."

While her new partner surveyed the expanse of open fields that stretched behind the house, the director pulled Nita aside.

"You're a bit of a yin and yang," he told her. "Bud's an operations genius, and our Havana man tells me you know more about these new electronic computers than any person in the Agency. We believe that's where the future lies—in carefully designed operations, supported by the best information we can amass to provide to our agents. And with the scrutiny we're getting right now, some of the most delicate problems will have to be solved by someone way below the surface. That will be you. I will know about you—and the president will, of course. But even he won't know who or where you are. And that's how it is going to have to stay."

It had stayed that way for more than half a century.

Bud had been assigned the code name *Fisher* and managed a small team of bright, independent, and committed mavericks who knew only in the vaguest way that there were others in the unit doing similar work. Fisher's people were loners. His organization was built around that autonomy and survived because of it. Five men and a single woman took their assignments from Fisher, called on Nita when they needed support information or materials, and let their handlers know when a job was complete. They were permitted, even encouraged, to initiate requests as they became aware of some damaging event or news item that had escaped the attention of analysts at Langley or was too hot for the agencies to touch. Bud screened the requests, leaned toward granting broad latitude, and kept the team at arm's length from one another and from Ashburn. None of the agents had ever met Fisher or Nita, and none had been to the yellow house.

For eighteen months after the director had left them at Ashburn, Nita and Fisher worked in collaborative isolation, shaping the land around the house into what appeared to be a heavily fenced and brightly lighted rural sewage-disposal plant. County authorities visited them once and fussed about government interference in county affairs. Bud gave them a brief and fictitious letter of explanation about how the plant supported the Langley facility twenty-five miles away. The officials were given a number to call and hadn't been back since. CIA directors came and went.

While sharing a meal of Nita's special *boliche* one evening just after the CIA chief who had started the operation was forced to resign, Nita had asked Fisher how long he thought they would be there.

He looked up from the plate of beef and sausage and shrugged. "I have no idea. No one ever gave us an end date."

"The director's gone, and all we get from the new man is the support information and equipment we ask for. I don't think he even knows who or where we are—or how many of us are here."

"I think that's true. That's probably a good thing."

"Then we could be here forever."

"We can always ask to be replaced," he said. "Would you like to be doing something else?"

"No—that's not it at all. I like being with you. It's just that if we're going to be here for a long time, just the two of us . . ."

"You're thinking I can't be much of a companion," he said, an embarrassed smile creasing his face. "I've thought of that . . . ."

"That's not it, either," she said uncertainly. "In fact, I think you'd be a wonderful companion—with a few minor improvements. You don't talk much, and I would enjoy a bit more conversation."

"About what?"

She shrugged her frustration. "*Anything.* I'd like to know what you're thinking. About this job we are doing. About our people.

About the job *I'm* doing. I never know if you think I'm good at what I do."

"You're wonderful at what you do. You amaze me."

"Then *tell* me sometimes."

Fisher smiled the first self-conscious smile she had ever seen on the man's face and rolled his chair up beside her, taking her hand.

"You are wonderful, and you amaze me," he said, lifting the hand to his lips.

"Thank you." She bent to kiss his forehead.

He held her hand for an extended moment, looking up into her inquiring round face, then began to release it. She didn't let him go, tightening her grip on his fingers.

"If we're going to be here forever," she murmured, "I would enjoy more from you than a little praise once a year and a kiss on the hand."

His gaze dropped to the floor, and he tried to back away.

"I couldn't be much of a companion," he muttered again, his voice almost too low to hear.

She dropped to her knees in front of him to let their eyes meet at the same level. "You would be all I want in a companion. I just wasn't sure you thought *I* would be."

He sniffed. "I think about it all the time. But *look* at me." He lifted his hands to draw attention to his withered lap and to the mechanized chair that was his life during the day.

"All I see is a man I've grown to care about very much. One who doesn't talk enough," she said playfully, "but someone I want to care for even more. Maybe we could find more to talk about."

He leaned back, frowning. "The chair's just a piece of it. I'm scarred from head to toe—with these on my face being the least of it."

Bud's face was a network of small scars from fragments of the windscreen that had exploded during his crash. She had stopped noticing them long ago, seeing instead the firm, determined set of his jaw when a problem caught his attention, the soft smile and light in his pale-blue eyes when he was amused, and the gentleness in his voice when he sensed one of her bouts of loneliness.

"We each have our scars," she said with a self-conscious laugh. "And I'm a little on the heavy side. But all I see in you makes me want to stay—for as long as they want us to be together."

He sat again in silence for a few moments, then waved an arm at the bank of electronic devices that filled the center of the room. "After dinner, why don't we turn off all of this stuff and get to know each other better."

In the years since, they had learned to love each other in all the ways their hearts, minds, and bodies could imagine. There were still periods of feeling isolated, but never alone. They had grown old moving anonymously from one director and one set of agents to another. Their operations had become increasingly complex, the consequences more potentially damaging to the nation. They had upgraded equipment to keep it state-of-the-art. And they had grown ever more deeply committed to each other.

"I'm not going to be around here forever, you know," he said after a long coughing spell left him breathless and leaning heavily forward in the chair. He had just turned ninety-two, and for months now, she had quietly witnessed his progressive decline.

"Neither of us will be," she said. "And they'll close us down if they know one of us is gone. They like to have us here when they need someone to clean the government's toilets, but I think we make them nervous."

He chuckled cynically. "Nervous and relieved. But when one of us goes, they won't need to know."

"Sooner or later, this place will go silent," she said. "They'll know then."

"It won't go silent. We'll replace ourselves."

"Without asking?"

He was sitting in front of the windows that opened onto the

fenced compound. She was at the central island of the long room that filled the back half of the house, hunched over her computers. He turned and smiled a wrinkled, tired smile.

"Yes. Without asking. They don't know who's here—or if we've ever been replaced. They hold their collective breath when a nasty problem develops and release it gratefully when the problem suddenly goes away. They feed our budget every year, and we have more money than we can possibly spend. If there's suddenly a new Fisher, no one will know the difference, and no one will care."

"Our agents will," she said, sitting back from her equipment.

"We'll use one of them. And do you think the others will care, as long as they keep getting what they need?"

"They like and trust you."

"I'm a voice on the phone who takes care of them," he muttered. "They'll like and trust anyone who does the same."

"Who are you thinking of?" she asked, but she already knew.

"Zak. He's smart, experienced, and levelheaded. And he has that friend who's almost as good as you are with this equipment."

"The Sason woman? After Zak wrapped up that Weavers affair and asked her if she wanted to team up, she said no."

"We'll have to change her mind. Neither of us is getting any younger."

The opportunity to ask had not come soon enough. Nita awoke one morning and knew from the absolute silence in the room that he was gone. No slow, labored breathing. No rustling as he tossed his weight to one side or the other to relieve the spasms in his shoulders. Just the silence of a peaceful death.

She had him cremated as he had asked and kept the ashes at the yellow house until she could take them back to Lindsborg. The Kansas town was, he said, the only home he had ever known aside from Ashburn. He didn't wish his final remains to be scattered about an artificial sewage plant. And the single regret that had accompanied his life with Nita was knowing that he had left a mother grieving a son who hadn't died until well after she was gone. "Take me back to Kansas," he'd said.

When the time was right and Nita learned that Zak had again teamed up with Sason, she invited her first guests to the yellow house. That had been one month ago.

5

Adam Zak and Dreu Sason had agreed to take over the Unit under two conditions: they could move its headquarters to Scottsdale, Arizona, where Adam had a ground-floor apartment in the Old Town Arts District; and Nita would agree to stay with them for two weeks to teach them about command and control.

Zak was tall and lanky, a man whose normal gait seemed to be a casual saunter. His long brown hair was pulled into a ponytail, his face chiseled and angular with a charming, lopsided grin that he used freely. Though Nita had known from his dossier that he had lost his left eye in a flying accident while an Air Force instructor pilot, the black patch that he chose to wear added an element of mystery that made the grin disarming, but not altogether approachable. When they met at the yellow house in Ashburn, he remembered having seen her before during an emergency equipment drop-off.

"The gas station in Remington," he said with a chuckle. "And you've been our contact voice the last few weeks?"

"The very same. Good to meet you more formally," she said.

Nita's second guest was new to her. Dreu Sason was hardly the image of a nationally respected computer-security expert. She was all that Anita Diaz was not: tall, slender, beautiful, the daughter of two Stanford physicists, and Stanford educated herself. She had created and managed her own security business that handled some of the federal government's most vulnerable agencies. The young woman had initially balked at the thought of sharing in the management of the unit, declaring that she couldn't possibly live the isolated, monastic life of the old Fisher and Nita. Nita could immediately see why.

"Your pictures don't do you justice," Nita declared self-

24

consciously. "You look like you should be in *Vogue*."

Zak flashed the disarming grin. "She was a few times. Mainly to spite her parents. But some psychopath became obsessed with her, and she retreated back into the veiled world of computers. I'm trying to drag her back out again."

Dreu initially had shown little interest in being rescued, if rescue meant living as Nita had for half a century. But given a little time with the systems the Latina had assembled and kept on the cutting edge of development, and assured that, with the mobility of the newest technology, the operation could easily be moved to Phoenix, she acquiesced.

"If I agree to this," she told Adam, "it has to mean one full day away from all this every week—and dinner out at least that often."

"Deal," he said.

Within a week, the Unit 1 nerve center had been relocated into an apartment just above Adam's in Scottsdale's Old Town. With the next encrypted request for information from one of their agents, Fisher's voice on the phone became Adam's. The director of central intelligence, who wasn't sure where they were and how many of them were in the unit, didn't know the change had occurred. Nita's two weeks of transition had become four, and neither Adam nor Dreu encouraged her to leave.

"We need to do something for Bud," the Cuban woman said one morning, sipping a cup of strong black coffee. She was gazing absently through the thin curtains that veiled their apartment from early morning Scottsdale exercisers who jogged along the pedestrian walk outside. It seemed to Adam that the streaks of gray in her hair had increased overnight, and that there was more slump to her shoulders.

"I know," he said over his own cup, a note of guilt in his voice. "I'll get you to Lindsborg sometime this month."

"No, it's not that," Nita said solemnly. She looked hesitantly over at Dreu. "You know . . . there was someone else . . . ."

Dreu and Adam exchanged glances. "Someone else in Ashburn?" Dreu asked.

"No. In Bud's life. Other than me. He tried to keep it from me, but in our business, there are no real secrets." She lowered her cup to her lap and returned her gaze to the veil of curtains.

"I think you must have been imagining this, Nita," Adam said. "As isolated as you were—and in his condition . . . ."

"Oh, this was well before me," she said, turning back to them. "Back in Norway during the war. Someone he must have been very close to. They kept in touch over the years." She smiled wistfully. "Coded messages that he thought I didn't know about."

Adam set down his coffee. "What kind of messages?"

"I really don't know. If he'd wanted me to know, he would have talked to me about them. I don't think they were anything that compromised the unit. Just private messages between two dear old friends."

Dreu set her own cup carefully on the table. "It may not have been a woman at all," she suggested. "He was involved in the Resistance, and I'm sure he developed friendships."

Nita smiled faintly. "Oh, it was a woman. I found out about them by coming across the file accidentally and opening a couple of the messages. I couldn't imagine a file I didn't know about—and the reasons were pretty clear. They talked to each other like old lovers."

"What do you know about the woman?" Dreu asked.

"Practically nothing. She now has family of her own, and her name is Kari. That's about it."

Dreu leaned forward with her chin on her hands. "And she doesn't know Bud's gone?"

Nita shook her head. "I thought of sending a note. But then she would know I had access to their correspondence. And . . . I opened another after he died. They had been exchanging information about something she thought Bud should investigate."

Adam reentered the conversation. "What made you think so?"

"Her message said, 'I think this *utlending* is a dangerous man. To us and to everyone else. I'm sure he is doing something related to the old *eksperimenter.*' *Eksperimenter* means just what it sounds like—experiments. And *utlending* means *foreigner* in Norwegian. I looked them up."

Adam leaned forward intently. "How long ago did you look at these?"

She stared thoughtfully into her cup. "A couple of months. Just before you came."

"And there's been no contact since?"

She shook her head.

"Any idea what she's referring to?" Dreu asked.

"No. But I know after Bud read one of her messages, he seemed troubled for a long time. Nothing he would talk to me about."

Dreu leaned back with her coffee cradled in her hands. "Well, she needs to be told. I'm sure she suspects something's happened to him."

"You've been insisting on your day out of the office," Adam said. "How does Norway sound?" He turned quickly to Nita. "If you don't mind covering the store for a few days."

"I took care of things on my own until I roped you two into this. I can handle a week. But you don't know where she is."

"They must have met in Ålesund, and she seems to be referring to something that happened there. That's where we'll start."

Nita nodded and lifted her cup, turning again to the window where she gazed with a tired sadness through the lace mesh at the walkers beyond.

"And we do need to get to Lindsborg," she murmured.

6

A response to Don Hendren's encrypted message to the person peddling the virus arrived within fifteen minutes. It was easily decoded using the key that had been included with the initial instructions.

The first round of bidding begins Monday, July 15, at 01:00 GMT. The bidding process will be open, with each bid period lasting for one hour. Bids will be posted by code names as they are received. At the end of the third round, I will provide the winning bidder with information needed to deposit two-thirds of the winning sum into a numbered account, with instructions about receiving the product. The remaining third of the purchase price must be deposited within three days of that exchange, or we will make our research public, including the process used to cultivate the most recent strain. Assuming timely payment, the winner will receive all existing samples of the product along with instructions for safe storage and cultivation. Prior to the first round of bidding, I will provide a demonstration of the product's effectiveness. Below, please find contact information for a certifying authority where each bidder can obtain a private key, allowing exchanges to be double encrypted. There will be no negotiations following close of the third round of bidding.

Hendren printed the message and handed a copy to Bedford, who sat expectantly across the desk. "What do you make of this?" he asked.

Bedford read through it quickly. "Clever," he muttered. "Three rounds of open bidding will create a frenzy of speculation and keep driving the price up. How are we going to guarantee we get this?"

Hendren looked up at him with a wry smile. "I guess we just make sure we outbid everyone."

* * *

The flight from Phoenix to Ålesund, Norway, took Adam and Dreu through Minneapolis–Saint Paul, from there overnight to Amsterdam, then north up the coast to the Norwegian fishing port. Dreu begged Adam to book business class for at least the eight-hour overseas flight. He finally relented after reminding her that a cardinal rule in their line of work was to remain inconspicuous.

"When first class boards, everyone else on the flight is standing there watching," he pointed out. "It's hard not to stand out."

"Only if you board when first class is called," she argued. "The way to be the least conspicuous is to have a first-class seat. Then you don't have to worry about overhead space and can board whenever you want. Get on late. In that forward section of the bigger planes, only the other first-class passengers see you. They'll all be using frequent-flyer miles but trying to appear casually wealthy. They won't pay attention to who else is sitting around them. And we can be first off."

He booked business class for the full sixteen-hour journey.

They spent the three-hour leg to Minneapolis talking about how they might find the mysterious Kari. Dreu had run census data on Ålesund for the past four decades. There were dozens of Karis—but none now in their late eighties or nineties.

"Bud was eighteen when his plane went down, and I suppose this woman could be two or three years younger," she reasoned. "But if she was involved in the underground at that point in the war, she would have to be at least eighty-five, and I didn't find any Karis over that age."

"Ålesund may just be a starting point," Adam suggested. "She may have moved when she married. We'll see if we can locate someone who was part of the Resistance. They may be able to guide us to her."

Dreu was seated by the window and turned, leaning back against the heavy, double-paned glass.

"Which raises a point I've been meaning to ask you about. Since partnering with you in the unit, I've learned that all of the field agents get new names and faces, and that their histories are essentially deleted from every paper file or database. We've known each other for what? Two years? And during that time you've been Randall Murch, Tom Russell, and who knows what other names. You always come back to Adam Zak. But is that who you really are?"

He looked over with a slight smile. "That's who I really am."

"And you were no one else before that? No 'Bud Liljigren' before he became Fisher?"

"As you say, we were all someone else before we joined the unit."

"And does the new Fisher's partner, with whom he has a relationship of complete trust and shares all things—does she get to know who you used to be?"

He leaned toward her across the armrest to keep the conversation private. "You know some of it. I was an Air Force pilot. Lost my eye when a sandhill crane came through the canopy of the T-38 I was flying with a student. Got picked up by the unit. End of story."

She also leaned into him, her lips inches from his ear. "You were Tom Mercomes, weren't you?"

His jaw tightened, but the thin smile remained. "So much for expunging all past records. I know you're very good at what you do, but where did you find that?"

"The student who was flying with you was killed," she said. "The newspaper in Enid, Oklahoma, where the accident happened, does seem to have lost all copies from the days following the incident. But not the paper in Marion, Ohio, where the student's family lived. There just weren't that many accidents involving pilots and sandhill cranes in the five years before you joined Unit One."

"So my partner—with whom I have a relationship of complete trust—has been investigating me." His smile flattened into an expressionless line.

"Partner, girlfriend, lover—whatever you want to call me. I knew you couldn't tell me and honor your security pledge, so I decided I'd better look it up myself. From the account in the *Marion Star*, you were quite the hero. Landed the plane with the canopy shattered, blinded in one eye, and the dead student in the front seat. Did you know there's still a record of Tom Mercomes being chosen as Instructor of the Year at the Air Force Academy two years later? It's very difficult to completely wipe out a lifetime. And I'm glad I know something about your past."

A flight attendant announced that the plane had been cleared into Minneapolis–Saint Paul, and they were about to begin descent. The passengers around them rustled in their seats, stowing tray tables and checking seat backs and belts. Adam continued to lean on the armrest, looking earnestly at Dreu.

"Does any of this make a difference to you?" he asked.

"It adds to my admiration—and raises a bucket load of other questions. I'm sure that our protocols don't require you to answer, but I'd like to know."

"Ask."

"Was Tom Mercomes married?"

"Yes. For a few years."

"Any children?"

"No."

"Your ex-wife?"

"Happily remarried—and wouldn't recognize me if she were seated across the aisle."

"So, you look different."

"Better, I hope. I was going bald. Had a crooked nose."

"Do you have other family?"

"None immediate. No siblings, and my parents are dead."

"And Adam Zak. Is that who you are all the time now?"

"All the time—except when I have to be someone else."

7

There had been times when Janet McIntire had also wished she were someone else. Now that she was, she wasn't all that enamored with it. She had continued to call herself Janet, but was now Janet O'Brien. The new Janet had arrived in Dublin as an American graduate student eager to reconnect with her Irish roots by pursuing a postgraduate diploma in Old Irish language from Dublin's Trinity College. To maintain the cover, she had enrolled in the introductory course and its accompanying tutorial and was spending as much time studying as she had as a first-year law student—a situation she had once pledged never to repeat.

Before law school, Janet had been an English major at the University of New Mexico, and the Bureau had arranged to have her transcript duplicated under the name Janet O'Brien. Two courses in early British literature were sufficient to qualify her for the Old Irish diploma program, but not to prepare her for the hours of work it was taking to memorize even the most basic structures of early Gaelic. As she sat at a table just inside the restaurant half of John Kavanagh's Pub and watched the evening crowd begin to filter in, she hoped British Intelligence had been right. Her assignment was to get close to a Dubliner named Patrick Flynn, a man MI5 believed to be the instigator of renewed activity by the Real IRA. They also believed Flynn had a personal fascination with the Celtic tongue. If that proved not to be true, she was driving herself to distraction with this language study for nothing.

She also hoped British authorities were correct about Flynn's occasionally careless interest in bringing new young acolytes to his cause. She had been studying at the table within view of his customary booth for more than two weeks and knew she had been noticed. She had chosen this evening to take a first step into Flynn's secret life. She waited until the five at Flynn's table were midway through their first pint of Guinness, then grabbed a pen and small notebook and, with a look of frustration, marched resolutely around the empty center table to where the men were seated.

"I really apologize for interrupting—and I know the pub is really big on privacy. But I've heard you talking when you come in, and you sound like native Dubliners. Do any of you happen to know anything about the early Irish language?" She carefully avoided looking directly at Flynn.

The men sat silently for a moment, then one of the younger members of the group gave her a cool smile. "You're right. We try not to be interferin' with others' conversations here. Sorry then, miss."

She nodded in embarrassment and started back toward her table.

"She's not botherin' us, Conor," an aged voice said behind her. "I might know a bit about it. What do ya want ta know?"

"No . . . I really *am* sorry," she said, turning back. "I knew better than to interrupt."

Flynn nodded his gray head toward the man he called Conor. "Get the girl a seat. Let's give her a listen. We don't have that much ta talk about, and this might be interestin'."

Conor pulled a chair over from the table in the center of the floor, and she slid cautiously onto it.

"I'm a new student at Trinity College in the Old Irish language program, and I'm having a devil of a time hearing the difference between the initial consonant sounds when a word changes usage," she said, this time speaking directly to the older man.

Flynn sat against the wall with Conor between them.

"What the bloody hell's she goin' on about?" one of the other men said with an amused laugh.

"I know what she's askin'," Flynn said.

She held her notebook out hesitantly. "Can I show you an example? Maybe you can tell me how these sounds are different."

He took the notebook and studied the page while she talked.

"They've been explaining what they call 'consonant mutation' when a noun is used differently. In that example I have there, if you say *toward a house*, the word *teg* for house is pronounced one way. But if you say *into the house*, it's pronounced with a different beginning sound. And *under the house*, still another. But I'm not sure I can hear the difference—and no one has been able to explain how you know which beginning sound to use."

Patrick Flynn chuckled and pushed the pad back across the table. "No rules, I'm afraid, miss. Ya just have ta memorize them. But in the first case y'er referrin' to there, the word begins with a *te* sound, as you said—*teg*. While in the second case, it's more of a *de* sound—like *deg*. And for *under the house*, it would be more of a *th*. The final vowel of the word that comes before it may tell you which to use, but not always. A bit like English. Lots of rules, always inconsistent, and often ignored."

Janet lifted the pad from the table, nodding and mouthing the *th* sound. "*Theg. Theg.*"

He acknowledged with a nod and a smile. "Very good. Now, lots of practice and memorization."

She rose and pushed the borrowed chair back to its table. "Thank you—and again, I'm so sorry to have disturbed you." She walked slowly back to her table by the door, practicing the consonant sounds as she went.

As the Flynn group left Kavanagh's an hour later, its leader hesitated until she looked up. "Lots of rules, meant to be broken," he said with the same smile.

The following evening, she did her best to ignore them. As the group rose to leave, Flynn gestured for his mates to go on ahead and stopped beside her.

"How's it comin'?"

She shrugged good-naturedly. "I'm sure I can learn it. But it's not like anything I've studied before."

"May I join ya?"

Her table had only a bench along the wall, so she scooped her books and worksheets aside and beckoned him in beside her.

"Patrick Flynn," he said pleasantly, turning toward her but not offering his hand. He looked very much like his file photos—a little older and closer to the seventy that was reported to be his age.

"Janet O'Brien," she nodded back. "Thank you for your help yesterday."

"I've seen you here almost every evenin'. This is a long way from Trinity College."

"I'm a little old for the college life—and came as much to soak up the culture as to study Old Irish. I'm a great admirer of Michael Collins. As you know, he's buried just beyond the wall there. So I got a flat out in this part of the city and take the bus in each day. It's only forty-five minutes and gives me time to get ready for my tutorial."

"I see we've already got ya sayin' flat instead of apartment," Flynn said with a chuckle.

Janet shrugged. "I'm doing my best to adapt."

"You from the US or Canada?"

"US. Wilmington, Delaware, to begin with. But I went to college in New Mexico and have been teaching there the past six years."

"Ah! New Mexico! Out in the wild west! And y'er a teacher."

She couldn't tell if she was hearing skepticism or admiration. "Was," she corrected. "I decided to give it up and come to Dublin to study Old Irish. My life wasn't exactly going where I wanted. When my father passed away, I thought I'd just take a break and learn more about the Irish heritage he was so passionate about. Collins was his hero more than mine, but just in the time I've been here, I understand why."

Flynn nodded. "I imagine I'm from your father's generation.

36

Collins meant a lot to all of us." He glanced over toward the bar. "Can I buy you a pint? Best Guinness in Dublin, right here."

She shrugged. "Sure. I'm living off my savings, so a free pint's always welcome. But at the risk of sounding sacrilegious to a Dubliner, I haven't quite developed a taste for Guinness. Could I have a Harp or O'Hara's?"

"Sure enough," he said, laughing. "Both good Irish ales. But you need to give Guinness a chance. You'll never speak good Gaelic until you've had a couple of pints."

While they drank, he asked about her family, and she reluctantly rolled out her backstory. English teacher. Messy divorce. Parents no longer living. No ties to Albuquerque or to Wilmington. Looking for something to add new meaning to her life.

"And you think you'll find it here at Gravediggers," he said wryly.

She sniffed. "I know they call the pub that. But if I don't find some kind of rebirth, maybe I'm in the right place. I come in here because I can't study in complete quiet. It drives me crazy. There are no cell phones allowed here—and no TVs on the walls. Just people talking quietly. I love this old place, and it's a great background for learning Irish."

"And you've got the souls of thousands of old Gaelic speakers whisperin' to ya from just beyond the stone wall," he said, pushing from the booth. "But I'm keepin' ya from gettin' your studies done. If ya need a bit o' help, I grew up down in Dingle in a Gaelic-speakin' part of the country. It's a particular interest of mine ta keep the language alive and healthy. When I'm in town, Gravediggers is where I spend my evenin's."

"You don't live in Dublin?"

"Partly here. Partly a village called Rothbury over in the north of England. I'm back and forth every few weeks."

"Well—when you're here, I'd enjoy learning from you, Mr. Flynn. You'll find me right here."

"I'll be watchin' for ya," he said, nodded, and left her to work through another list of mutated consonants.

8

The airport serving Ålesund filled nearly half of the island of Vigra and connected to the main peninsula by a series of tunnels and causeways. The approach to runway 25 brought landing aircraft in low over the water onto a seventy-five-hundred-foot strip of concrete that jutted out into the sea. As their plane reached what Dreu thought must be close to ground level and she could see nothing but choppy, cobalt-blue water, she clutched Adam's arm, pressed back hard into the seat, and squeezed her eyes tightly shut. He was an ex-flier and didn't seem at all nervous. But then, he wasn't seated by the window. She felt his hand on her arm, the jar and squeal of tires against concrete, and she relaxed forward, glancing sheepishly across at her seatmate.

"Reminds me of Logan in Boston," he said, grinning over at her. "It makes me nervous every time I land there, even when I know the runway's right in front of us."

They deplaned down rolling stairs directly onto the concrete apron. The scenery that surrounded them quickly wiped away any tension she still felt from the landing. Steep, green islands rose from the sea in three directions, and the blue waters of the fjords glistened under a late-afternoon sun.

Adam had rented a car online through Europcar and within an hour they were guiding a silver BMW toward the Ellingsøy Tunnel for the eighteen-kilometer drive into the city.

They checked into the Clarion on the harbor, a five-story mustard-yellow building that hugged the water's edge. Its long central foyer with exposed timber beams evoked images of an ancient Viking longhouse.

Each had learned over time that the other had habits when they entered a hotel room that bordered on ritual. Adam found the TV remote and checked channels until he located a news station that served as background noise while he turned the thermostat down to the equivalent of 68 degrees Fahrenheit and hung shirts and pants in the closet. Dreu went straight to the window, pulled the drapes and sheers fully open, and surveyed whatever her new view had to offer. Below, white sailboats floated motionless on the mirrored water of the harbor, their masts and rigging extending well above the steeply pitched roofs of the buildings around her. Opposite, across the narrow inlet, a row of Art Nouveau homes and shops in white, rose, lemon, and salmon reflected in the water in unruffled perfection. A gaggle of yellow and blue kayaks floated below them as if painted on the still surface.

"Beautiful place," she murmured without turning. "It's hard to imagine that sixty years ago, this city was the heart of the Norwegian Resistance."

Adam interrupted his routine to drop a pair of twill pants on the bed and move beside her.

"The city almost burned to the ground at the beginning of the twentieth century," he said. "Everything was rebuilt in about five years in this same style. Pretty impressive."

She gave him a sidelong smile. "And you just happened to know that interesting bit of trivia?"

"I always research the places I'm going before I get there. The fewer surprises, the better. Anything else you want to know?"

"Population?"

"About forty-five thousand. Another three or four on the islands around."

"If our lady's here, it shouldn't be hard to find her."

"I think the men we're meeting tomorrow morning will be able to help," he said. "But I still have no idea how many will show up."

"They have to be old."

"All in their nineties. But I was told there are still eight or ten."

"And this evening?"

He wrapped an arm around her waist and pulled her tightly against his side. "I could use some dinner, then thought we might walk around the harbor a bit. Then maybe we can come back here and take advantage of Nita not being down the hall."

"Just what I was thinking," she said.

9

The dugout was as long as a school bus and half as wide, carved from a single fallen tree by Mongo tribesmen two generations before Andrew was born. He sat at the stern, watching the thin trail of muddy water slip behind the boat's small gas motor and fade into faint ripples on the brown surface. His mother sat cross-legged in the center of the wooden hull with the village girl beside her. Six other people, three large shapeless cloth bundles, and two bleating, trussed-up goats separated her from her son at the stern. Another group and their belongings filled the front half of the dugout. The motor was now idle, its three-bladed propeller raised above the water. Two black boatmen with long poles worked their way barefoot along the sides.

Every few minutes Andrew glanced down at the Rubik's Cube that turned endlessly in his hands, checking to ensure that the algorithm he had memorized was producing the desired result. When the colored sides all aligned, he looked away, twisted randomly at the block until the small squares were thoroughly mixed, squeezed the cube between his knees while he flexed his hands and fingers, then started through the solution sequence again. By the time they returned from the village, his goal was to shave at least five seconds from his best time—possibly even beat thirty seconds. The end goal—solve the puzzle in less than fifteen.

The boat was headed downriver to the town of Wendji Secli, but he and his mother would be dropped off midway at a Bantu village on the west bank. The village girl had arrived that morning, asking for the doctor lady.

"Please!" the girl pleaded when his mother brought her into the family's living room. "My sister is having a baby. It has started but will not come. You will know what to do."

Andrew's mother had convinced him that accompanying her to

42

the village was a better way to spend his Saturday morning than sitting on the balcony of their Mbandaka home, endlessly spinning what she called "that infernal cube." So he was perched in the bow of a dugout instead, twisting the puzzle through the steps of what was called the Fridrich method, a layer-by-layer solution that he had almost mastered.

With his shaggy blond head bobbing in a sea of closely shorn black ones, Andrew had gone early to the fish market looking for his friends Deo, Sese, and Pelo. But Pelo's older sister had been buying fish and told him her brother was not feeling well. Pelo had wakened during the night with a severe headache and by morning was feeling too weak to move. Andrew knew better than to ask to visit his friends at their homes. They were too ashamed to have him see where they lived. So he had gone back to the white-stucco house in the mission clinic's compound. The messenger from the village was at the house when Andrew returned.

"This girl is only fifteen," his mother said. "Only three years older than you. It will be good for you to see what happens when children have children."

They were hugging the east bank of the river, staying close to the shore controlled by the Democratic Republic. Across the wide, murky expanse, impenetrable jungle pressed tightly against the water's edge on the western shore—the Republic of Congo side. This far upriver, no one worried too much about who crossed between villages. As they approached the cluster of huts where the girl was having the baby, the boatmen would pull oars from inside the dugout and row them across, steering clear of barges and larger motorized boats that used the Congo as the major transportation link in the central river basin.

To their left, an occasional cart or motorbike moved along the dirt road that ran from Mbandaka south to Wendji Secli. It was July, the dry season, and Andrew could see a low cloud of red dust moving northward beyond a screen of tawny head-high reeds that separated the river from the road. He shifted on the pile of blankets that served as his seat and watched until a chain of four white pickups emerged from behind the grass cover. The trucks looked new, an oddity on roads coming into the Congo basin. They were traveling together. Four armed men in the blue uniforms of the state police sat in the bed of each truck.

"Look there!" he called forward to his mother, pointing toward the row of vehicles.

She looked back at him, then toward the near bank.

"*Police Nationale*," she murmured, her voice reflecting the suspicion that followed every major police action in remote parts of the country. The other passengers fell silent and hunched more closely together as if the slightest sound might somehow attract the attention of the passing vehicles.

"And look ahead, madam," one of the boatmen said, lifting his pole to point downriver. Two gray powerboats, each carrying a front-mounted machine gun and six black-uniformed sailors, rounded the broad sweep of river in front of them. One steered left toward a flat, rusty barge that lumbered upriver in the middle of the channel. The second boat turned toward them. One of the sailors waved for them to pull alongside. The passengers bunched even closer, and a mother pulled her toddler to her, partially hiding him behind one of the mounds of cloth.

The powerboat eased alongside, and one of the sailors held the dugout against the launch while the boats drifted slowly downstream.

"Are you from Mbandaka?" a man wearing the cap of an officer called in French to no one in particular.

One of the boatmen answered nervously. "Yes. We are going to Wendji Secli."

"You must return to Mbandaka," the officer said. "We have orders that no one can leave the city."

Andrew's mother straightened on her pile of blankets. "*Je suis *médecin*," she said in French. "I am a doctor. I need to see a patient across the river in the next village. It is an emergency."

The officer shook his head vigorously. "No one can leave Mbandaka. Are you with the General Reference Hospital?"

"With the mission clinic," Andrew's mother said.

"Then you may not know," the officer said. "Two patients came to the hospital late last night. The doctors think they may have Ebola. The city is quarantined. No one may enter or leave until more is known about these patients."

The passengers in front of Andrew seemed to melt into the mound of cloth bags. A whispered chorus of "Ebola" rippled through the dugout.

"We are from Wendji Secli," one of the men said. "We must get to our homes. To our families."

The officer waved abruptly back upriver. "Anyone who has been in Mbandaka must return. You must return now."

"A woman needs medical help in a village across the river," Andrew's mother repeated, looking at the girl beside her. "Let them drop me off. I will return as soon as the baby is delivered. I will be needed at the clinic, and one of your men can stay with me if you wish."

"We have orders that all are to return immediately," the officer snapped. He gestured at the lead boatman. "Start your motor and turn around."

The boatman looked back at his huddle of passengers. "And if we continue?"

The answer was quick and direct. "If you continue, you will be shot."

When the dugout squeezed between two others and scraped bottom against the bank below the fish market, Andrew's mother waited until the other passengers had clambered ashore with their wares. She then helped him out of the boat with the village girl and

45

led them up onto the dusty road that skirted the docks. Two of the white pickups were now parked at the market. Nervous shoppers scattered from the normally crowded stalls with their woven baskets half-filled, less interested in which direction they took than in being away from the gendarmes. When finally alone, his mother squatted in front of the two children.

"I must go to the hospital," she said, looking at the village girl. "You may go to our house and wait with Andrew."

The girl shook her head. "One of my sisters lives here with her husband. I will go to them." Before his mother could object, the girl hurried off across an empty field.

His mother gripped him tightly by both shoulders, looking directly into his pale-blue eyes.

"I don't think your father will be allowed back into the city today. I have to get to the general hospital and see what's going on. Then I'll return to the clinic. I need you to go directly home. Don't stop and talk to *anyone.* When you get there, tell Belvie that there may be a reported case of Ebola. She should get home to her family. Stay in the house and keep the doors locked until I return. The other satellite phone is on the counter in the kitchen. I'll call you when I'm coming back. Can you do that?"

There was nothing complicated about the instructions, but he could hear the alarm in her voice. And she was speaking to him in French—something she rarely did when they were by themselves. He quickly nodded that he understood. They skirted the market where a rush of people still hurried back toward the city. As his mother separated to go toward the town center, she gave him a quick hug and an encouraging push on up the river road.

"Remember," she called after him, "send Belvie home and lock yourself in. I'll be home as soon as I can. If your father calls, tell him I'm at the clinic and have him call me there."

Belvie was hanging clothes on the line that stretched across the bare patch of red earth Andrew's family called its backyard. When

46

he told her of the rumor, she dropped her handful of clothespins into the plastic basket that held the waiting laundry, wiped her hands on the hips of her loose green dress, and looked back toward the house in nervous confusion.

"Mother said you should go home," he said.

She nodded mutely and hurried toward the passageway along the fence that led to the front of the house. He heard the gate open and snap shut, looked at the basket of unhung clothes, and wondered if he should put them on the line. Instead, he dropped his cube in among the damp clothing and carried the basket back into the house.

From the kitchen, Andrew could hear the satellite phone rattling on the countertop. He dropped the basket and sprinted to answer it, breathlessly stammering, "Hello."

"It's Mom." She was speaking in English, her tone even more charged with concern. "Are you in the house and by yourself?"

Andrew nodded. "Belvie was hanging clothes, and I sent her home. I just came in."

"How are you feeling?" Her voice sounding as if it were about to break.

"You mean, am I scared? Or am I feeling sick?"

"Do you feel ill? Any headache or feeling really tired?'

"No. Pretty much like always."

"When were you with your friends last? With Sese and Pelo?"

"Last week. Thursday after we finished school. What's up?"

"I'm at the hospital, and both are here. The two of them and five new babies. You need to stay inside and make sure no one comes in unless it's your father. I'll be home as soon as I can."

For the first time since being stopped on the river, Andrew felt cold fingers of fear work their way up his back, forming a lump deep in his throat.

"Are they sick, Mom? Do Sese and Pelo have Ebola?"

There was silence for a moment, then she said, "The doctors are quite certain they do. Do the boys live together?"

"No. I haven't been to their houses, but they live a long way apart."

"Do they get together often?"

"About every afternoon. And all day on market day. We meet and play soccer in the street with some of the other guys while you do your shopping. But the four of us are the only ones who still get together after school."

"Then you need to think about where and when you were with them last," his mother said. "All four of you together."

10

By her own admission, Dreu Sason was hardly an experienced lover. Until she finished college, she had been so intent on meeting the career expectations of two obsessively overachieving parents that she rarely dated, and then with a firm commitment to avoid anything akin to attachments. During her postbaccalaureate period of rebellion—the years she spent modeling in New York—she had found the men around her either gay, and fun, dependable companions, or too narcissistic to be taken seriously. After the attack, she had been too ashamed of her body to let it be seen.

Lonnie Marchisio had become obsessed with her without Dreu being aware that the two had ever met. He served bagels at the deli near her New York apartment where she stopped for a morning cinnamon raisin with cream cheese and coffee. Before she could put a face to the name, a note slipped under the door of her apartment let her know that someone named Lonnie had been waiting for a long time for God to make known to him who was intended to be his soul mate and partner for life. That revelation had come when he saw her "at the shop." When she came in again, he would let her know that she was his intended, and they could plan from there.

To Dreu, the most frightening part of the note was that she had no idea where "the shop" was, or how to avoid it. Before she could think through whether to take this to the police, her stop for morning coffee answered the question and brought her face-to-face with her new beloved.

"I'm Lonnie," he said quietly as he handed the bagel across the glass countertop, pressing his hand against hers as they made the exchange. "Pick up your coffee and wait for me over by the door. We can decide what we want to do."

The man who looked across the counter at her was a few inches shorter—five-nine or ten—with a beaked nose and small, wide-set eyes that stared at her with the intensity of a hunting falcon. His hair was bristle-short with a dark widow's peak that added to his avian stare. The voice was deeper than she expected from the narrow, lipless mouth that was separated from his chin by a black, triangular soul patch. She pulled the hand quickly away, a chill running up the touched arm and shuddering through her chest.

"I'm sorry. I think you must have me mistaken for someone else," she said and bolted from the deli.

He came up behind her the next morning when she was only a few steps from the outer doors of her apartment building on East Seventy-Seventh Street, stepping beside her as she walked to the corner to hail a cab. She had decided to skip her bagel.

"You don't need to be afraid of me," he said, the deep voice relaying a confident certainty. "If we can just talk for a few minutes . . . ."

"Please," she said. "I don't wish to be rude, but I'm not interested in a relationship of any kind."

His hand was around her arm so quickly that she shrieked involuntarily. The few passersby on the walk glanced at the couple uncertainly, then hurried on.

"Neither is the man without the woman, nor the woman without the man, in the Lord," he whispered against her ear. "God has selected you for me, and there is no power greater than God's."

"If you don't let go of my arm, I'll scream until you do," she hissed, twisting away as she felt his grip lighten. "Now, you leave me alone. If I see you again anywhere close to here, I'll call the police."

She called them, anyway, as soon as she reached the studio, directing them to the man named Lonnie at the deli. All the court could do was issue a restraining order. It restricted him to fifty feet, just enough to allow him to follow her from the other side of the street wherever she went in the city. She had the order changed to prevent him from coming near her apartment.

The afternoon of her attack, Dreu had just stepped into her bedroom and was loosening her belt when he caught her from behind, one hand wrapped tightly over her mouth and the other pressing the tip of a long knife between her breasts. Dreu closed her eyes, clenched her teeth, and wondered fleetingly what it was going to feel like when the knife plunged into her heart.

"I'm going to take my hand away from your mouth. But if you scream, I'll kill you," he said without emotion.

She jerked her head forward into a quick nod.

"We are meant to be together," he whispered, his mouth only inches from her ear and his hand still tight across her mouth. "Will you listen to me?"

Again, she nodded.

He released her and sat her on the bed, pulling a white Jacobsen swan chair close to face her. He bent forward, the bird eyes piercing her own. She knew she couldn't look away if she wanted to live. The knife twitched nervously in a hand that rested on the arm of the chair a few feet away.

"Since I found Jesus, I have asked him to make known to me who I should marry. Who I will spend my life with and raise children unto the Lord." He studied her face to see if she was understanding, his head moving nervously side to side. She tried to look attentive and mask the terror that stiffened her body to the point of aching.

"When you came into the deli with your friend—the black woman—He spoke to me as if he were standing by my side. 'Lonnie,' he said. 'This is the one who was prepared for you from before the foundations of the Earth. She is the one who will be your bride.'" He leaned farther forward, cocking his head as a hawk might and peering up at her as if reading her thoughts.

He's completely insane was all that ran through her mind,

51

followed by a realization that if she were going to survive the night, she needed to pacify the man.

"And what God has ordained, no man can put asunder," he said, shaking his raptor head and waving the knife a few inches beneath her chin. "Don't you understand that?"

She waited until he lowered the knife and nodded slowly. "This is all so new to me," she whispered, licking her lips to keep the words from sticking in her mouth. "God hasn't said anything to me about this . . . ."

"This is a patriarchal order," he said dismissively, but seemed to calm. "The man will serve as channel and mouthpiece."

Work him, she thought. *Let him be the patriarch.* "Mmmm," she said with a nod. "I guess that makes sense. And what are we to do?"

"I can marry us myself," he said. "God has ordained me through a personal manifestation of the Holy Spirit."

Time, she thought. *I need to convince him I need some time.* She reached slowly forward and placed her hand on the one that was free of the knife, searching about in the recesses of her mind for something that sounded scriptural. "His will be done," she murmured. "And when will this take place?"

He leaned forward and kissed her chastely on the cheek. She froze against the shudder that surged along her spine.

"We can do it this evening. *Now!*" He bolted from the chair and looked frantically about the room. "Not in here. In the living room."

Dreu's mind raced. "Do you have a ring? It doesn't need to be much. But a ring has always been something I've dreamed about. Just a simple one . . . ."

He looked down at his hands in confusion and fumbled with his free hand at his pockets.

"I don't have a ring. I wasn't expecting you to agree to this tonight."

"Can we get one? I have some money in a jar in the closet."

"Where would I find a ring this late?"

"Pat Areias. It's only a block away over on Madison. There's about five hundred dollars in the jar. We can get something simple for that. I don't want much."

He looked at her narrowly, the hawk again eyeing his prey. "If I take you out, you'll run."

Dreu looked at him with what she hoped was shocked disbelief. "Do you believe that God has ordained this union?" she asked.

"I know He has."

"Then how can I run? I could not escape God."

He stood and studied her in silence for a long moment, looked about the room, then lifted a bathrobe from a hook on the open bathroom door and stripped out the terrycloth belt.

"I'll have to tie you. I don't trust in your faith."

She pulled her hands behind her and pressed the wrists together. "Tie my hands with that—and there's another robe in the closet. You can use that belt on my feet. You'd better hurry."

She shifted on the bed while he tied her hands, then stretched out on her back as her feet were bound.

"How did you get in?" she asked. "The doorman won't let you back in unless he calls me."

"I used the service door in the back," he said.

"Those have alarms on the crash bars . . . ."

"Not a problem if you know what you're doing. Just like your door lock."

"You'd better hurry," she repeated. "I just want a plain wedding band. Nothing fancy. That money should buy what I want."

He disappeared into the closet. She heard him sorting through the jar on her dresser. He stepped back into the bedroom, clutching a handful of bills. He looked at her thoughtfully for several seconds, then disappeared down the hall. She heard the door open and snap shut. Then silence.

When Dreu entered the apartment, she had dropped her purse on the table by the door, taken out her cell phone, and slipped it into the hip pocket of her jeans so she would remember to plug it in when she changed. She slipped her fingers down into the pocket and eased the phone out, clasping it firmly between her bound hands. She pressed the On button, swiped a finger across the face to bring up her security screen, and felt downward along the touch screen for the bottom-left corner. If she remembered correctly, there was an emergency-alert icon.

It took four blind presses on the screen before she heard the connection click and phone ring. She hurriedly tossed her hands to the side and released the phone, then rolled onto her stomach and slithered downward on the bed until the phone was next to her cheek.

"This is nine-one-one," the woman's voice said. "What is the nature of your emergency?"

"My name is Dreu Sason," she yelled into the phone. "I live in the . . ." She felt the knee press into the bed behind her as his hand reached across her face, lifted the phone, and shattered it against the floor behind her. He rolled her roughly onto her back and stood above her, his small eyes narrowed to dark slits. The knife rose above her in his right hand, and with his left, he tore away her blouse, snapped her bra between the cups, and pushed it aside.

"You have chosen a life that puts your body on display," he hissed. "I will show unto thee the judgment of the great whore." The knife slashed down across her chest, and she felt the blade pass through her right breast, cutting just below the nipple from side to side. Pain seared through her as if the blade had been on fire, and she began to swoon.

"If you cannot accept the will of God, no man will ever desire this body," she heard him scream above her own agonizing cry. He ripped at the waist of her pants, and she tried to twist away. But the bindings still held her hands and feet. Then the searing heat passed across her abdomen. She felt the skin and muscle on her belly separate. As she screamed herself into unconsciousness, the wail of sirens echoed against the canyon walls of downtown Manhattan.

Adam had been the first man she had allowed to view the devastation. New York and the runways of Fifth Avenue were long behind her, and she had established herself as a computer-security systems designer of some reputation. As their relationship had moved from friendly to flirtatious to serious fondness approaching intimacy, she knew she had to tell him about her attack and the thick, roped scars that remained.

"He broke into my apartment and attacked me with a knife," she confessed one evening as they sat together in her apartment. "Didn't want to kill me. Just punish me for, as he put it, 'putting my body on display.' So he cut me up so no one else would want me."

"I'm so sorry," he had murmured in a way that she knew meant "so sorry for you" and not "so sorry for me."

"How badly?" he asked.

She had raised her left hand to her right breast and placed her other across her stomach. "He slashed my breast almost in half—this way." She drew her index finger from under her right arm over to the middle of her chest. "And he cut across my stomach where he thought my uterus was. Got more intestine than uterus. Some amazing surgeons were able to get everything stitched back together and in place. But he did manage to ruin the uterus. There are some pretty ugly scars."

To her surprise, he had not shied away and not suggested it might be time to bring the evening to a close. He had straightened on the couch and moved his own hands to his lap. "May I see?" he asked.

All she remembered feeling at the time was an overwhelming sense of relief. She had slowly unbuttoned her shirt and lifted her bra. Her right breast, otherwise nicely shaped, had a pink, thick-edged crease that ran horizontally just below the dark circle of her nipple, with visible marks where the skin had been stapled together.

"They could have done more cosmetic surgery, but I didn't want it," she told him, looking down at the rope of scar tissue. "It is what it is, and I was getting sick of New York, anyway. The pressures of schedule, the paparazzi that hovered outside every place I went, and the constant, simpering attention of almost everyone. Plus, though most of the women who worked with me were intelligent, interesting people, we were treated as if we never had an original thought and were no more than underfed, pretty faces who had learned to strut."

She had replaced her bra and buttoned her shirt, then pushed her hips forward on the sofa and unzipped her jeans, wriggling her red underwear low enough to reveal another knotted scar that ran from hip bone to hip bone.

"He cut me top and bottom," she said, pulling the jeans back up and giving him a "Well, there you have it!" look.

Adam had remained silent for long enough to begin to make her uneasy, then raised his elbow to the back of the couch and rubbed his fingers across his chin. "Well, you're in luck," he said, reaching up to lift the black patch that covered his left eye. Beneath it, the prosthetic eye was perfectly matched in color and had a lifelike shine that made it almost indistinguishable from the right—but not quite. She looked back and forth between the eyes, then raised a questioning brow.

"This one," he said, pointing to the prosthesis, "happened to be my judgmental eye. It saw flaws in people that shouldn't have mattered. You've never asked about it—and I guess now I know why. I'll tell you sometime." He lowered the patch and pointed at the other. "This one is my 'thing of beauty' eye. It's all I have left . . . so when I look at you, and I mean *anywhere* on you, that's all I see."

Now, when they made love, he sometimes traced a finger along the scars until he found some especially sensitive spot, but she always knew he was seeing them through that remaining eye. She still found it uncomfortable to completely undress, wanting subconsciously to cover the marks that were such clear signs of imperfection. But Adam was the perfect lover: patient, playful, easing her through the self-consciousness until raw passion took over, and they could completely lose themselves in each other.

They had had such a night in the Clarion overlooking the Ålesund harbor—and such a morning. He had ordered in breakfast, and they had taken a long shower together. They now sat on the deep-blue sofas of the hotel's central longhouse atrium, waiting for their guests and looking completely satisfied, but a little worn.

"These men are all members of *Veteranenes Landsforbund*?" she asked, shifting slightly to be able to watch the door for the aged veterans.

He nodded. "The organization's dwindling as World War Two veterans die, but there's still a small chapter here. We'll see who comes."

As if on cue, the doors at the end of the hall opened. Two ancient men shuffled in hand in hand, a third following in a wheelchair being pushed by a young male attendant. Adam and Dreu rose, waved a welcome, and invited the men to matching sofas that faced theirs across a long, glass-topped table.

"I am Gunner Carlson," the man in the wheelchair said. "I am not one of the *Veteranenes Landsforbund*. But these men are not confident of their English. Our generation did not learn it like the younger people do." He introduced Arne Landvik, a thin stick of a man with a full head of silver-gray hair, and Kjell Vollen, whose round, age-spotted head was completely bald.

"Thank you. Thank you so much for meeting with us. My associate and I are journalists and are anxious to learn more about Norwegian Resistance activities in Ålesund during the Second

World War." He needed say no more. The old men's faces brightened. For the next hour, he and Dreu listened attentively as each told his story.

Arne Landvik explained that the Norwegian government had not prepared the country well for the outbreak of hostilities when the war began, and the army was easily overrun by Nazi forces. He had fought in the Battle of Narvik that had initially pushed the Germans back to the Swedish border, then escaped to England when Allied troops evacuated Norway in June, 1940. He had then served as a member of Norwegian Independent Company 1, operating out of Dumfries.

"We were basically a branch of the British Army," he said. "When the Allied forces returned to the continent, we fought with the British."

Kjell Vollan had served as part of the Second Mountain Company that in 1944 began a campaign against occupying Nazi forces from the northeastern county of Finnmark along the Finnish and Russian borders.

"We were supposed to be under Russian direction," he said with a broad smile that spread across most of his pale, stubble-covered face. "But they were too busy to give us much attention. We operated mostly on our own with support from the *Hjemmefronten*—the Home Front."

Mention of the Resistance movement gave Adam the opening he had been waiting for.

"I believe Ålesund played a major role in the Resistance," he said. "What can you tell me about what was happening here?"

Gunner Carlson entered the conversation as more than an interpreter.

"I was a boy of ten living in the city then. Some Norwegian soldiers had chosen to fight with the Germans, so there was great secrecy about who was with the *Hjemmefronten*. Do you know about the man they called Northern Lights?"

Adam and Dreu both feigned ignorance.

"He was an American airman who had joined the RAF before America came into the war," Carlson said. "He crashed his plane near the end of one of the fjords and was badly injured. The people from one of the villages brought him here. When he recovered, he broadcast German troop movements in Norway to British and American warships. The *Hjemmefronten* finally had to evacuate him when the Gestapo discovered where he was hiding."

"I would like to know more about this man," Adam said enthusiastically. "Is there anyone still living in the city who knew him?"

The three Norwegians spoke for several moments in their native tongue, punctuated in every other sentence by what the Americans understood to be the name Kari.

"You should visit with Kari Eikram," Carlson said finally. "She knew the American very well."

"And she's here in Ålesund?" Dreu asked.

Gunner pointed in the general direction of the sea. "She now lives on Giske Island. Arne knows her best."

"I haven't seen her for several years," the old soldier said. "But I know she is still living. Whether she can see you—or whether she remembers—who can say?"

11

Andrew waited until he could hear the compound's generator rumble to life beside the clinic before reheating half of a sweet potato and eating it with a banana and a cup of hot tea. He was scraping the orange potato skin into the trash bucket when the satellite phone buzzed at the end of the counter. Pushing the peel quickly into the metal container, he snatched up the phone.

"Andrew, this is Dad. Is your mother there?"

"She's at the city hospital. Have you heard about the Ebola? They stopped us on our way down to the village . . . ."

"There's a roadblock here on the Bolombo road. All they told us was that the city had been quarantined. Where did you hear anything about Ebola?"

"The soldier who stopped our boat said Ebola. They weren't sure, but Mom called from the hospital and sounded scared. I think it must be true."

"Is Belvie with you?"

"No. Mom said to send her home. What are you going to do?"

There was a long pause. He could hear his father talking to other men.

"We're going to try to cut through the bush to the airport road. It's been dry for a week. Kasim thinks there's a track the Rover can take that will bypass the barricade. If we join the road on the city side of the airport, we might be inside the zone they've blocked off. Are you doing OK?"

"Yeah. I'm OK."

"I'm going to try to call your mother. Sit tight until you hear from one of us."

"I'll be OK. Just try to get home."

"As soon as I can," his father said, and he was gone. Before

Andrew could put down the phone, it buzzed again in his hand.

"Dad?" he said quickly.

"This is Mom, Andrew. How are you?"

"I'm OK. Just talked to Dad. He's stuck on the road from Bolombo. They're going to try to cut across out by the airport road to get home. He's trying to call you."

"Are you feeling OK?"

He thought again about how he felt and answered truthfully. "Yeah. I'm fine."

"I need to ask you again to think about where your friends might all have been together. About three days ago."

"How're they doing, Mom? Are they going to be OK?"

"The doctors here are doing everything they can, Andrew. But they're very sick. And a few minutes ago, they brought Deo in. They're all here. Can you think of someplace you were together on Thursday or Friday after school? Maybe some place they did something that you didn't?"

"Naw. When we're together, we all pretty much do the same stuff."

"Well, if you think of anything, call me. Or if you start getting a headache. Stay there, and one of us will get home soon. I think your father's trying to call, so I'd better go . . . ."

When she was gone, he grabbed his Rubik's Cube from the table and threw himself into an old overstuffed armchair that, with a matching green couch and two straight-backed wooden chairs, served as furnishings for their sparse living room. He and his friends had spent most of the week together after school and had been over half the city. He started to twist through the steps of the Fridrick solution, closing his eyes and working down through the puzzle layer by layer. Tuesday was layer one. They were all students at Frere Illo's Catholic Institute on Revolution Avenue. On Tuesday after class they had walked through the back lot to a soccer field and played until dusk. Andrew spun the final row until a yellow cross appeared on the face he was working.

Wednesday? They had wandered through the city of low, block buildings and dusty streets all the way to the administration ground on Avenue de la Justice, thinking they might catch a bus from there down to the river market. There had been an aid truck there—some agency he didn't recognize—and they had helped the guy pass out boxes of baby formula to mothers who had somehow learned about the giveaway. There were no newspapers in Mbandaka and no radio station, but word-of-mouth moved news through the city like a brushfire. When the small panel truck pulled onto a patch of brittle, brown grass beside the dirt-packed drive leading to the administration building, there must have been thirty mothers waiting. They squatted flat-footed in their long, brightly patterned dresses, babies strapped across their chests with wide shawls or bouncing on ample hips. The man had asked Andrew and his friends to carry boxes of the free formula to a cluster of women huddled in the shade of an okoume tree. Pelo had dared them all to open a bottle and try some of the chalky liquid.

"It will be like sucking on a woman's tit," he'd said with a grin, unscrewing a tight ring, popping the metal cap, and reversing a rubber nipple that extended down into the bottle. He screwed the ring back around the nipple, tilted it upward, and sucked noisily.

"Tastes like your sister Anisa," he said, handing the bottle to Sese. Sese frowned and drew a long gulp from the bottle.

"No. This tastes like Sister Mary Claire," he said, referring to the young nun who taught them science. They all laughed, and Deo took the bottle. He sucked for a moment, looked thoughtfully up into the cloudless sky, and rubbed his chin dramatically.

"This came from that girl Pelo likes who sells cassava in the market. I milked her myself to get it . . . ."

Behind them, the man distributing the formula yelled across the open grounds. "Get those boxes to the women, and get out of here!" he shouted. Deo thrust the open bottle back into the box, and they hurried their cargo toward the waiting mothers.

"You'll have to wait until we go to the market on Saturday," Deo said, grinning at Andrew. "Maybe Pelo can convince her to give you a taste."

Andrew sat up in the armchair, his fingers frozen on the sides of the cube. Pelo, Sese, and Deo were at the hospital, his mother said—along with a bunch of babies.

Andrew snatched up the phone and punched the autodial number for his mother. He knew where the sickness had come from.

12

Giske Island was a small patch of pastureland at the mouth of the Ålesund fjords, centered by a quaint, whitewashed village. It was connected to the peninsula by a high-arched bridge that joined it to the island of Virga, then by tunnel to the mainland. Kari Eikram's white-clapboard cottage sat on the windward side of the island along an isolated stretch of rocky beach, separated by a broken hedgerow from a meadow where a pair of shaggy brown ponies grazed among a dozen equally shaggy rust-colored cattle. Harsh winters and incessant sea breezes had warped and twisted the wooden siding until the house's sides seemed to ripple like the breakers against the shoreline a hundred yards away. But the siding and window frames were freshly painted, and the thick-bladed grass in the small front garden was neatly clipped.

Adam knocked loudly on the solid spruce door, then stepped back to study the face of the cottage. Dreu stood a few steps behind along the gravel path.

A thin, indistinguishable voice came from somewhere beyond the door.

"Hello," Adam called. "Mrs. Eikram?"

"*Hvem er der?*" the voice called.

Dreu stepped to the door. "Hello? My name is Dreu Sason. We're from America and are friends of Bud Liljigren."

For a long minute, there was nothing. Then in faltering English, "Come in. The door is not locked."

Adam eased the door open and beckoned Dreu through in front of him. They entered a heavily curtained sitting room that contained an over-stuffed chair and sofa and a wooden rocker with a small side table. In the muted light from the open door, they saw a tiny woman encased in the rocker by red pillows, gazing up at

64

them with wide, milky eyes, an uncertain smile brightening her pale, crinkled face. A white knit cap nestled snuggly down across her ears, showing only a tuft of even-whiter hair that peeked out across her forehead. From neck to waist, she was wrapped in a knit shawl, her lap and legs tucked snuggly under a blue-woolen blanket. Although a lamp sat beside her on the table, it was not lit and no other light brightened the room. The woman had been knitting in the dark when she heard the knock and her hands, still holding the needles, rested across a partially completed scarf that draped over her knees onto the floor.

"I am sorry I can't get up to greet you," she said in the same wispy voice. "Once my granddaughter puts me in this chair, I stay here until she comes to make my lunch. Are there two of you?"

Dreu stepped forward and crouched in front of the rocker, laying a hand on the woman's frail wrist. "Yes. There are two of us. My name is Dreu. My friend's name is Adam. You must be Kari Eikram."

"I am," she said. "Please—turn on the light—and sit. The switch is there by the door." She freed a hand and waved it generally in front of her. Dreu perched on the arm of the larger chair where she was close to the old woman. Adam flipped the switch, illuminating the table lamp and another behind the easy-chair, then lowered himself onto the plain brown settee.

"We had a difficult time finding you," Dreu said, leaning forward and again taking Kari Eikram's hand. "We looked in the records for a Kari of about your age who lived in the Ålesund area and didn't find anyone."

The woman's smile saddened, and she blinked her pale eyes. "Bud has died, hasn't he?" she said. "He would have told you my name is really Katharine. But I have always been called Kari. It can be confusing."

"I understand," Dreu said. "I am partly Indian, and my given name is actually Dhriti. But when I was in school, my friends

65

called me Dreu, so that's what everyone knows me by." She smiled over at Adam, enjoying the moment of surprise on his face. He wasn't the only member of this team with a different name.

"And yes," she said, giving the woman's hand a light squeeze. "Bud passed away a few months ago. We just learned about you and wanted to come tell you personally."

Kari Eikram closed her eyes and leaned her head against the back of the rocker. Her visitors sat silently until she spoke again.

"I knew he must be gone. I always heard from him every week." She opened her eyes and looked blankly across the room. "Did you work with Bud?"

"Yes. Adam and I are taking over the work he was doing."

"Did the other woman know about me? His Anita? He loved her, too, you know."

Dreu glanced again at Adam. "She was the one who learned about you when she was going through Bud's files. She had known there was someone. And I think she knew it was someone very special to Bud. Can you tell us about his time here?"

Kari's dim eyes brightened as her memories took her back to a time when she was the only woman Bud Liljigren loved.

"When he crashed, they brought him to our home. My family were Haugens. I became Eikram when I married. My father was a fisherman, and we lived in Ålesund—right by the water. Bud was almost dead, and I was assigned to care for him. You might say I brought him back to life." She smiled at no ne in particular. "I taught him to be a whole person again when he thought he was only half a man."

She dropped her knitting needles into her lap and lifted Dreu's hand to the arm of the rocker, continuing to hold it as she spoke. She told of nursing the broken airman back to health, improving the English she was learning in school while she taught him Norwegian. Her parents were members of the *Hjemmefronten,* her mother spending her days traveling inland to scout German troop activity on the mainland while her father used his trawler to track maritime movement. When Bud was well enough to play a role, he took over command of the radio. It was kept on a sailing ship in the harbor, where the antenna could inconspicuously be run up a mast, the tallest point in the city. Each morning, Kari wheeled him to the pier and along a wide gangway that had been constructed just to accommodate the radioman. As reports came in from sea and countryside, the man who became known as Northern Lights broadcast information on troop strength and movement, naval activity, and successes of the *Hjemmefronten* to American and British warships. Kari Haugen was always at his side. After a year together, they pledged they would never be separated.

"But the war intervened," Dreu prompted.

"My parents went inland together one morning when there were reports of increased German activity in the mountains," Kari said, her voice barely above a whisper. "The Gestapo had been trying to track the broadcasts and had been into the city before, looking for the transmitter. When we knew the Germans were coming, the ship went to sea. But that day, my parents and several others from the city were captured and tortured. I didn't see them again. Those who got away came to the house and told us the Gestapo were coming for Bud."

Kari looked quickly in the direction of her visitors. "My parents didn't break," she added hastily. "Someone in the group did, and we carried Bud out through a door that went down to the docks only minutes before the Germans broke through the front. I stayed on the boat with him until he was moved to a hiding place over on Godoya, then to an American ship. He promised he would be back—but as you say, the war intervened."

Dreu leaned forward, looking into her pale eyes. "He continued to love you all these years. Even Anita said so. And you managed to stay in touch . . . ." Dreu looked around the simple sitting room for some indication of how the woman might have communicated.

Kari Eikram seemed to read her thoughts and gave a slight nod toward a low door that went into the back of the cottage. "There is a small kitchen and bedroom in the back. I have a computer on the kitchen table. My granddaughter, Sofi, sends messages for me. The island is very flat. We get good reception here."

Adam stepped into the conversation. "We were told that in some of your messages, you said you feared that foreigners had returned to Ålesund who were continuing what you called 'the old experiments.' And you thought they may be very dangerous. Can you tell us about them?"

The old woman's face sagged into a troubled frown.

"I learned that they were back from Sofi. Late in the war, the Germans built a large house near Hoffland, across the fjord. But the people who came there weren't military officers. They were scientists. They were very secretive about what they were doing in the house. One of the men became friendly with a friend of mine— a girl named Eva. She said he once told her that if they were successful with their experiments, they could end the war. That the weapon would never have to be used, but countries would surrender at the mere threat of its use."

Adam pushed himself forward to the edge of the sofa. "I know the Germans were doing a lot of work with rocket technology. And were making some progress on an atomic weapon. But I can't imagine some of that work being done here."

"I don't believe so," the woman said quietly. "From the way the scientist talked, Eva thought they were working on what we would now call a biological weapon."

"I didn't think the Germans got involved in germ warfare," Adam said. "The Japanese, yes. In fact, they experimented on some of their Chinese captors. But if the Germans were, that would be something new."

"After the war, the men all left, and the house was sold," Kari said. "It was searched by local police, but nothing was found. Then, about twenty years after the war, one of the men came back and purchased the house. A man from Yugoslavia. He said he was using it as a summer place. He was the son of one of the scientists, and the house has now been passed along to his son."

"And you suspect they are continuing the experiments?" Dreu asked.

"I was a married woman by the time they returned to the house but continued to write to Bud." Kari smiled to herself. "He didn't ever tell me what he did, but I knew it involved security and intelligence work. So I continued to be a suspicious person— especially when the son of an old scientist from the Reich moved back to the city. And I recognized a coincidence that I thought Bud needed to know about."

She paused until she could feel the full attention of her guests.

"The Yugoslav was from Belgrade," she said, as if the announcement carried more meaning than either of them recognized. The old woman tilted the rocker forward. "But he told people he worked in Marburg."

Dreu looked over at Adam and could see that his mind had ratcheted into another gear.

"When did the man return to the house?" he asked. Kari's smile revealed that she knew he was following her.

"Nineteen sixty-five."

Adam grunted. "And there were outbreaks of Marburg virus in both cities two years later."

She nodded with satisfaction.

Dreu turned in her chair to face Adam. "You'll have to catch me up here. I'm guessing you're suggesting this virus may have come from here. But I don't know about the outbreaks."

"Would you like . . . ," Adam began to say to Kari, but she waved a thin hand, letting him continue the explanation. He turned to Dreu.

"In 1967, there was an outbreak of a virus very similar to Ebola

69

in two cities in Europe—Marburg in Germany and Belgrade in Yugoslavia. Since then, it's been referred to as the Marburg virus, though it was eventually attributed to some test monkeys that had been imported into labs in both countries from Uganda. I don't remember the death toll, but it was several dozen. I think what Kari is suggesting is that the virus didn't arrive with the test monkeys but was given to them by scientists who had been working here. Is that about it?" He turned back to the Norwegian woman.

Kari nodded. "That's what I told Bud," she said.

"I don't want to minimize the seriousness," Dreu observed, "but several dozen isn't exactly an epidemic. It doesn't seem like a very effective biological weapon."

"It's controllable as long as you can keep people from direct contact with the exposed," Adam explained. "The disease is transmitted through bodily secretions of various kinds, and only when the sick are displaying symptoms. The virus is also very vulnerable to antiseptics. Even soap and water. So you can isolate the infected and wait the disease out. But among those who have it, the mortality rate is very high. You've read about the outbreaks of Ebola in Africa."

"All the more reason it isn't a very effective bioweapon," Dreu said. "Quarantine the sick, and the disease kills itself."

"Unless . . . ," the frail voice interrupted from the rocker. "Unless it can be modified. Bud called it 'weaponized.' He said if a mutation could be created that survived prolonged exposure to the air, it would mean airborne transmission. Then it would be extremely difficult to stop."

"And your fear," Dreu guessed, "is that the work is continuing with a goal to weaponize the Marburg virus."

"Have you been listening to the news?" Kari pointed at a pedestal flat-screen TV that sat on a low table opposite her in the room.

"We didn't see it this morning." Dreu glanced at Adam and

reddened slightly. "We got up a little late."

"There's been a new outbreak in the Congo," the old woman said. "They're still calling it Ebola. But there is fear it may be spreading through the air. I think that when they get it under a microscope, they will find it is Marburg."

13

The call from his mother awakened him just after 5:00 a.m. He had slept fitfully but finally slipped into deep slumber a few hours before the buzz startled him awake. The calm in his mother's voice was even more alarming to Andrew than the note of concern he had heard the previous night. He knew the tone. It was the voice she used when she had to pass along very bad news to a patient. She would spend a few moments preparing herself before she went into the room, eyes closed and drawing a few deep breaths. Sometimes, he thought she was praying.

She first asked if his father had made it to the house, then said in her trying-not-to-sound-alarmed voice, "There's been a new development here. I may have to stay longer than I expected. At least through today and possibly for another night. If your father doesn't find a way home, you'll still be on your own. Can you do that?"

"What's happened?" he said, looking with different eyes about the house that seemed even more silent in the early hours of morning.

"We've had some new patients come in overnight. Some that we can't trace to any direct contact with someone who is ill."

"So—what does that mean?"

"Well, in cases of this disease that we've seen before, transmission has depended on actual physical contact between two people. It's not like the flu or measles—or at least, it hasn't been. We need to make sure that hasn't changed before I come back to the house."

Andrew's heart sank into his stomach. "You're not sick, are you, Mom?" He tried to control his own panic.

"This is just a precaution." From the smoothness in her voice, he could tell she wasn't certain. "I've sent a message back to the States letting them know about my concern and that you may have information about how this got started. Someone may be calling you."

"So—if you aren't back tonight, do I go to school tomorrow?"

The calm in her voice disappeared. "*No. Absolutely not.* Don't leave the house for any reason. And don't allow anyone inside unless it's your father. Are you finding something to eat?"

"Yeah. I'm doing OK. When are you going to know anything?"

"I'll call you tonight and will know more then. Keep the phone charged."

"Are my friends doing OK?"

She paused long enough for him to know that they weren't. "If you are right about where this came from, they were the first to be exposed. They aren't doing well. I'll tell you more when I see you."

The phone buzzed against Andrew's ear, and he glanced at the "incoming call" message.

"Dad's calling," he said.

"OK. I'll call you later. Remember—stay inside, and don't let anyone in." Her pause this time told him she was struggling for composure. "I love you, Andrew," she said, and hung up.

Andrew blinked tears from the corners of his eyes and pressed the green Connect button on his father's call.

"Dad? Where are you?"

"Still at the airport. We tried again to get around the barricades but were stopped before we reached the outskirts of the city. They have the whole town sealed off. We'll try some other routes, but more soldiers are arriving every minute. You OK?"

"Yeah. I was just talking to Mom. She's not going to make it home 'til late—and maybe not tonight . . ."

"I spoke to her just before she called you," his father said. "She's just being careful." His mother hadn't mentioned that she had spoken to his father, and Andrew now heard the same concealed concern in his father's voice. He slumped slowly into a chair.

"There's a lot of canned food in the pantry, and we just had a water delivery, so you should be fine. Did your mother tell you to lock all the doors?"

"She said to not let anyone in."

"Lock the doors," his father repeated. "And don't open them for anyone but me or your mother."

"This is really bad, isn't it?" Andrew murmured.

"It could be. But if you stay inside and don't let anyone in, you'll be all right."

There was nothing in what Andrew was hearing that sounded all right in any way.

14

The white Ford Transit left the A513 on the north edge of Lisburn, Northern Ireland, following signs that directed prospective home buyers toward an openhouse in the new Ralave Meadows Estate. The first half mile wound through undeveloped land, the roadside bordered by thick gorse as high as the van's windows. Before a row of newly installed street lamps indicated that the area beyond was under development, the driver checked his mirrors to ensure no other vehicles were close behind, then turned left into an open field. He crossed to where a thick patch of heath remained untouched by the town's northward expansion and steered the Transit along a narrow track through a screen of bracken, bilberry, and bell heather until the path opened into a grassy clearing.

Leaving the van running, the man walked back along the track until he could again see the main road. Confident he hadn't been followed, he returned to the Transit and swung open its rear door.

From the cargo area, he drew what appeared to be two sturdy, folding music stands, extended them to a height of five feet, and placed them back-to-back a yard apart beside the van. He opened a case on the van's floor and, lifting out a spindly, black-metal apparatus, carefully unfolded its six arms. With a finger, he tested the tension on twin propellers mounted, one above the other, at the end of each arm. A gimbaled video camera, usually suspended beneath the xFold Dragon drone, had been moved to its top, leaving four open clips suspended from the arms on the craft's underside. The man carefully lifted the unfolded drone and balanced its five-foot frame across the two braces, returning to a second case to retrieve its payload.

Aside from a wire that extended a few inches from its side, the rectangular bundle in the smaller case appeared to be no more than a nondescript block of green clay, tightly wrapped in clear plastic. A metal loop protruded from the top of each corner. The man hunched beneath the drone, snapped the loops into four dangling clips, and ducked back out to inspect his work. Satisfied everything was in order, he drew a remote unit from his pocket, activated the camera, and returned to the back of the van where he booted up a thin laptop. Within seconds, the screen displayed a head-high view of the clearing in front of the van. As he rolled a control ball beneath his thumb, the drone's camera swept in a smooth arc, rolled forward to scan the ground around the stands, then swung upward to pan across a sky streaked with wispy horsetail clouds.

A second controller from the drone's case brought the twelve propellers to life. With a practiced hand, the operator lifted the machine smoothly from the stands. He swept it out over a vacant field to the south of his hiding place, returned it to hover immediately above him, then guided it west over the head-high gorse. He again held the drone in place until a camera sweep assured him the road was still clear. The craft crossed Magheralave Road at fifty feet, then dropped to ten until the camera showed it to be above a brush-covered wash.

Turning south, the Dragon skimmed above the draw until a small stream at its bottom emptied into a long, narrow lake. The pilot hovered the drone momentarily and swept the camera over the lake's surface, looking for boats and fishermen. Seeing none, he pressed the lever in his right hand gradually forward and sped the craft south over the water, then across a second tree-lined lake. At its far end, another streambed disappeared into thick woods.

The pilot eased the craft a hundred yards into the trees where a footbridge crossed the stream. Again, he hovered the drone until the camera picked up two joggers who had stopped to inspect the strange, six-armed hovercraft. Certain that it had been seen, the operator again lifted the Dragon to fifty feet. Swinging the camera to the east, he guided the drone out of the trees and across Duncans

Road, crossing the concertina wire that topped the high chain-link fence guarding Thiepval Barracks.

Using the broad football pitch in the center of the military installation to get his bearings, the drone pilot whirred his craft across the main street that divided the compound and lowered it slowly across the parking area in front of the headquarters building of the British Army's Thirty-Ninth Brigade. Responding to a practiced touch, the Dragon descended with its lethal cargo to eye-level a few feet from the building's main doors. Holding the craft steady, the operator snapped back a safety cover on a third controller that held only a button the size of a five-penny coin. "*Tiocfaidh ár lá,*" he muttered under his breath, and pushed the button.

The ensuing explosion shattered every window within two hundred yards of the entryway and demolished five offices that framed the doorway on two floors. Six military personnel and four civilian workers died instantly in the blast. Seven others were seriously wounded. Ninety seconds following the explosion, news outlets throughout the British Isles received the same three word tweet in Irish: *Tiocfaidh ár lá—Our day will come!* Everyone who saw it immediately recognized the old battle cry of the Provisional Irish Republican Army.

15

Adam stood on the gravel walk in front of the cottage and watched the grazing cattle as he relayed his conversation with Kari Eikram to Nita in the Scottsdale control center. Dreu had stayed inside with the old woman, seeing if she could nurse additional details from Kari's story about the Serbian's return to Ålesund.

"The man who's there now is a grandson of the original scientist and is known around Ålesund as Sava Gavran, though that may be an alias," Adam relayed to Nita. "See what you can learn about him. Almost all of Kari's information about the man came from her granddaughter, Sofi, who says he claims to come here to vacation. He doesn't seem to spend a lot of time in the old German house but is a real player. Loves the women. He's hit on the granddaughter a couple of times, even though she's married. Kari thinks the best way to find out what the guy's up to is to bring in someone who can seduce him—get the man involved in a little pillow talk."

Nita chuckled into the phone. "Our only female agent is Dee Quinly. I haven't met her personally, but you've seen her profile and photo. She's hardly the seductress type. Five-four. Solid as an iron post. Described as having the personality of a cornered bobcat. You might remember that she was one of the few women to make it through Special Forces training." Nita was silent for a few seconds, then said, "You know who the seductress on the team is."

"No way," Adam said sharply. "After that night in the cave in Budapest, Dreu's had enough field work. I won't even ask her."

"Just saying," Nita said. "But I have a suggestion. And I think it may be related. I track most of the high-level communication that goes on inside both the Bureau and the Agency. On the Agency side, there's been chatter about a highly effective biological weapon that's being offered for sale on the international market.

The CIA's working to set up a shill bidder to try to identify others who are interested, and possibly even acquire it themselves."

"How did you learn all this?" Adam asked, grinning at the shaggy cattle across the hedgerow. "I can't imagine this would have been discussed, even in encrypted e-mail."

"With internal communication, they're more careless than you'd like to believe," Nita said with the same humor in her voice. "I receive the daily encryption codes, and in this case, it was a coded interagency exchange. Once they encrypt a message, they aren't at all careful about what's said. A week ago, an FBI agent in Illinois sent a limited-access message to her Washington office, telling them a confidential source had informed her that organized crime in the state had been invited into the sale. The Mafia people not only didn't want to be players but wanted the federal security community to know about the offer."

"Protecting the national interest," Adam muttered.

Nita chuckled. "Since the seller is supposedly some foreign source, the Bureau passed the information along to the CIA, who immediately told the Bureau to get the agent to back off. Forget the whole thing about the bioweapon *and* the sale. In an exchange between directors, the CIA said they were putting together a team to track the sale and asked NSA to see if they could follow the cyber trail. That's the communication I've been able to follow so far, but I'm working on seeing what's being exchanged inside the Agency."

"If the CIA has some surrogate buyer in the game, it's a clear violation of the Biological Weapons Convention," Adam said. "But how does this relate to our seduction?"

"Some of the communication about the Illinois agent who reported the tip suggests she's being watched internally by the Bureau. They suspect she either collaborated with a professional killer during a recent kidnapping and murder, or was at least aware that he had been hired by the victim's family. There's even some suggestion that the two have a romantic relationship."

"The agent and the killer?"

"Yes. The Bureau's essentially banished her to Ireland to fill some request MI5 made for a female agent. But I did some checking on the woman. When Bud saw someone who seemed smart, capable, independent, and unhappy with a job in the armed forces or with one of the agencies, he liked me to work up a profile. That's where all of you wonderful people came from."

"And you've worked one up on this agent?"

"I haven't tried to find out anything about the boyfriend yet, but the woman has a great record, good training, and the kind of face you might be looking for. If the body matches, and if she's had her fill of the Bureau, she might be our seductress."

One of the cattle wandered over and gazed at Adam across the top of the hedge through a heavy thatch of matted hair, chewing contentedly.

"Name?" he asked, returning the cow's stare.

"Janet McIntire. Very nice-looking redhead. And a runner. So probably pretty fit. As I recall, she just turned thirty."

"Can you get me some contact information?"

"She's operating out of Dublin under the name Janet O'Brien. For reasons that may have been confirmed today, MI5's concerned about a resurgence of IRA activity in Northern Ireland, and they're trying in infiltrate. Contacting her might put her in jeopardy."

"I haven't been staying on top of the news. What was today's confirmation?"

"There was an explosion at British Regimental Headquarters south of Belfast. A bomb brought in by drone. Check tonight's news. It will be top story."

"Kari said there'd also been an Ebola outbreak. Sounds like a bad news day. I'll check out both stories. We're about through here. Get me what information you can on the agent. If she looks like our kind of woman, I'll figure out how to get to her without putting her at risk."

"I'll have something to you this evening." Nita paused, then asked, "Tell me about Kari Eikram."

Adam couldn't resist a smile. "She's a very tiny, blind old lady. But she's still got the heart of a Resistance fighter. You'd like her, Nita."

"I think I would," Nita said.

* * *

Adam and Dreu flew Norwegian Air from Ålesund to Dublin with a brief stopover in Oslo. Adam had booked a room at Dublin's Best Western Skylon in the Drumcondra suburb, a short drive from Glasnevin Cemetery and John Kavanagh's "Gravediggers" pub. As they sat in the Oslo airport waiting for the second leg of the flight, he and Dreu worked through their contact plan.

"Nita's message says we'll find her at Kavanagh's every evening after six," Adam said, opening the encrypted text on his phone. "Patrick Flynn and his people come in about six thirty. Janet leaves shortly after they do, about eight. Once last week she stayed later just with Flynn, and another evening they went elsewhere to have dinner together. So far, they seem to still be in the 'getting acquainted' stage."

"I could approach her in Kavanagh's before Flynn arrives," Dreu said. "Arrange for a meet between the two of you somewhere that's more private."

He frowned skeptically. "If Flynn's starting to take an interest in her, I don't think we can assume she isn't being monitored. Not just who she talks to, but what she says. The approach is going to have to be casual, natural, and on the surface, completely innocent."

"I could just be another American visitor who's been steered to her to get a perspective on what's worth seeing in Dublin. I can slip her a note asking her to come to the hotel—or any other place you want to meet."

"If they're at all suspicious, she might also be under video surveillance. She apparently sits in the same place every evening. I don't want to take the risk of slipping her a note."

For the thirty minutes until their flight was called, they looked over a rough diagram of Kavanagh's and talked through alternatives until satisfied with a plan.

"That should work," he said as their flight to Dublin began to board. "We'll just have to count on her being able to shake a tail if she decides to meet with us."

"If she can't, we don't want her," Dreu said.

16

The knocking was at first timid, then became insistent. With the windows covered, Andrew couldn't see who was on the porch. His first thought was that his father had found a way through the ring of soldiers that surrounded the city. He hadn't heard from either parent since morning, and it was now late afternoon. When he had tried to call, no one answered, and he had shuttered and barred the windows of the two-story block mission house. But his father wouldn't knock. He had a key and would try to let himself in before finding the keyless deadbolt in place. Then he would call to Andrew from the porch.

"Who's there?" Andrew shouted through the door in English, then followed in French. "*Qui est là?*"

The response came in French. A woman's voice. "We need the doctors. Are they here?"

Andrew backed away from the door "My dad's gone out of the city, and Mom's at the community hospital," he shouted. "Go to the clinic at the end of the compound. Dr. Degan should be there."

"There are hundreds of people there. All of the city is sick. Even the doctor isn't well. We need medicine."

"We don't keep any medicine in the house. Go to the hospital. Mother should be there and will try to help you."

"Can we have food? There is no food anywhere. All of the shops are empty."

"I can't let anyone in," he called, followed by a weak, "I'm sorry. I just can't let anyone in."

There was silence, then footsteps on the porch and steps. He waited until he heard the metal gate snap shut in the compound wall, then went to the pantry. He loaded a cardboard box with as many cans of fruit, vegetables, and Vienna sausage as he could lift, adding three boxes of crackers to the top. The house was a simple rectangle divided in half by a hallway that ran from the front entrance straight through to a rear door that opened onto a fenced backyard. One side of the lower floor was taken up by a sitting room and small parlor. The other was divided between a front dining room and rear kitchen. The pantry was a long, narrow room that separated the kitchen from the rear hallway. Across from it, a set of steep stairs climbed to the second floor that held three bedrooms and what had once been a sewing room. The family now used it for general storage.

Andrew struggled up the stairs with the heavy box, placed it on the floor beside his bed, and made his way down the upper hallway to the storage room and to a tall cabinet that was absolutely off-limits. It was secured with a heavy padlock for which he had no key. But he had always thought of the lock as no more than a minor inconvenience to anyone who really wanted to get in. It was looped through the eye of a tarnished hasp, held in place by four short wood screws.

Andrew retrieved his father's toolbox from the corner of the musty room, found a heavy flat-headed screwdriver, and thrust the end down behind the hasp arm. Three hard tugs ripped the screws from the wood, and he swung the cabinet open.

He knew he would find only three things in the case, three things he had been forbidden to use: a long machete with a razor-sharp edge that his father used to thin a stand of bamboo that invaded one corner of the dusty backyard; an ancient Mauser M 98 rifle; and a box of 8 × 60 mm cartridges. Andrew hoisted the heavy weapon from the cabinet and carried it with the box of cartridges into his room, placing them carefully on the bed.

He went to the window and pulled back the slatted wood shutters. The dirt road beyond the front wall of the compound was eerily quiet, the usual steady flow of carts and aged pickups reduced to an occasional passerby on foot headed in the direction of the clinic. From the river, he heard what sounded like gunfire, and he glanced quickly back at the bed.

He had fired the rifle only twice—a few practice rounds after a departing missionary gave the weapon to his father to carry into the countryside when he visited villages in the bush.

"Most of the wildlife want to stay away from you as much as you want to avoid them," the man said. "But once in a while, you'll stumble across something that's just feeling ornery. This will stop most things. But if you encounter an angry elephant or rhino, just get the hell out of there."

The test firing in a secluded clearing east of the city was part of what his father called "learning something you should know as a young man." His dad had shown him how to press the long cartridges down into the top of the breach, lift and throw the bolt to chamber a round, then brace his feet and steady the heavy gun tightly against his shoulder.

"Now—take a breath and let it out as you aim. Then smoothly squeeze the trigger," his father instructed. The first shot had jarring Andrew backward onto his seat, and he had suggested one practice round might be enough.

"Give it a try in a sitting position," his father urged. "Put your heels together, knees apart, and brace your elbows against your knees." Andrew had reluctantly agreed, wanted to show his father that he was worthy of learning what a young man should know. The second blast had still rocked him backward, but he stayed upright.

"Lesson for today," his dad said as they drove back into the city. "These weapons are not toys and must always be handled with respect and care."

Andrew didn't remember the Mauser ever being taken from the cabinet since. But he remembered how to load the rifle, how to throw the bolt to put a cartridge in the chamber, and how to brace himself. If he needed to . . . .

Down in the dusty street, two men paused outside the compound wall to study the house, then pushed open the black-iron gate into the narrow front yard. Both carried machetes. Once inside the wall, they split up: one moving around the side to Andrew's left, the other climbing the steps to the front door. The pounding on the door sounded like the man was driving the handle of his machete into the thick wood.

"*Ouvrez!*" the man shouted. "Open! We need food and medicine!"

Andrew quietly closed the shutters and threw the latch. Slipping off his shoes, he crossed to the bed and peeled open the box of cartridges, tipping them onto the bedspread. He lifted the heavy Mauser, forced the bolt up and back, and sat back on the bed, the rifle across his lap.

Below him on the porch, he heard the man throw his shoulder against the locked door. It cracked against his weight, and Andrew knew the deadbolt was breaking through the frame. At the rear of the house, the second man slammed against the door in back. Andrew grabbed a cartridge from the spread, seated it in the open breech, and pushed downward. The bullet moved, then jammed in the narrow slot. He clawed at it desperately as the man in front slammed again against the breaking wood.

Andrew managed to pry the cartridge loose, this time pressing his fingers against the outside of the magazine as he tried again to push the bullet smoothly into place with his thumbs. It snapped down securely. He pressed a second in on top of it, then a third. In the hallway below, he could hear the front door breaking in its frame and another crash against the rear.

He pushed off the bed with the old Mauser pressed across his chest and padded in stocking feet to the head of the stairs. Channeling his session with his father in the clearing, he dropped into a sitting position, back against the wall, the stock firmly seated against his right shoulder, feet together, and elbows propped between his knees. He heard the back door open and the two men push into the pantry. They spoke in muffled French, gathering up what food Andrew had left on the shelves, then moved back into the hallway where they divided to search the lower floor. Andrew gripped the stock of the Mauser until his hands ached, his heart pounding so loudly he feared the men could hear it over the din of their ransacking the lower floor.

The looters met again in the hallway below. He heard one of the men say something about medicine, then "*en haut.*" They were headed upstairs. The pair stepped together into the bottom of the stairwell and began to climb without looking up, their arms holding the few cans and boxes they had scavenged from the pantry.

"*Arrêtez!*" he shouted in a voice that broke on the second syllable. The men froze in place, looking up at the boy with the ancient rifle propped between his legs, its black barrel pointed at them. A wide grin spread across the face of the man on the right, and he muttered something to the other in a dialect Andrew didn't understand. Together, they took another step upward. Andrew remembered suddenly that he had failed to put a round in the chamber.

As the men eased up another step, he grabbed the bolt, drew it back quickly, and slammed it forward. The action seemed to jar the men into motion, and they surged upward. Andrew closed his eyes, gritted his teeth, and squeezed the trigger. The hallway around him seemed to explode. The rifle butt slammed him back against the wall like he had been hit by a full swing from a ball bat.

17

From her station beside the door, Janet noticed the woman the moment she walked into Kavanagh's. She wasn't a woman who was easily overlooked—tall, slender, and strikingly pretty. Her raven hair fell in loose waves midway down her back, and her large dark eyes were set under brows that, even at a distance, looked like hours had been spent shaping them to perfection. The woman passed her table and went first to the bar, spoke casually to Fiona, the barmaid, then turned toward her as Fiona pointed her way. The dark eyes took her in with what appeared to be approval, and the woman smiled and nodded. A moment later, she was standing across the table from Janet.

"Excuse me," the woman said in American English, "but I'm looking for someone who can tell me what to see in Dublin from an experienced American perspective. We're here for a couple of days, have seen the tourist highlights, and are looking for those hidden treasures that the locals might overlook because they're so familiar with them. I understand you've been here a couple of months and wondered if you would help us?"

"Us?" Janet said, looking past the woman at the mainly empty tables in the pub's small dining area.

"My friend and me. It embarrasses him to just stop people and ask like this. I'm willing to risk looking a little foolish. He's over on the other side in the bar. One of the men there said I'd probably find you here."

Janet nodded at the bench beside her. "Have a seat. What kinds of things are you interested in?"

"It's more what *he's* interested in. He has some Irish ancestry from Leinster and I think is looking for a genuine taste of old Ireland."

"His people came from Dublin proper? Or from one of the outlying areas?"

"He thinks maybe Dalkey, which I guess is now a southern suburb."

"Pretty harbor town," Janet said. "With an interesting old castle. Have you been down there yet?"

"Probably tomorrow morning. We were looking for other things to catch when we went that direction. By the way, I'm Tanvi Russell." The woman extended a hand. "What brings you to Ireland?"

"Janet O'Brien," she offered. "I'm a grad student studying Old Irish language."

"No kidding!" the woman said, straightening on the bench. "Tom's grandfather knew some Gaelic and used to try to teach it to his grandkids! Have you got a second? I'd like you to meet him. Will your things be all right here for a minute? Come over and let me introduce you!"

Janet glanced down at the time block in the corner of her computer screen. The Flynn bunch shouldn't be arriving for another half hour, and she should probably act like any grad student who'd been away from home for a few months.

"Sure. Nobody will touch things here. I'm here every day, and if someone messes with my things, Fiona will jump all over them." She slid from the bench after Tanvi and followed her outside and down the short walk to the tavern side of Gravediggers. The pub had been built just beyond the walls of Glasnevin Cemetery the year after the graveyard opened in 1832, and the tavern side didn't appear to have been touched since. Its old wooden tables and narrow benches were scarred and stained by a century and a half of spilled pints and by the calloused hands of the gravediggers that gave it its nickname. The woman who called herself Tanvi led her to one of the half dozen tables where a nice-looking man of about thirty-five sat nursing a Guinness. His light-brown hair was shoulder-length and pulled into a thick ponytail. He stood as Tanvi brought her toward him and gestured to the opposite bench.

"I see Tanvi's found a victim," he said with a light laugh. "I'm Tom. Please join us."

"Janet," she said by way of introduction and slid onto the bench across from him to the spot against the wall. It was early, and there were only three other customers clustered together at the rear corner table, arguing about Irish football.

"I understand you have some ancestry from down the bay at Dalkey," Janet said. "And a grandfather that spoke some Gaelic." Tanvi had pushed in beside her.

Tom leaned forward onto his elbows. "True on both counts," he said, his smile broadening. He slid a partially unfolded map across in front of her. "Could you take a glance at this map and suggest which of the highlighted places we ought to visit?"

Janet knew instantly that it was not the map she was being asked to examine and that this conversation wasn't about what to see in County Dublin. She resisted the urge to stand and push past Tanvi. Keeping her expression unchanged, she slid the map closer in front of her. A printed note was taped across central Dublin.

We are with a national security agency of the US government other than the FBI. We would like to visit with you privately at a place of your choosing about having you join our team. We have backgrounded you thoroughly, believe you would be a good fit, and would enjoy the kind of work we do. If interested, give me a call by midnight tonight at the speed-dial number on the phone I will give you. If not interested in hearing the offer, don't call, and that will be the last you hear from us.

What the hell is this? she thought, reading the note over a second time. The safe and wise thing to do would be to excuse herself and walk away right now. Were these some of Flynn's people trying to get her to break cover? Some kind of loyalty check from the Inspector General's office at the Bureau? She looked back up at the tall man across the table, noticing for some reason that she couldn't imagine that the pupils of his eyes were not exactly the same.

She slid the map back toward him. "There are so many options here, it's hard for me to make an immediate recommendation."

"I understand," he said. "Give it some thought. If you think you might have something that would be of interest to us, give me a call." Janet felt the woman beside her slide a small phone against her hip.

"I'll do that." She reached down and slipped the phone into her jeans pocket. "Now, I'd better get back to my studies."

The woman who called herself Tanvi stood and allowed her to slide from behind the table. "I hope we hear from you. We'd be very interested in your suggestions. And by the way, we may have a mutual friend—Michael Bond."

Janet hardly noticed the Flynn group as they ambled into Kavanagh's a few at a time, casually swept the area around their booth with an electronic sensor, and settled around the table. Patrick arrived last and gave her a friendly nod, politely returned, but without any real thought about the man she knew had probably planned the recent bombing at Thiepval Barracks. She was still completely engaged in trying to figure out what had just happened with the woman who called herself Tanvi and the Tom with the prosthetic eye.

They weren't part of Flynn's operation—or if they were, she was in deep shit. Whoever they were, they knew about Michael. If it was Flynn, she doubted he would take her through this charade. He'd just have her disposed of. And his group had seemed perfectly normal as they arrived this evening. Though the dining side of Kavanagh's served only tapas after six thirty, it had become something of a tradition for the cook to save Flynn a bowl of Irish coddle that he ate while his men talked. Since he and Janet had become more friendly, he now began his meal by saluting her with a spoonful of the steaming soup and *"Bain taitneamh as,"* the Irish equivalent of *bon appétit*! As he did so this evening, there was no trace of suspicion or uncertainty.

The FBI's office of the Inspector General? Why would they be messing with her now? She'd reported her suspicion that Flynn and his men had planned the Ulster bombing, recounting how one had even mimicked the flight of the drone with his hands, including a culminating blast, as she watched from her table. Her contact at MI5 was increasingly impatient with the speed with which she was establishing a relationship with Flynn. But from what contact she had had with the Irishman, she was convinced that trying to force her way into his inner circle would be disastrous. Flynn was cautious by nature, liked to handpick his acolytes, and took great pride in carefully wooing them to his way of thinking. British Intelligence had tried to force people in before, and they had all been discovered. Now they were trying to push her into making the same mistakes. She had refused, but as far as she knew, she was the British agency's only set of eyes on the ground. Why would the Bureau want to mess with her now?

The other possibility, of course, was that this was exactly what it was presented as being: a contact by another agency that was interested in her services. Members of the American intelligence community certainly weren't above recruiting from one another. She was feeling less and less loyalty to the Bureau, and that was probably not a secret. But who else might be interested—especially if they suspected she had a relationship with Michael? She knew that if she didn't call, the uncertainty would drive her crazy. And if she did, what was the worst that could happen?

She placed the call during her late-evening run through Glasnevin Cemetery. The expansive graveyard was circled and crisscrossed by wide, paved paths. She could run for a mile without covering the same ground. And she found that running through the ghostly shadows cast by regiments of towering Celtic crosses and the breeze-rustled branches of century-old yews gave a boost to her adrenaline. She usually finished her five-mile run both exhausted and completely alert. Making the call simply added to the rush.

She paused for a moment to push the autodial, then listened through a small headset as she resumed her pace. Tom answered immediately with a perfunctory "Yes?"

"I'm interested in hearing what you have to say," Janet said without formalities.

"Where are you?"

Janet glanced around at the tall granite crosses that lined both sides of the path. "I'm about halfway down the main drive toward the back of Glasnevin Cemetery. I run here every evening."

"So, you're a runner."

"Runner. Rock climber. Skier. Anything outdoors. But my graduate-student status here hasn't given me much opportunity to do anything but run."

"I assume you're alone and can't be overheard?"

"I'm pretty confident no one can overhear. But just to be safe, you talk, and I'll listen."

"Fair enough. I'd like to make you an employment offer. I represent a small group that takes care of problems for the US government that are either too messy or too sensitive for the visible federal agencies to handle. We think you'd be right for our team."

"Not the group I'm with now?" she asked, quickly checking a cross path to insure no one was nearby.

"No, but very indirectly connected to the CIA. We use their systems for much of our information."

"Is this call encrypted?" Janet asked, concerned that even the mention of central intelligence on an open channel might attract attention somewhere.

"Yes. That's why we gave you the phone. Is this something that would interest you?"

She had reached the path that divided the cemetery running east-west and turned left, working her way toward the wall opposite the gate that exited beside Gravediggers. "Give me an example of the kind of work you do."

"Most of what we do, you don't hear about because we stop it before it happens. In other cases, the final result is credited to some other group. But the power outage in the Northwest a year ago was designed to be nationwide. We got to the perpetrators before it could fully be implemented."

Janet ran in silence for a moment, considering what she was hearing. "Why do you think I might be interested—and be any good at the kinds of things you do?"

"We know about your conversation with the deputy and about his concern that your friendship with Michael Bond might be compromising your commitment to duty. That's one of the reasons you're attractive to us. Our group is made up of people who have a history of not playing by the rules."

"I've always played by the rules,'" Janet said testily. "What Michael Bond does is his business."

"Even when you're aware of it?" the man asked. "We've looked into Bond's background, and frankly, we don't have major problems with what he does. In every one of his cases we've been able to follow, he was cleaning up for failures of the judicial system. We're not in altogether different lines of work."

Again, Janet paused. "So, you like Michael. But what makes you think *I'm* right for you?"

"You were a brilliant law student at the University of New Mexico, chose to go into law enforcement instead of practice law, and were one of the top Academy graduates at Quantico. Your service in Dallas was stellar, and you showed real nerve and common sense in breaking up that bank heist. Since the Curren kidnapping and the suspicion that surrounded Bond's role, you've been something of a pain in the ass to the Bureau. I know you're fond of the guy, but mainly, you're protecting him because you believe he did the right thing. Those are all traits we like in our people."

"You've done your homework. What do you know about my current assignment?"

"Almost everything. Including that MI5 is impatient with your pace."

She turned right along the western edge of the cemetery. As she moved toward the back, the markers became simpler and the grounds less well kept. In places, headstones had fallen into the high grass. Some of the oldest graves had sunken into shallow pits.

"And what do *you* think of my pace?" she asked.

"Our agents all work independently and determine their own pace. We figure they know the people and situations better than we do. So they make the calls."

"And what kinds of things do you expect of them? Principally intelligence gathering and surveillance, or more active intervention?"

"If you mean assassination? Seduction? Those might be expectations from our people. As long as we're confident that we are achieving the right result, we have an open playbook."

"And who determines what the *right result* is?"

"The agent and our manager—a man we call Fisher. Between the two, they decide on the appropriate resolution."

"Without approval from elsewhere?"

"Only internal approval. That's our mandate."

"And I assume the 'appropriate resolution' is that which best protects the national security interests of the United States," Janet suggested. She had turned along the path that separated the cemetery from the national botanical garden. An eight-foot gray-stone wall pressed against the pavement on her left. Much of the back of the cemetery looked as if it had been neglected since the markers were placed in the mid-1800s.

"Protects national security and supports the public good," the man corrected.

"Not always the same?" Janet challenged to see what he would say.

He was silent for a moment, then said, "The situation you reported to the Bureau—about the biological agent. Suppose it were determined that our government was trying to obtain that agent. Possibly good for national security. Potentially not in the best interest of the public. In those cases, the agent and Fisher determine the best solution."

"You *have* done your homework!" Janet chuckled. Just past a large cedar, the path and wall took a sharp right, and she turned along what she judged to be a crematorium.

"That's one of the reasons we're interested in you," Tom said. "We think we may have inadvertently linked into this bioweapons case. There's some possibility that our government might be thinking about becoming a player—an idea that may have occurred to you, but that we don't think much of. As far as we're concerned, bioweapons shouldn't be in anyone's hands. Even ours. We need someone like you to help us find and eliminate them."

Janet snorted into the phone. "This is beginning to sound more like an IG loyalty check. And I have nothing to do with the bio-threat deal anymore . . ."

Adam interrupted. "We're not Bureau, McIntire. Do you want a quick review of all we know about you? Bank account balances? Relatives back for three generations? Your father's record as a police detective? How each of your parents died? This is no IG investigation, and if my offer has no appeal to you, we can end this conversation now."

More silence. "If I were interested, what then?" she said finally.

"We need to talk again. Personally. And at greater length. We need to bring some resolution to your current situation, and you

Allen Kent

need to disappear. Even as far as the Bureau's concerned."

"You can get that done?"

"I have a suggestion as to how we can accomplish both. But Janet O'Brien disappears, and Janet McIntire with her. Your records will all be purged, and you'll be given a new identity. A little help to alter your appearance, but probably not until this bio-threat issue is resolved. We need to move quickly on it and will need your help immediately."

This time the silence lasted for a full minute as Janet absorbed what she was hearing. She knew Tom would hear that she was still connected by the sound of her breathing and footfalls on the paved path.

"And all former associates?" she said finally.

"If you mean Bond, I'm not certain. We might find his talents useful. Everyone else, there are no former associations."

"Can I think about this?"

"I need to know within an hour. If you're not in, I need to find someone else. But you're the person we want."

"I'll call within an hour. This number?"

"Yes—and no consultations. We'll be monitoring your activities."

Again, Janet sniffed into the phone. "I'm sure you will," she said.

97

18

In the stairwell below, one of the men screamed. Andrew heard him tumble backward down the steps, cans and boxes clattering after him.

The boy opened his eyes and stared at the second figure who had frozen in place ten feet in front of him. Without conscious thought, Andrew jerked back the bolt and rammed another round into the chamber, the empty shell casing sounding a metallic alarm as it hit the floor beside him. He swung the barrel to center it on the second man's chest.

The man raised his hands and backed slowly downward. Behind him, his partner struggled to his feet, his right shoulder bleeding heavily and arm hanging limp. With the uninjured man propping his partner's good arm over his shoulder, the intruders eased sideways into the rear hallway. Andrew heard the back screen door bang behind them. He sat motionless, his breath trapped and his hands gripped like vises around the ancient Mauser. In the backyard, the wounded man screamed as he was dragged around the corner of the house. Andrew scrambled quickly to his feet and dashed through the bedroom to the window, throwing back the shutter and watching as the men stumbled through the gate and fled down the road toward the clinic.

Andrew refastened the slatted window cover and made his way quietly back to the top of the stairs. He had to seal the front again and close up the rear more securely. If more came—a few at a time—he could defend the windows, but not the doors. He needed the toolbox and . . . . The thought jolted through his mind like the slam of the rifle against his shoulder. *What if the men were already infected—and the disease was in the blood that covered the wall in the stairwell and coated the steps? And what if it spreads through the air? Was the house already contaminated?*

He propped the Mauser against the wall, retrieved the toolbox from the storage room, and went into his parents' room. In a bottom drawer in their bathroom, he found green surgical masks and a box of disposable latex gloves. From a drawer in his own closet, he dug out a long-sleeved shirt and the pair of goggles his father made him wear when they sprayed outside for mosquitos. With mask, gloves, and goggles in place, he returned to the closet for a bottle of bleach, a mop, and a plastic bucket. He filled the bucket from the shower, poured in a third of the bleach, and edged slowly down the staircase, mopping as he went.

The Mauser had blown a baseball-size hole in the wall after passing through the man's shoulder. At arm's length, he sloshed disinfected water into the gap. He emptied the bucket into the tub and refilled it. When the second bucket again flushed pink with blood, he hopped from the bottom step across a pool that covered much of the rear hallway and started working from the sink in the kitchen. He had seen four more bottles of Clorox in the pantry, a six-month supply his mother brought back from their rare trips into Kinshasa. When the hallway had been scrubbed, he emptied the remainder of a second jug into a half bucket of water and went over everything again.

When satisfied he had thoroughly washed every splattered surface, Andrew again closed and locked the back door and hoisted the front back into its frame. He forced a heavy hall table in front of it and jammed a chair from the kitchen under the edge of the table, wedging it more tightly against the shattered entrance. There were nails, a hammer, screws, and a hand drill in the box, but he needed lumber. His first thought was the leaf of the dining table, but he thought it might be teak. He'd never get a nail through it. Then he remembered the gun cabinet upstairs. With mask and eye covering still in place, he left the Mauser and toolbox in the kitchen, remounted the sanitized stairway carrying a hammer and short pry bar, and went to work on the tall wooden chest.

An hour later, he'd nailed three boards across each of the exterior doors and stacked whatever furniture he could slide across the bare floors tightly against them. What little light he could see through slats in the shutters was beginning to fade. Gunfire still echoed from the river. Andrew tried to hoist one of the five-liter water bottles onto his bruised shoulder, but had to settle for cradling it in his arms as he again struggled up the steps. With a pillow from his bed propped against the hallway wall at the top of the staircase, he sat cross-legged and leaned back into the cushion, pressing three more rounds into the Mauser. His shoulder ached where the rifle had slammed him against the wall, and he rolled it gingerly and massaged the bruise with his other hand. Arranging his favorite cube, the Mauser, and the satellite phone beside him on the hall floor, he hunched back against the wall, adjusted the mask and goggles, and gazed forlornly down the stairs.

19

When he met her at the door of the room at the Best Western Skylon, the man who called himself Tom had covered his prosthetic left eye with a black patch. He ushered her into the room where his partner, Tanvi, quickly patted her down and swept a wand over her body.

"I can see we've already achieved a high level of trust," Janet said dryly.

"We haven't achieved anything yet," Tom said. "You're certain you weren't followed?"

"Certain. And you're confident this room is secure?"

"No one knew we were coming here. We scheduled the hotel on the way, asking for two rooms at the end of the hall. And we've swept them both. Please—have a seat."

The room offered only a desk and armchair. She took the desk chair, swiveling it to face the pair. Tanvi settled into the armchair, and the one-eyed agent sat facing her on the edge of the bed. He came directly to the point.

"You've had a few hours to consider our proposal. What do you think?"

"I'm intrigued, but I'd like to know more about how you think you can take care of my current situation and make it—and me—disappear."

"You're quite confident that Flynn and his group are responsible for the explosion at Thiepval Barracks?"

"Yes. Very confident. They have what's almost a private booth at Gravediggers and protect their little table area about as well as you protect this room. Fiona—the barmaid—keeps the booth open until one of them arrives right at six thirty. He sweeps it every time he comes in with some kind of handheld device, and they keep a sensor live on the table while they meet. But as you saw, the place is small. I've been able to pick up bits of conversation with an amplifier in my computer. And I can see and record everything that goes on in the booth—like their hand gestures. I'm confident they sent in the drone."

"How do you listen without raising suspicion?" Tanvi asked.

"I'm a language student. I study with headphones on all the time."

"How deep is Flynn's organization?" Tom asked. "By that, I mean, if he were gone, what other leadership is there?"

"That's pretty hard to judge. I've had dinner with him a few times, and we've just started to touch on the subject of Irish independence. I'm letting him do all the initiating. It's important, I think, that he see me as a reluctant recruit. But if I had to venture a guess? I'd say it's pretty much his show at this point. If he weren't running the operation, I don't think he has anyone in a position to step up, if that's what you mean."

Tom leaned back loosely onto his hands. "Then my suggestion would be that the next time Mr. Flynn works on putting a bomb together, he makes a fatal mistake."

"We kill Flynn?" Janet knew her voice reflected surprise, if not shock. "I said I was quite certain, but I don't have any real evidence."

"I hear a lawyer and FBI agent talking," Tom said, cocking his head to one side. "How certain are you that he planned the bombing?"

"Certain."

"But not certain enough to pronounce judgment?"

Janet stared intently into the one exposed hazel eye. It didn't seem to be challenging her as much as assessing. Was she certain enough? And comfortable with a death sentence? This was exactly the kind of judgment her friend Michael made all the time, and she had condoned it on two other occasions.

She nodded. "Certain enough to pronounce judgment."

Tom leaned forward with elbows on knees. "Then you need to go with him."

"Go with him?"

"Be blown to smithereens."

She stared again into the single eye, working through what she knew he was suggesting.

"I'm not sure he's willing to let me get that close yet."

"He doesn't need to. You're a US agent. You discover him making the device. Perhaps he triggers it as a suicide and to eliminate you."

"We'd need to catch him alone—and not in some public place where others would be injured."

"Does he ever go anywhere alone?"

"He has a retreat in northern England where he spends about half his time. A farmhouse outside a village called Rothbury. I don't know if anyone goes with him. He doesn't talk as if they do. But he's about due to head back."

"Rothbury—the name sounds familiar," Tanvi said.

"There was a major manhunt there a few years back. A man who'd murdered a former girlfriend and her lover—and a police officer, if I remember. It received a lot of international attention because England doesn't have many multiple murders and manhunts."

"Sounds like a good place to take care of our Mr. Flynn," Tom said. "But there will need to be a second party—someone we can have formally identified as you. That's going to be the challenge."

Tanvi inserted herself into the conversation. "The DNA samples that are sent to MI5 after the explosion aren't important. It's what shows up in Washington that we need to worry about. I think Nita can arrange for it to be Janet."

"Change the samples after they reach MI5?" Janet asked. "You can get that done?"

"It will be much simpler to revise your records in Washington," Tanvi said. "We'll type your stand-in and substitute that data for yours. That, I know we can do."

"Are you good with this?" Tom asked, his hazel eye studying her intently.

"I'm good," Janet said. "What kind of time do we have?"

"None," he said. "If he doesn't provide us with an opportunity within a few days, we'll have to create one for him."

20

Two months after the outbreak of World War II, a small German settlement on the eastern fringe of French Equatorial Africa was decimated by an unknown plague. The colony of forty families had been established on the west bank of the Congo River in 1915 while Germany briefly held a piece of the Congo basin, a concession from France in a deal that solidified French control of Morocco. The Germans had hoped to turn the river into a commercial conduit that could move rubber, lumber, and minerals to ports on the sea and from there into Europe, which was still struggling to recover from the first Great War. The settlement, called *Neukamerun* after the German name for the region, served as a supply station along the three thousand miles of Congo waterway.

When a medical team finally reached *Neukamerun,* they found a village of corpses. Most lay in their beds, soaked in their own blood. A few had died in the streets, seemingly watching for a savior that hadn't come. At the edge of the settlement, the team found a survivor—a man in his early twenties leaning against the stained wall of what had been the community school. His eyes were blood-red, and open lesions covered his ravaged body. After burning the dead, the team stayed with the survivor until he showed no signs of the illness, then took him back to Berlin where he became the subject of intense study.

In the man's blood and semen, scientists discovered a virus: a pathogen that previous studies had speculated existed but had been too tiny to be seen with existing microscopes. Using a new German development, the electron microscope, epidemiologists were able to distinguish the disease-causing agent from what at that time had been thought to be the primary cause of infectious illnesses: bacteria. Two years after the man carrying the tiny rod-shaped killers in his body was rescued from the banks of the Congo, samples of his bodily fluids left Berlin for a secret laboratory built beneath a home outside the Norwegian city of Ålesund. Two of the Reich's most talented pathologists carried the samples: a woman named Lena Maier and her Yugoslav husband, Vilim Gavran. Their charge: to see if the lethal hemorrhagic disease from the Congo could be turned into a weapon of war.

* * *

The passport that Sava Gavran presented when he passed through customs in Kinshasa, Democratic Republic of Congo, identified him as Dieter Roth, a German doctor from Heidelberg. He informed immigration officials that he was a specialist in tropical diseases, on his way to a medical station in Kananga, and expected to be in the country for two to three weeks.

There was, in fact, a Dieter Roth, and he actually was an MD. He and Sava had been in medical school together in Heidelberg and had remained in touch after Roth joined the school's faculty of medicine. Sava knew that for the past five years his colleague had been battling ALS, and that for at least the past ten, he hadn't traveled outside the European Union. The Serb simply applied for a passport on Dieter's behalf, using his own photo. The two men's lives were so similar that assuming Roth's identity had been relatively simple. Both came from medical families and were specialists in internal medicine. Both had completed their training in Heidelberg and were similar enough in appearance that a written description of eyes, hair, height, and weight wouldn't distinguish one from the other. And Sava had been raised in Marburg, Germany, where his father was employed as a researcher for Hoechst AG, a German chemical and pharmaceutical company. His German was as fluent as his Serbian.

What did distinguish the two physicians was that while Roth had chosen to return to the academy after several years of practice as an internist, Sava Gavran had elected to follow a line of research his father had passed down to him from his grandfather. Upon the death of Vilim Gavran, his son Josif had discovered in the scientist's locked cabinets detailed descriptions of experiments conducted in the Norwegian lab—trials that had been abandoned when the war came to an end. According to the notes, no means had been found to broadcast the deadly test virus to a wide population. In the state the virus existed, mortality rates were so high and so rapid that infected subjects died before the disease spread with epidemic effect.

If Vilim Gavran's journals were correct, stored quantities of the live virus were still secreted in a vault beneath the house near Ålesund—a scientific opportunity that Josif Gavran could not resist. In 1965, he was able to reacquire the home and, following directions in the journal, locate the hidden laboratory and the preserved specimens. But were they still viable?

When the Hoechst Company imported thirty monkeys from Uganda for pharmaceutical research, Josif Gavran saw his opportunity. While the animals were still in quarantine, he secretly inoculated half the shipment with his mystery virus. Two days later, he came to the lab to find that the animals had been divided into three groups, with two shipped that morning to laboratories in Frankfurt and Belgrade. Within a week, he knew that the virus had survived. Thirty-seven people were dead of the newly christened Marburg virus. Two months after the outbreak of hemorrhagic fever at the Hoechst labs, Josif resigned from the company to start his own pharmaceutical research group that he simply called Gavran. At his father's retirement, reportedly due to ill health, Sava inherited the company along with the family-held secret—the secret, he believed, to wealth beyond imagination.

21

The rattle of the phone on the floor beside him jarred Andrew awake. He was still propped against the wall with the Mauser between his feet. He grabbed instinctively at the weapon before realizing it was the phone that had startled him. The incoming number wasn't one he recognized. He lifted it hesitantly to his ear. His "hello" was barely audible.

"Is this the Martin residence?" a woman's voice asked.

"Yes. This is Andrew."

"Are you Dr. Martin's son, Andrew?"

Andrew wasn't sure he wanted this woman to know. "Who is this?"

"My name is Dr. Grace Hailey. I am with the Centers for Disease Control and Prevention in Atlanta, Georgia. We received a message to contact your mother at the hospital there, but when we returned the call, she wasn't available to speak with us. The message said she believed her son had information about how the outbreak in Mbandaka began. The hospital gave us your number. Would you be the son she was referring to, Andrew?"

"Why couldn't Mom talk to you?"

There was a silent moment that added to Andrew's concern. "I'm not certain. They just said she wasn't able to come to the phone and gave me this number. Is your father there?"

"Not yet. He's trying to get home, but the city's all blocked off."

"Are you the son your mother was referring to? The one with information about what might have started this epidemic? We could really use your help."

"Yeah. I think I know. I was playing with some friends down by the administration building. Some guy was passing out free baby food to women who'd come for it. My friends tried some, and I didn't. They got sick—and a bunch of babies, too. So I figured it was in the baby food."

"Was this baby food in jars? Like puréed meat and vegetables?"

"I don't know what puréed means. But it wasn't meat and vegetables. It was like baby milk."

"Bottles of formula?"

"Yeah. With an end that was upside down under the cap that the baby can drink from."

"And your friends tried some and you didn't—and they all got sick?"

"That's what Mom said. When she called yesterday, she said all three of them were at the hospital and not doing too well."

"Did you know the person who was passing out the formula, Andrew?"

"No. I'd never seen him before. He had this van with some NGO name written on the side. He was passing it out from the van."

"Do you remember what was written on the van? The name of the NGO?

"No. It was in French and not one I recognized. All I remember is *Agence*. I think part of it was covered by the van door."

"Was the man African?"

"No . . ." Andrew tried to remember the features of the stranger at the administration grounds. "And from listening to him talk, not French or American—or English or Australian."

"Would you say European or Asian?"

"Not Asian. Maybe European."

"An old man? Young?"

"Not too old. I'd say about my dad's age."

"Would you recognize the man if you saw him again?"

"Yeah. I think so. But I don't think he was from Mbandaka. I know I'd never seen him before."

The woman spoke softly to someone who was in the room with her, then asked, "How are you feeling, Andrew? Are you feeling sick?"

"No. I'm OK. I wish my mom or dad would get home."

"We'll try to get someone to you. Stay inside. Don't let anyone in unless it's your father or they tell you Dr. Hailey sent them. Can you do that?"

"What if Mom comes home?"

Again, Dr. Hailey paused. "You can let her in, of course. I'll try to call you later. Keep the phone charged."

Andrew again laid the phone beside him on the floor and gazed about the empty house. He unwrapped a package of crackers and pushed onto his feet to pour a cup of water from the heavy jug. A low rumble that had been no more than background noise suddenly ceased, and the light above his head flickered out. The clinic had lost its generator.

22

The night following her recruitment, Janet again met the Russells at the Skylon. It was about four miles from the cemetery, and she started her run as she normally did, but jogged directly to the gate by Kavanagh's and cut down an alley to Saint Mobhi Street. By 9:30, she was sitting again in the desk chair, dressed in her running sweats with her hair pulled back into a tight ponytail.

"You don't look like you broke a sweat," Tanvi commented. "I envy your conditioning."

"It's a cool evening," she said. "And I was chilled by the thought of being blown apart."

They grouped around the bed where, laid out across the spread, Tom had satellite imagery of the farmhouse on the outskirts of the English village of Rothbury. The detailed photos showed that it was under heavy video surveillance. Cameras on posts surrounded the property and covered every approach to the brown stone building.

"Our first task is going to be getting past this security," Tom said, laying out a schematic of the Northumberland property. "There are no fences or gates—nothing too visible to suggest this is anything other than a typical farmhouse. But the electronic surveillance is heavy. Tanvi's tried to find a data link that will allow us to hack in, but no luck. Our guess is that it's hardwired. That's good and bad. We can't disable it remotely, but hardwiring means those who are monitoring the system are somewhere on the property or nearby. Probably in the cottage beside the house. So we need to work out a way to get into the house and incapacitate Flynn without alerting his security."

"Or we need to take them out, too," Janet suggested.

"Or that," Tom agreed.

Janet tapped a finger on the photos of the house. "I may have a partial solution. Pat took me to dinner this evening at the Washerwoman up on Glasnevin Hill. He's going over to Rothbury this weekend. When he first told me he had a home in northern England, I mentioned that it was a place I'd always wanted to see. He asked tonight if I'd like to go with him."

Tanvi frowned. "That's almost too coincidental. Do you think he suspects anything?"

"I don't think so. We've been getting more friendly with every one of these little dinner dates. But I can tell he's nervous about having any kind of relationship here in Dublin. In fact, he asked if I'd be willing to fly over separately and meet him in Newcastle."

"As long as we're not setting you up for something, this could be perfect," Tom said. "If you can get into the house and disable him, we'll need to figure out how to draw the security person or people out of the cottage. It will have to be fast. I suspect they have backup that's close by. But if we plan this well, we can create our accident and have you out before anyone can get to the house."

"And the other me? The one that needs to be in the house with Flynn?"

"If we know the time, I can have a body delivered."

Janet tried not to sound surprised. "I'll be going over day after tomorrow. Getting there about nine thirty in the morning. I'd prefer this be taken care of that day—before things get too friendly. Can you get a body that quickly?"

Tom glanced over at Tanvi. "Fisher—the man you'll be working through—is watching for one now."

"And bodies that match my description show up with that kind of regularity? Or do you go find someone?"

"About sixty-two hundred people die in the United States every day. Three hundred are shot, half that many die in traffic accidents, and about that many of drug overdoses. Over two days, somewhere in that bunch is an unclaimed thirtysomething Caucasian female, five-six to five-eight with a decent body." Tom ran an appraising eye over her figure. "After the blast, there shouldn't be enough left of the victim to ID her other than through DNA analysis. And we'll have you change clothes so the pieces of clothing that are scattered around are what people may have seen you in when Flynn picks you up at the airport."

"The other woman's hair will be all over the place."

"The other woman won't have hair by the time she arrives. And we're including an added incendiary with the device to create as much burning as possible. But as Tanvi said last night, by the time the report reaches offices in Washington, the DNA will match your file."

"You make it sound so simple. I just get him into the house, incapacitate him, and call you. You bring everything else we need."

"It's never simple," Tom said grimly. "In fact, it's always much more complicated than our plan anticipates. That's why we go out looking for very bright people like you. You'll have to improvise."

"And how do you want me to incapacitate him? An injection of some kind? I went through training in which we used a mixture of propofol and remifentanil that puts a person under almost immediately."

Tom shook his head. "Can't do that. MI5 will be thorough. We can't leave chemical traces. This will have to be a physical blow."

"With whatever I find available, I presume."

"Ideally with your hands. We also don't want a weapon around that might have trace evidence on it. Your record shows you did well in hand-to-hand combat. Here's your chance to see if it really works when the chips are on the table."

Her memory flashed to the sessions during which she had practiced half a dozen ways to incapacitate a person with a headlock or skillfully directed blow. In each practice scenario, they had pulled punches, taking the instructor's word that the blow would have the desired effect. This seemed like a pretty high-stakes way to find out.

"I'll find a way," she said. "And I'll try to draw the security people out of the cottage. But you will need to be ready to intercept immediately. How do I let you know I have Flynn down?"

"The same phone we used yesterday. No message. Just a call."

"And you think you can get past the cameras to be outside the cottage door when I draw them out?

"I have an idea about that as well," he said.

* * *

After she was gone, Dreu poured them each a glass of a red cabernet they had picked up from a local vintner during a morning drive into the countryside to maintain their tourist identity. Adam took a sip and raised an appreciative brow.

"Not too bad for a country of whiskey and stout. What was this called?"

"Lusca—after the village of Lusk where they make it. The man said he thought it might be the only true Irish wine." She swirled the deep-purple liquid and held it up to the light of the table lamp.

"They picked the right person to get to Flynn," she said. "She's very pretty, in a tough, Irish kind of way. And she's certainly bright."

Adam chuckled. "In a tough, Irish kind of way? You mean in contrast to a more elegant, Judeo-Indian kind of way?"

Dreu raked him with a dark Judeo-Indian glare. "You know what I mean. To use your terminology, the woman's 'cut'—not an ounce of fat on her anywhere."

"And you could tell that from seeing her sit there in a sweat suit?"

"Trust me," Dreu muttered. "There's a lot of power in that little body. Are you going to tell her our names? If we're bringing her in, I think she deserves a little more trust."

"Do any of the other agents know our names? We survive on separation."

"So when this operation's over, we disappear back into the woodwork and leave her to think there are a Tom and Tanvi Russell out there somewhere?"

"I think that's best."

"You don't fully trust her yet, do you?" Dreu said with a thin smile.

Adam shrugged. "She seems a little too taken with this Patrick Flynn. Not romantically. Just a kind of heroic admiration."

"Do you think she may really have some Republican sympathies? She has the genes—and maybe this immersion in old Irish has gotten to her."

Adam took a deeper sip of his Irish cabernet. "We'll find out this weekend. And on second thought, if she performs well, we'll probably have to tell her our names. Kari Eikram knows them."

"Do you really have a plan that will have you at the cottage door, undetected, if she's able to lure the security people out?"

He laughed and raised his glass. "You mean, get *us* to the cottage door . . ."

23

Tom had been right about there being nothing simple about her new assignment. Janet's forty-five-minute flight to Newcastle had been on time. As the plane taxied to the terminal, she had seen a smaller unmarked jet at a hangar beside the runway off-loading what could easily be a box holding her body double. Patrick Flynn had not been on the flight but had asked that she text him, once on the ground. As she exited the modern, glass-fronted building, he pulled into the passenger pickup lane in a blue Mini Clubman that looked like it had just been driven off the lot. She realized as she slid in beside him that the pickup had been planned to minimize chances of them being seen together in Newcastle.

"Did you come in yesterday?" she asked as they left the terminal drive, heading north away from the city.

"Yesterday mornin'. Had a bit of business in Bradford. So I just flew in there and rented the car. We'll take the A-1 north, and you can see a bit of the countryside."

"Thanks for inviting me. I needed to get away from the studies for a few days. And I've always been fascinated by this part of England."

"You won't be wantin' to practice some old Irish phrases as we drive, then?" he asked, smiling over at her.

"A few. But let's not make this weekend just another tutorial."

The drive to the village of Rothbury took only forty minutes. Flynn spent most of the time in a running commentary on the history of the area.

"The countryside up here is dotted with stone circles like Stonehenge," he told her. "Not on the same scale, mind ya, but just as mysterious. And because this has been a border area for centuries, there are more castles in Northumberland than in any

English county. Tomorrow I'll run ya up to Alnwick and over to the coast to see Bamburgh. Two of the very finest. And that will give ya a peek at the North Sea."

They turned off the main motorway onto a narrow, two-lane road that wound through low wooded hills along the river Coquet.

"There's a right lovely old Tudor country house up through the trees there to our right," Flynn said as they passed a sign that said *Cragend Grange*. "It was built by Lord Armstrong and was the first house to be lighted by hydroelectric power. If you like, we can stop by there during our drive-about tomorrow."

"I'd like that," Janet said, wondering as she said it why the man couldn't just come across as completely evil. But as soon as the thought occurred, it was replaced by a realization that none of the criminal minds she had encountered had been completely bad actors. Still, it would make her new assignment easier if Patrick Flynn weren't so disarmingly charming.

They entered Rothbury from the east along its High Street, past rows of picturesque stone shops and a lichen-stained war memorial topped with a Celtic cross. The village was different from most she had seen near Dublin: the same two- and three-story shops and homes under slate or tile roofs, but in a creamy, brown stone rather than the whitewashed stucco common to Ireland. Rows of subcompact cars nosed against the curb in front of shops with bright awnings selling flowers, textiles, and baked goods. The main street bustled with vacationers.

They continued through the village and a mile beyond before turning right onto a lane dappled by the morning sun's play on overarching branches. The farmhouse, solidly built of the same light-yellow-brown stone, was another hundred yards through a break of pines and hardwoods. As Flynn eased the car into its unpaved courtyard, he slowed and leaned from the window, waving at a camera that covered the open ground.

Tom was right. Someone's here monitoring these, Janet thought as they pulled to the front of the weathered, L-shaped home. A smaller cottage of the same square-cut stone stood in front of them, forming a third side of the farm's courtyard. Although no visible cables connected the buildings, thick conduit sprouted from the ground on both sides of the cottage, disappearing through the stone walls at knee height.

"Is this a working farm?" she asked as they climbed from the car and the smell of fresh hay and manure teased her nostrils.

"There's a barn in back and a coop full of chickens," Flynn said. "I keep a few horses. Behind us, there's only open fields up to where the heath begins." He nodded toward the cottage. "I have a couple of men who keep an eye on the place and take care of the animals. Do you ride?"

"I haven't since I was a kid," Janet said, noting that the caretakers hadn't come out to meet them. A new Land Rover was tucked in behind the smaller building.

The interior of the old farmhouse was just as Janet had imagined. Its heavy front door opened into a great room with a low, open-beamed ceiling and raised fireplace that filled half of the wall to her right. Horse brass, a copper warming pan, and ancient leather bellows hung from the walls on either side of the hearth. The furnishings were of plain varnished oak with heavily cushioned seats and backs. The only things that looked out of place were two conspicuous black lenses that blinked at her from beams in two corners of the room.

"Oh, I love this place!" she murmured, turning back to Flynn with a delighted smile. "Very homey—and very English!"

His eyes shown with pleasure. "This is where I find peace," he said. "Let me show you your room." He led her up a steep open staircase that climbed the wall opposite the fireplace and pushed open a door at the top left, beckoning for her to enter. The room was equally rustic with brown, vine-embroidered curtains framing a high double window that looked down over the cottage. A thick white eiderdown covered a plain four-poster bed. A three-drawer dresser in the corner held a porcelain pitcher and basin.

Flynn nodded toward an unpainted side door. "There's a bathroom with shower just through there. Make yourself comfortable. I thought we'd go into the village to the Queen's for an early lunch in about an hour. They've a pork-and-apple stack that's smashing. We'll walk, if you don't mind. It's about twenty minutes, and the morning is perfect. Just come on down when you're ready."

When the door was closed behind him, Janet walked slowly around the room, examining each piece of furniture and wall hanging with an amused smile fixed to her face for the benefit of anyone who might be watching. She found the tiny camera lens in the center of an ornate brass sunburst that decorated the arched top of a mahogany clock. The clock was centered on the wall opposite the foot of the bed where it provided a wide sweep of the room. She moved on past without looking directly at the black dot and continued her inspection.

Surveillance or voyeurism? she wondered, turning back to the bed to unpack her small case. Possibly both for the person in the cottage. She stripped off her jeans and blouse as if unaware she was being watched and pulled on a casual navy tank dress that fell to midthigh.

Flynn was seated in one of the pillowed chairs when she descended the stairs, thumbing through texts on his phone. He glanced up, smiled approvingly, and tucked the phone into the breast pocket of his shirt. "Ready to go?"

"I think we're ready," she said.

The restaurant in the Queen's Head was exactly the choice she would have made had she known the town better. Like Gravediggers, it had a well-stocked bar and tavern area that was separated by a main entryway from the dining room. The Queen's displayed a little more formality than a place called the Turk's

Head they had passed on their walk through the village, the pub Flynn pointed out as his favorite place to have a pint.

"Good Guinness there," he announced, "but when I want a bite, I prefer the Queen's."

The tables were laminated wood on metal pedestals with a wall-length bench along one side and padded captain's chairs on the other. But the Queen's insisted on cloth napkins. Janet found the food excellent and the locals friendly. Flynn was much more comfortable with her company than he had appeared at the airport. He drank more freely than he had at Kavanagh's, having a pint before his meal and another to wash it down and keep conversation moving freely. By the end of the meal, Janet knew that many in the village would remember the Irishman and his lunch partner.

As they visited over their meal, she leaned more intimately toward him, softening her voice and eyes and keeping a hand on the tabletop as if barely able to restrain her desire to touch him. They talked about her studies until she insisted they move to something less tedious. "Tell me about your family," she said. "One of your mates told me you were widowed."

"Goin' on fifteen years now." He beckoned a waitress in a short black dress with white apron over to take their double order of the pork-and-apple stack.

"Do you have children?"

"The Good Lord saw better than to force any *leanbh* onto a difficult man such as me," he said with a wry smile. "Heaven knows what they would have grown to be. Ireland's my family now."

"You seem very devoted to her," Janet said, spreading her fingers slightly to inch them toward his hand.

"Heart and soul." He seemed not to notice the gesture.

"It surprises me that as a Republican, you spend so much time in England."

He shrugged. "Enjoying this country is no reason to wish Ireland to be part of it. You enjoy being here, but I'm guessin' you wouldn't choose America to still be a colony."

The lunch was leisurely, followed by a whiskey for Flynn and a second light ale for Janet. When he excused himself to visit what he called the jax, she stopped a passing waitress and emptied most of her drink into a glass on the girl's tray.

"Would you like to try something else?" the girl asked.

Janet smiled up at her. "I think I've had enough for tonight."

* * *

They walked back through the village and down the lane to the farmhouse with Flynn weaving just enough to occasionally brush her side. On the third bump, she wrapped her arm about his, and they walked hand in hand across the courtyard.

In the timbered great room, Flynn dropped heavily into one of the chairs, still holding her hand.

"I think I'll go up to my room for a minute," she said. "I won't be long."

He released her with a slight squeeze. She climbed to the bedroom, slipped off the tank dress and her underwear, and fished a lacy black teddy and matching panties from her case. Turning toward the wall clock, she smiled seductively at the camera, winked, and hung her light dress over the clock. From the door, she called down to Flynn.

"Pat, could you come up for just a moment?"

"You'd like me to come up there?" She heard suspicion in his voice and stepped out onto the landing where he could see her from below.

"I have something I'd like to show you," she murmured, seeing that at least two other cameras were watching her.

"Oh—I like what I'm seein' from here!" He pushed unsteadily out of the chair.

As he staggered upward, she backed slowly into the room until she stood in the space between the foot of the bed and the draped camera. As he stepped through the doorway, his eyes moved to the covered clock and his brow furrowed.

"I couldn't help but notice there are cameras everywhere in this house," she said, smiling seductively. "I guess if you want to record this, I'd be OK with it. But I can't imagine you'd like something to show up on the Internet." She reached for him to come to her, and his brow softened.

"I don't think either of us would like the publicity," he said with an inviting grin and stepped toward her. She moistened her lips with her tongue and urged him closer with extended fingers. When a step away, she threw her weight forward, directing every ounce of strength into her right hand that fired into his throat like an exploding piston, knuckles first into his larynx. The voice of her instructor echoed in her memory. "Don't pull the punch. If you aren't being attacked, the urge will be to strike and pull back. But if you intend to kill or incapacitate, drive through like you want to go straight through the neck. No mercy!"

She heard the cartilage crunch and saw Flynn's eyes fly open in desperation, fear, and anger. His mouth gaped wide for a breath that refused to come. One hand went to his throat, the other reaching for her as he staggered forward. She stepped back and twisted away, coiling like a taut spring. The coil released, unleashing a two-fisted blow to his temple that sent him crumpling across the foot of the bed, his hands grasping futilely at his crushed throat. The bedsprings squeaked loudly, and she turned to face the covered clock.

"Ohhh—that's nice!" she said in an airy whimper. "That's so *very* nice!"

24

In the cottage beside the farmhouse, Flynn's two security men rocked their chairs back in front of the array of video feeds and grinned at each other.

"The boss ain't pullin' the pig on that one," the stockier of the men said. "Nice bit of Yankee quim. You think he told her to cover the camera?"

The second man, thinner but solid, leaned forward and switched camera views to the great room.

"We can see the bedroom door, but not what's inside. My guess would be he wants this private." The syncopated squeak of the mattress and occasional grunts and moans poured from the bedroom microphone.

Movement on a screen to their far right turned both of their heads as if pulled by a single cord. A black Ford Mondeo rolled up the drive and stopped midway between the front of the farmhouse and the cottage. A tall couple climbed hesitantly from the car, the man in a dark wool suit, white shirt and tie, the woman in a conservative ankle-length gray dress. Both clutched Bibles. The man held a handful of tracts. They studied the two buildings, spoke briefly, and the man waved the woman toward the larger house. He turned toward the cottage.

"Bloody Mormons," the heavier man said.

"Not Mormons," the thin man said. "They send kids. These are Witnesses. The boss is going to be pissed when she beats on the door."

The thick man leaned into the screen. "She's a bit o' all right herself. Wish she was coming this way. I might get a bit o' religion."

A muffled scream came from the bedroom microphone,

followed by a clear shout for help. The bedroom camera suddenly came to life, and the redhead stood in front of it, naked and clearly terrified.

"*Help me!*" she pleaded. "Something's happened to Pat! I think he's had a heart attack!" She turned aside, and the men could see Flynn's naked form sprawled behind her on the bed.

"Bloody hell," the thin man muttered as the male visitor rapped at the door. "Get those bloody Bible thumpers out of here, and go see if you can give him CPR. I'll call for an ambulance."

His partner was already at the door. As he pulled it inward, two prongs jammed into his chest and a million and a half volts coursed through his body, dumping him into a heap at the intruder's feet. As he fell, his partner rose from his chair, fingers paused above the keypad of his phone. Before he could hit the second "9" in the emergency call number, the man outside raised a laser-sighted M26 Taser and fired two probes into the guard's chest. He spasmed uncontrollably as the phone clattered to the floor, his limp body slumping on top of it.

Adam drew a short leather sap from the inside of his jacket and swung it hard into the fallen guard's temple. Stepping over him, he did the same to the man in front of the console. A row of black switches controlled the cameras and screens. He ran down the column, snapping each into the off position. When the panel in front of him was black, he again pulled the phone from his breast pocket.

"The guards are down," he said without having to dial. "Tanvi has clothes for you. Get dressed, and help her carry the body in from the car. You'll need to put your clothes on the woman. Is the rear door unlocked?"

"I'm on my way down now, dragging Flynn with me," he heard through the phone. "I'll get the back door, but we'll need to dress him again."

"I interrupted the nine-nine-nine call. We should have plenty of time. Let's just be careful and keep everything clean. I'm bringing the first man over."

He struggled the heavier of the guards onto his shoulder, checked the drive to insure it was clear, and carried the security man around the back of the farmhouse and through the rear door into a rustic kitchen. Four chairs surrounded a distressed oak table. He propped the unconscious man in one of them. Patrick Flynn lay naked in the kitchen doorway, his face blue and eyes bulging.

"I'm getting clothes on in here," Janet called from the great room. "We'll have him dressed in a few minutes."

The team worked in silence, Adam retrieving the second guard and returning to the cottage to gather recorded disks for the last twenty-four hours, replace them with blanks. When he reentered the kitchen, Flynn was propped in another of the chairs, his clothes neatly tucked and belted. Dreu pulled the Mondeo around to the rear. He helped her lift the wrapped body from the trunk and carry it in to be laid on the table. As they unwrapped the foil blanket, the pale corpse was still cold to the touch. The woman appeared to be in her early thirties, thinner than Janet but otherwise close to the same size. Her body had been completely shaved.

"Nita said they were able to get her into cold storage within twenty minutes of death," Adam said. "She was an abuse victim whose partner beat her nearly to death, then shot himself. The police had been called to the place before and tried to get the woman to leave, but she said she had no family and nowhere to go."

"She doesn't look badly beaten," Dreu observed as she worked with Janet to dress the body in the blue tank dress. "The guy must have been one of those stealth batterers who knew how to do serious damage without it showing. Somehow it seems sacrilegious to use her like this."

"Think of it as revenge against men who kill and injure innocent women," Adam said. "Nita's arranged for her to have a headstone.

If next of kin show up, they'll have a place to visit. Now—let's get our group arranged and the charge in place."

* * *

With the bodies clustered tightly about the table, Flynn and the woman sitting opposite each other, leaned forward until almost touching, Adam placed an M185 demolition kit between them and inserted a remote detonator. The team did a final walk-through to insure they had left no trace evidence and met again beside the staged table.

Janet examined the demolition pack. "That's a huge charge. Aren't you worried about residual damage?"

"There's nothing behind this place for miles. Same to the west. The closest home is a quarter mile back toward town, and there's a bit of a rise in between. Flynn picked the place to be remote, and that works in our favor. Some people will lose windows. We'll just have to hope that's the extent of the damage in the village." He nodded toward the door that led back through the living room. "Tanvi drove a van up from Newcastle with the body. It's parked about halfway up the drive. I'll be taking the Ford. You and Tanvi are driving the van back to the airport where one of our planes will fly you to Ålesund in Norway. I'll give you about fifteen minutes after we're on the road before I detonate the charge. Tanvi will brief you as you go."

Janet followed him out to where the Ford stood behind the house. "Will we have a chance to talk again? I feel like I'm learning what I need to know while I'm doing it."

"That's not likely to change for a while," Adam said. "Maybe never. Get your hair cut short as soon as you can, and send Tanvi some photos. You should have new documents by late tomorrow. Until this next assignment ends, you're going to be Anna Eikram. Now, let's get moving."

Adam waited until the van disappeared along the road heading west toward Thropton, then turned the Ford back into the village. Just beyond the town's center, he turned right on Bridge Street and crossed the Coquet over the arched stone bridge that gave the street its name. He turned left and wound south through hedge-lined pastures into the low, rugged Northumberland hill country, the fields on either side broken by long stretches of rocky fell. At a barren patch in front of a farm gate, he pulled the Ford to the side and quickly changed into dark corduroy pants, a checkered long-sleeved shirt, and plain, dark, quilted vest. Two miles beyond, a row of towering white wind generators loomed above the hilltop. He slowed as he crested the rise and descended into a lush river valley. In front of him the road divided, branching right toward Newcastle and Hexham, left to the town of Morpeth.

He parked beside a gray stone building that looked very much like the Rothbury farmhouse. In an open courtyard beyond a low stone wall, a busy lunch crowd clustered around wooden picnic tables. A green sign on the pub's wall identified the place as the Gate Free House. Adam pushed through the gate that gave the place its name into a paved patio and took one of the few remaining seats beside a young woman in torn jeans and a baggy, high-necked sweater. A round, red-faced woman with orange hair pulled up into a tight knot was immediately at his side.

"What can I get you, luv?" she asked, her accent the broad Jordy of England's northeast.

"Do you have a local beer?"

"Oh, aye. One for every taste."

"Something in a pale ale. Fairly light."

"I'd suggest a Galatia. Brewed right down the road in Newcastle."

Adam nodded. "I'll give it a try." When the woman was back inside the pub, he pulled the phone he had used to speak to Janet from his breast pocket but this time entered another number and pressed the "Call" button. Four miles to the north, the clear summer sky flashed suddenly as if lighted by a second sun. Seconds later, the air about him shook as a shockwave rolled across the sparsely covered heath. The young woman beside him leaped to her feet, banging her thighs against the table and tumbling backward. He squeezed from beneath the table and helped her untangle. They gazed toward the rising plume of gray smoke.

"My God," he sputtered. "That sounded like one hell of an explosion!" He joined the girl and the rest of the lunch guests in a rush out onto the country road that fronted the inn. As Adam stood at the back of the crowd, another phone in a pants pocket tickled his leg. The display showed a text from Nita.

There may be a witness who can ID whoever's developing the virus, the message said. *Fly ASAP to Libreville, Gabon.*

25

Andrew had been alone in the house for four days and had not heard from either parent for two. The generator that provided backup power to the clinic had gone silent the day before, as had the city around it. Andrew stood at the window of his second-floor bedroom and watched the street, begging to see life beyond the mangy dogs and molting chickens that roamed about, scratching for any morsel of food. For some reason, the dogs left the chickens alone, either aware that the wary birds could fly to the wall-top or out of respect for their shared misery. Andrew felt the misery. But more than anything, he felt a crushing loneliness. At the same time, he knew that he would be terrified if some unknown person tried to enter the compound. The Mauser stood ready beside him against the wall.

The clinic was no more than two hundred yards down the road, and it also had fallen silent. Without the generator, he guessed the staff had moved everyone to the main hospital in the city center. His mother must have gone with them. Andrew had tried to call her once since the generator died but had then decided to keep what charge he could on the battery and wait for his parents to call. The thought occasionally flitted through his head that his mother may no longer be able to call, but he pushed it quickly aside. And his father—he must have been stopped by the police trying to bypass the barricades. They might even be holding him. Both parents, he was certain, wanted him to stay inside for a life-and-death reason. Nothing was going to draw him out until he saw them at the gate beckoning for him to open up.

Through the window, the scents of the city had changed. Normally in the morning, he could smell the river. In the later parts of the day, when the sun was steaming hot, the city smelled of dung, stale water, and the smoke and spices of cook fires. During the rainy season, the damp, earthy smell of jungle closed in across the city. But now it smelled spoiled—like meat that had hung too long and was turning putrid. It was at once sour and bitter, even through his protecting mask. Andrew knew that the city was dying.

To keep himself alive, he had devised his own rationing plan: a half cup of water with each of two daily meals. Dry crackers and a half can of fruit in the mornings. Part of a package of macaroni and cheese that his mother had taught him how to prepare in the afternoon with the rest of the fruit. Two tablespoons of powdered milk stirred into his water. The milk was thin and chalky and left a bitter taste on his tongue. But he knew it must add something to his diet that would be better than plain water. He had discovered a package of Oreos hidden behind plastic containers of rice and beans in the pantry and allowed himself one with each meal. His mother must have forgotten they were there. The cookies were stale and soft but added a touch of sweetness to the end of each day.

Tonight he had decided to try to cook some of the rice. There were no instructions on the plastic bag, but he thought he could figure it out. Rice, water, and maybe a little salt. He wasn't sure about amounts but thought a cup of rice to a cup of water should work. He was still getting propane from the tank and wanted to eat something hot.

The phone buzzed on the floor beside him. His heart leaped as he scooped it up, then dropped heavily in his chest when he didn't recognize the incoming number. His "hello" was barely audible.

"Andrew Martin?" a woman's voice asked.

He remembered his father's warnings about identifying himself when home alone. "Who's calling?" he said.

"My name is Anita, and I'm sending someone to pick you up." The woman had an accent he didn't recognize.

"What about my mom and dad? They told me to stay here until one of them came."

"Do you remember when Dr. Grace Hailey called you? She said we would try to come get you. We don't know when your parents will be able to reach you, and we need to get you out of there. We're looking for them, too."

"Who are you?" Andrew asked hesitantly. "I won't leave with someone I don't know."

The woman's voice was clam, but firm. "I work for the president of the United States. We received a call from the clinic telling us you might know who brought this disease to Mbandaka. We need to be able to talk to you as soon as possible. We'll be trying to locate your parents at the same time and bring you all together outside of the country."

"I don't think they'll let you come get me. My dad tried, and they stopped him. We saw police trucks along the river, and they'll stop everybody."

"Are you at your home? The one by the clinic?"

"Yeah. Mom told me to stay here and not let anyone in."

"She was right—and you need to continue to do what she said. We can't come for you until tomorrow night. Do you trust me enough to let us come for you, Andrew?"

He wished he could talk to one of his parents and tried to decide what they would tell him to do. Someone from the clinic had called these people, so his mother must be OK with it. He had to get out of the house before he ran out of food and water—and it would be best if he could get out of the city.

"Yeah. I think I can trust you. How will I know it's you?"

"Well, listen carefully," the woman said. "There are some things we need to have you do so we can pick you up and get you out of the city without creating more problems. Are you ready?"

"Ready," he said. "I'm pretty good at remembering a bunch of instructions."

Perfect," she said. "Here's what you need to do."

26

If she could master the changes in identity, Janet was certain she could handle the rest of her assignment. In the course of twenty-four hours, the woman who had once been Janet McIntire had transitioned from being undercover agent Janet O'Brien, to being fragments of a corpse in an obliterated English farmhouse, to becoming Anna Eikram. During the drive to Newcastle, the woman she had known as Tanvi reintroduced herself as Dreu Sason and told her that Tom Russell was actually Adam Zak. As the private plane that had been awaiting them at the Newcastle airport flew them toward Ålesund, Dreu suggested Janet begin to think of yet another name, the one she would assume after this Norwegian operation was complete.

"This new name. Will it be permanent?" she asked.

"I'd say semi-permanent," Dreu said with amusement. "During the time I've known Adam, I think he's gone by three or four names . . . sort of like you being Anna Eikram for the next few weeks."

"And he said something about altering my appearance. I hope it works as well as it did for you!"

Dreu's smile turned to a laugh. "I'm generally not in operations, so I didn't have to disappear. This is the face I've always had. We'll need to alter yours just enough that you won't be recognized by people who have known you. You're a beautiful woman and I'm sure won't want to give that up, but we can make some slight changes that create uncertainty. And that's all we need."

"If I stay away from Albuquerque and Quincy, Illinois, there's not much chance of being recognized," Janet had said with a sniff. "That's where I've spent my life since I was twelve. And I haven't been back in New Mexico since my parents died seven years ago."

"You spent time at the Bureau's academy at Quantico with people who were trained to remember and recognize faces. And you were with the Dallas office for three years. With the kinds of things you'll be asked to do now, it's likely you'll run into some of those people. After they ID you as having been killed in the Rothbury blast, your records will be purged and prints, photo, and DNA information removed. So think of a new name to use when not on an assignment like this one."

"I always liked Brittany," she said, remembering an argument during her early teen years with her mother over what an uninteresting name Janet was. "I was named after an aunt and never really liked the name—or the aunt. And I think she'd be happy to have me called something else."

"Brittany suits you," Tanvi said. "Come up with a last name, and we'll start working on documents. But for now, you're Anna Eikram. A passport, Minnesota driver's license, and a few other random bits of ID will reach us tomorrow."

Her new persona, she learned, was as the grandniece of a ninety-two-year-old woman named Kari Eikram who lived on an island at the mouth of a Norwegian fjord. The woman had been a member of the Norwegian Resistance, was now blind, and was cared for largely by her granddaughter.

"The granddaughter's name is Sofi. She's about your age and believes you are actually her cousin, several times removed," Dreu told her. "Kari's brother-in-law Carl immigrated to the States shortly after World War II and died about fifteen years ago, leaving two sons. Both are now also dead. The Norwegian family's pretty well lost track of any American relatives. If they do some searching, they'll find you as a daughter of Carl's son, Peter. You grew up in Saint Paul." She handed Janet a folder.

"This outlines the mission and has a basic bio for you. You can pretty well make up the rest. There's no good way for them to check."

"And what does Kari think of all this?"

Dreu chuckled softly. "She really initiated this investigation. And she's excited about having a new niece, though she knows you're not the real thing. You'll like the old lady. She's a real-life kickback to the Norwegian underground from the Second World War and is pretty caught up in being back in the game. You'll need to spend enough time out there with her to sell your cover to the granddaughter. But you'll be staying at the Hotel Brosundet on the harbor in the city."

Janet flipped open the folder and looked at the eight-by-ten photo that sat on top.

"I gather this man is our reason for being there," she said.

"Yes. Your assignment is to learn all you can about a Serb who goes by the name Sava Gavran. He spends most of his time in Ålesund and stays at the Brosundet. Kari thinks he's continuing some kind of chemical or biological experimentation that was started by the Germans during the war. She'll tell you all she knows about it. You'll find in the brief everything we've been able to learn about the man since she made us aware of him."

"So, this is Patrick Flynn all over again. I'm to befriend this man and learn what I can."

"Exactly."

"Why are we doing this and not some other security group?"

"There's nothing that gives them reason to suspect the man," Dreu said. "And in some ways, this is a favor. Kari helped one of our people in the past."

"Other than her suspicion, do *you* have reason to be concerned about this Gavran?"

"There seem to be a lot of coincidences right now, and we haven't been able to connect the dots. Kari thought the men were experimenting with some strain of an Ebola-like virus called Marburg. Then, as you know, we learned someone is offering what is being billed as a highly lethal bio-agent on the world market.

Now we have that outbreak in the Congo. Lots of dots. No connecting lines."

"And you think this Gavran might be able to connect the dots?"

"That's what we're counting on you to find out."

27

The explosion in the quiet Northumberland village of Rothbury made the front page of the *Times* of London beneath the headline "Blast Kills Suspected RIRA Leader." Adam's flight had departed Heathrow for Gabon before the early edition made the newsstands. He found a copy in Paris during transfer to his Air France flight to the African capital. As the airbus climbed south toward the Mediterranean, he read through the article, marveling at how quickly Northumbria's Special Operations Unit was piecing things together. The article stated:

> According to Northumbria's Police and Crime Commissioner Wilma Giles, officials have determined that the owner of the property, Real IRA activist Patrick Flynn, was killed by the blast. DNA evidence indicated that at least three other persons, two men and a woman, also perished in what police initially described as an unintended detonation of a large explosive device.
>
> A source within the Northeast Regional Special Operations Unit, who asked not to be identified, indicated there is speculation internally that the blast may have been an attempt by other parties to kill Flynn. Video surveillance of the farmhouse and its property had been turned off, and recordings covering the time period of the incident were either missing or deleted.
>
> "It may simply be that those killed in the explosion didn't want their work to be recorded," the source said. "But it may also indicate someone else triggered the blast."
>
> Flynn had been seen earlier in the evening in the village with a woman who is thought to be the

female victim of the explosion. Associates of the RIRA leader in Dublin told the *Times* that he had been accompanied to England by an American graduate student at Trinity College. The identity of the student has not yet been disclosed.

The explosive device was similar in both size and composition to one used in an attack on the headquarters of the British Army's Thirty-Ninth Brigade at Thiepval Barracks near Belfast a week ago. *Times* sources in Belfast suggest that members of the Provisional IRA may have been interested in keeping Flynn from reigniting sectarian and political violence in Northern Ireland and could be involved. Forensic evidence indicated, however, that Flynn and his party were working in very close proximity to the explosive when it detonated.

Adam tucked the paper into his canvas backpack and leaned comfortably back in his seat. Before boarding in London, he had received a message from Nita confirming that Janet's prints, blood type, dental records, and DNA in the Bureau's files in Washington had been replaced by those of the abuse victim. Evidence from Rothbury should reach her FBI superiors within the week. Janet McIntire would be presumed dead.

* * *

At CIA headquarters in Langley, Don Hendren felt the buzz of a secure phone in his breast pocket and saw that a text had arrived from the only person who had this number. Hendren lifted the receiver of a desk phone that connected him to offices within the complex and punched in an extension. The call was answered immediately.

"Bedford," the voice said.

"Jay, a message just came in. Running it through decryption now. You have a minute to come down?"

"On my way," Bedford said. In less than two minutes, Hendren's colleague was standing beside his desk. Don placed the phone on the desktop and opened the message.

I trust you have appreciated my demonstration in Mbandaka and are all trying to cultivate the strain. This test was conducted with an early prototype using an aerosol-droplet nucleic life of only a few minutes. Yet the mortality rate, as you have witnessed, has been above 70 percent. Our research and testing are now several generations and several years beyond the time that strain was developed. We are now measuring airborne-droplet nuclei life in hours rather than minutes. The newest strain is known to be resistant to all of the latest antiviral drugs. It has been modified in such a way that anything developed to resist the Mbandaka strain will not be effective.

Bidding to exclusively acquire the new strain will begin Friday, five days from today. We repeat, this is an open bidding process, and each of you is assigned a bidder's code name that follows this message. I do not know who you are beyond your code names and wish to keep it that way throughout. Seven parties have responded to my invitation. When bidding begins, the site link where bid amounts are posted will allow you to see bids as they come in, listed by code name. There will be three one-hour rounds, one day apart. The highest bid when time expires in the third round will receive the virus upon payment to a numbered account. There will be no opportunity for further negotiation after that round. Receive what authorizations you need before the bidding begins.

Below was an additional message:
Your code name is Bulldog.

Hendren glanced up at Bedford. "You seen what you need to see?"

"Yeah. The only information we really need to remember is that bidding begins Friday and we're Bulldog. Go ahead and delete the thing."

"Seven bidders. Who do you see filling those spaces?"

"China. Russia. A couple of the terrorist groups. Probably ISIS and Al-Qaida, though I don't know that Al-Qaida will have the resources to stay in past the first round. Israel. That would make six, with us."

Hendren nodded. "Maybe India or the Saudis. I can't see any European countries or Japan coming in."

"Even to buy and destroy?"

"I doubt it. They'll count on us to do that. And this is going to take big money. I'm guessing a hundred, two hundred million."

Bedford glanced toward the door. "Can we get that kind of authorization?"

"Hell," Hendren scoffed. "We're spending six hundred *billion* on defense each year. That's as much as all the others we've listed combined. They're going to authorize whatever we think it will take to make sure we get the stuff."

"Any word from upstairs about efforts to find the source? It could save us a bucket load of cash."

"They're looking. So far, no joy. These messages are being routed through a pretty sophisticated chain of zombies, and we haven't been able to isolate the host." Hendren glanced over at his partner with a cynical grin. "Plus, I'm thinking Defense would rather own the virus. The scuttlebutt is that we've been trying to get Ebola to survive in aerosol form for years without success. The virus is pretty fragile."

"Could this guy be shitting us about the viability time? The CDC said it believes the virus in Mbandaka has been lasting only ten to fifteen minutes in droplet form. Maybe that's all he's been able to get out of it."

Hendren shrugged. "Maybe. But I think the experts believe that if you can get it to survive for ten minutes, there's a way to increase that time. And the CDC's working their asses off to develop an antivirus. I don't think our man would have staged that demo without something more potent in his back pocket. He had to know every major lab in the world would get a sample and start working on an antidote."

"Or this guy is one hell of a bluffer."

"Or that," Hendren said. "But we can't take that chance."

28

Janet sat alone in the dining room of the Brosundet, waiting for Sofi Eikram to join her for a late supper. When she and Dreu Sason had landed in the Norwegian coastal city, Dreu hadn't even accompanied her from the terminal—just ushered her to a waiting car that drove her into the city.

"We've checked you through customs and passport control," Dreu said. "Your passport as Anna Eikram will be waiting at the hotel desk. Just ask for an envelope in that name before you check in."

If she was supposed to look like an inexperienced traveler, bumbling her way through her first foreign travel experience, she had done the job well. When living in New Mexico, Janet had been to Juarez a few times with friends who wanted to buy cheap tequila and get antibiotics without a prescription. But until she went to Ireland, that had been the extent of her international travel. Acting like a novice was coming naturally.

As the car crossed the arched causeways that joined the island airport to the mainland, she marveled at the deep blue of the sea and the rugged, pine-studded coastline the surrounded the fjord. There was something surreal about being a member of a deep-cover intelligence and security unit but feeling more like a child walking for the first time down Main Street at Disney's Epcot.

And Ålesund! The city looked as if it had been built as one of those Disney attractions. Neat rows of white and brightly colored homes, each with a gray roof of what looked like overlaying palm-shaped tiles. The buildings nestled side by side along brick-paved streets that led to a harbor, where freshly scrubbed fishing boats bobbed at anchor, waiting to be photographed by entranced tourists. She almost expected little Dutch-looking children to stream into the street singing, "It's a Small World After All."

The dining room in which she now waited was also a step or two above what Janet had been able to afford in her previous life. But a credit card was waiting with the passport. Dreu had indicated it was essentially without limit.

"Be responsible," she had said. "But you are now a woman of comfortable means. Learn the part. And remember your PIN. The Europeans use only chip-imbedded credit cards and almost always want the PIN."

The passport had been at the desk as promised. The clerk didn't even look at her picture when she checked in. The hotel's Maki Restaurant where she now waited was clearly Scandinavian, with heavy timbers bracing an exposed-beam ceiling. But the tables were linen-draped with white-porcelain tableware, candles complementing what looked like contemporary gaslights that hung overhead, and a wait service that was unnervingly attentive. Her room was similarly Scandinavian modern, furnished with what she thought must be some upscale version of IKEA. She had selected a cabernet that seemed ridiculously expensive and sipped at it while she waited.

Janet had checked into the hotel in midafternoon but was able to find an open salon and get her hair done. It had never been this short, and the new look added to the sense that she wasn't sure how comfortable she was in her new skin. The short hair made her face more severe, with larger eyes and a sharper jawline. If she had on a pair of glasses, she might not need further work to disguise her face. The thought made her chuckle. Glasses on—Clark Kent. Glasses off—Superman. And no one ever guessed.

In a trendy women's clothing shop, she had found three new outfits more fitting a comfortably independent traveler than the graduate-student clothing that had been blown to pieces in her suitcase in Rothbury. She had changed quickly in her room into a new pair of figure-hugging jeans, a gray pullover shirt, and tan leather jacket with matching boots, then added a leopard-spotted scarf. Half an hour later, she had been on Giske Island, sitting with Kari Eikram.

She couldn't help but like the old woman. Kari welcomed her like a true niece and guided her about her simple clapboard cottage from her rocker while Janet made coffee. When both were comfortably seated with steaming cups, the blind woman's face had begun to glow with anticipation.

"Would you mind if I touched your face?" she asked in her quiet voice. "It will help me see you better."

Janet had moved over to kneel in front of the woman and closed her eyes uneasily while the thin fingers gently felt at her hair and made their way down over her eyes, nose, cheeks, and mouth. With one hand feeling carefully down one arm and side, Kari pronounced judgment.

"You are a very pretty woman, Anna Eikram. And very fit. Not in the same way as your friend, Dreu. You do know Dreu, don't you?" She didn't wait for an answer, and Janet didn't offer one. "Her face is more oval. You have higher cheekbones and a more heart-shaped chin. And very fine hair. Is it red?"

Janet smiled against her hand. "You have an amazing sense of touch," she said lightly. "Yes. People tell me it's copper-colored, if that helps."

"And your eyes?"

"Distinctly green."

"Ah! I suspect you have . . . what do they call the little spots on your face in English?"

"Freckles? All over," Janet muttered. "Leave that part out of your imagination."

"I was with the *Hjemmefronten* during the war, you know," she said, her pale eyes seeming to brighten. "It was my job to observe, and I have made a habit of it since. That's how I got to know Bud. And that's what first got me concerned about the *eksperimenter*—

what they were doing in the big house on Ellingsøya."

Janet backed across the cottage to her chair. She had no idea who Bud was but guessed he must be the member of the unit that Kari Eikram had helped at some time in the past. She saw no reason to display her ignorance and listened as the woman told her everything she knew about Sava Gavran and the *eksperimenter*.

"I need to connect with the man when he comes next time," Janet said. "What can you tell me about him as a person?"

"He likes women," Kari said. "And from what I can tell about your appearance, he will like you. You must meet with Sofi. She is excited to meet you, and the man has made advances toward her in the past. If you can hand me that phone, I will call her."

It was that call that now had Janet waiting awkwardly among the white china and candlelight of the Brosundet's dining room.

* * *

Sofi Eikram was a pixie of a woman with short-cropped blonde hair, large blue eyes, an upturned nose, and delicate hands that waved excitedly at Janet from the dining room's reservation desk. She greeted her new American cousin with an enthusiastic hug and stood for a moment, studying her up and down.

"Grandmother said you are very pretty," she said with a laugh. "You must have undergone her touch test. And she was so right! I would love to have your hair. That red didn't come from the Eikrams!" Her English had only the slightest trace of an accent, and Janet wondered if the woman had lived for some time in the States.

"From my mother's side—the McIntires," she said, creating a history she would be able to remember. "Your English is so good! Did you live in the US for a while?"

"No. We learn it in school and from American movies and TV. It's really a second language to us."

144

"I'm sorry," Janet improvised, "but none of the family insisted on us learning Norwegian."

"You won't need it. Everyone speaks English. And Grandmother is so excited to have you here. So am I! We hadn't heard anything from Carl's family since he went to America. No one knew what had become of them."

"My grandfather died quite young, and so did my father," Janet said. "There wasn't a lot of time to pass along family history. But I became interested and was able to find Kari through Ancestry.com. Are you familiar with it?"

"Yes. The family history website. Well, we are so happy to be connected." She beckoned again for Janet to sit and slid onto the armless chair opposite her. "I want to hear all about you. Let me treat you to dinner, and you can tell me about your family. How long are you staying?"

"Dinner's on me," Janet insisted, "and I really don't have a schedule. I got an open-return ticket and hoped to stay long enough to get to know everyone well. I won't be an imposition on anyone and plan to travel a bit around the area. I'll be here at least a few weeks, I hope."

They talked for an hour over a delicious creamed cauliflower soup and pan-fried redfish with apple and portobello mushrooms. As conversation turned back to Kari Eikram and her lonely cottage on Giske Island, Janet was able to raise the subject of the Serb.

"When I visited her earlier today, she seemed obsessed with some man she thinks is carrying out secret experiments of some kind near Ålesund."

Sofi's blue eyes turned cold. She placed her fork neatly across her plate, wiping her delicate hands on her napkin.

"Oh, Grandmother can't let that rest. She's obsessed with Sava Gavran." She leaned forward secretively. "If you are here for more than a week, you will meet him. He stays here when he comes, likes to eat in this restaurant, and I'm sure will introduce himself.

He likes pretty women—especially those who are just in town for a few days."

"You sound like the voice of experience," Janet said with a teasing smile.

"I was eating here with friends. He followed me out when I left and asked if I would like to go somewhere for drinks. I told him I was married, and he said that didn't matter to him if it didn't to me. I made it clear that it *did* matter to me. A few months later, he tried again. He is always looking for a new conquest."

"What does he come here for?"

Sofi shrugged. "He says to care for the house on Ellingsøya. And maybe that's it. But I wouldn't be surprised if he is up to something." She shivered involuntarily. "How do you say it? He gives me the creeps."

Janet chuckled. "Perfectly said. And thanks for the warning. I'll try to avoid him."

Sofi shook her head. "You won't be able to. If he sees you, he will make sure you meet."

29

Captain Jim Vaughn flew the UH-60 Black Hawk gunship as if he had been born with it attached to his body. Although all of Adam's Air Force experience had been in fixed-wing aircraft and his instructor time had been in jets, he recognized the relaxed ease with which Vaughn maneuvered the helicopter and the smooth anticipation with which it responded. It stirred a desire within Zak that he hadn't felt for years. He was tempted to beg the captain for a quick lesson and ask if he could take over the controls for a portion of the flight. But the urgency of the mission and his recognition that they couldn't afford a misstep kept him strapped in his seat in the open bay behind the pilots.

Vaughn and a warrant officer named Frost had met him on the tarmac when his plane landed in Libreville. Their uniform patches identified them as Eighty-Second Airborne. Without any pretense of processing him through customs or passport control, they hurried him to the waiting chopper. The interior of the passenger area had been stripped down to four mesh seats that hugged the back wall, facing the cockpit. Within minutes, they were airborne, skimming east over what looked like a collection of long, dilapidated greenhouses and metal-roofed buildings until suddenly the city ended and they were over a thick carpet of jungle.

"We're headed for a small base at Franceville," Vaughn said into the mic connected to headphones that shielded Adam's ears from the drumming rotor noise. "We'll pick up the hazmat suits you wanted, refuel, and take off from there about twenty-three hundred hours. We're about two and a half hours from Franceville. It will be another hour and a half from there into Mbandaka—all over jungle. We'll be flying blacked out. Should reach your target about zero one-thirty."

"Thanks for taking care of whatever needed to be done to process me into the country," Adam said. "At least, I didn't see anyone tearing after us."

Vaughn grinned back at him. "Gabon's one of our few friends in this part of Africa. We run joint jungle-warfare and emergency-medical exercises with their army all the time. You're cleared through as one of our technical people in disease control. As far as officials here know, we're going into the back country to pull out a kid who's got some kind of viral infection the CDC wants to study. The Gabonese are more than grateful to have us hauling him out of the country."

"He's going to look pretty white for a backcountry African kid."

"I was told you'll have a company plane waiting when we get back. We'll have some of our people meet us with a gurney and will roll him to your plane in the suit. No one else will see him."

"So when we get back to Libreville, a sick kid in a hazmat suit gets on a plane with me, and we're gone with no questions?"

"Should be that simple," Vaughn said. He glanced back at Adam's black eyepatch. "I saw you studying the instruments. You an ex-flier?"

"Air Force. T-38 instructor. We took a crane through the canopy that ended my time in the cockpit."

"That's why we're up here at six thousand feet," Vaughn said. "There are millions of birds down over the treetops. When we cross over into the Republic of Congo tonight and all the way into the DRC, we'll need to drop down to a few hundred feet. I suspect we'll take a few hits, but we're only going about one fifty and shouldn't hit anything very big."

That didn't make Adam feel more comfortable. "What about your intakes?" he asked.

"They're shielded. We do a lot of low-level work as part of the warfare and medevac training. Don't worry. She'll stay in the air."

The crew asked nothing about his mission, and he offered

nothing. As the sky began to darken over the jungle, they talked about the capabilities of various military air operations in the region and what they might encounter.

"The Republic of Congo only has three or four fighter aircraft and about as many attack helicopters. They're all stationed at Brazzaville. There's nothing up in the north where we'll be flying. Even if we're heard on the ground, no one's going to raise the alarm. The people in the backcountry are scared of authority and try to stay out of things. Once we get across the river into the DRC? They have a pretty sizable air force with a couple of tactical fighter wings and some Russian Mi-8 choppers they use as gunships. Each has a KV-4 machine gun in the nose and outrigger pylons that carry up to six pods of rockets. The rockets are air-to-ground and just point and shoot. Nothing guided. So the only real danger is the KV-4. Our recon tells us there are a couple of them patrolling over Mbandaka. We'll need to get in and out without being spotted. If the kid's located where you said he is, we should be able to do that. Any other attack aircraft that isn't already in Mbandaka won't be able to get up there before we're back in Gabon."

"Is this thing armed?" Adam asked.

Vaughn shook his head. "One condition of us going over into the DRC was that it had to be stripped of all armament. If something goes wrong, we don't want an armed American gunship in one of those countries."

Adam grunted. "Flying blind to an uncertain target. What could go wrong?"

* * *

The station at Franceville was no more than a six-thousand-foot concrete airstrip and apron with a collection of rusting metal buildings squatting along one edge and jungle lurking on every side. A second Black Hawk, this one heavily armed, sat on a pad in a yellow circle of light cast by a flood on the corner of one of the buildings. While Vaughn's aircraft still hovered, its rotors throwing waves of hot air across the ground below, two other US Army airmen emerged from a door in the building, carrying a pair of white, plastic-wrapped biohazard suits and a green duffel. They waited until Vaughn killed the twin engines, then ducked under the blades as Adam opened the chopper's side door.

"This one might be a little large if you're going after a boy," a black lieutenant whose name strip read *Robertson* said. "It's for a woman, and the smallest we could get."

"It'll work," Adam assured him. "We haven't seen the kid, but he says he's five-four."

"And the bag has masks for Vaughn and Frost," the second airman, a warrant officer, said. His name tag identified him as *Taggart*. "HQ wants both of you in masks as soon as you reach the river."

"We might be flying with night-vision equipment," Vaughn said. "I'm not sure the goggles will work with the masks."

Taggart shrugged. "I'm just telling you what we were told, sir. Masks once you reach the river."

An ancient fuel truck rattled onto the apron and pulled up beside the Black Hawk. An African in a loose, sleeveless T-shirt and khaki shorts climbed from the cab and dragged a heavy hose to the chopper.

"Pretty loose operation," Adam said with a wry smile.

Vaughn glanced over at the fuel truck. "You'd be surprised. These guys are amazingly efficient and damn good soldiers. Their pilots don't get much training, but the ground forces are first-rate."

While the African fueled the chopper, Adam followed the four Americans into a small briefing room in one of the buildings where a dripping air conditioner rattled in one window, struggling unsuccessfully to cool the place. On a table in the corner, cans of

Coke sat in a bucket of ice. A large platter steamed with fried bananas and a sweet-smelling chicken dish.

"Looks like Mama Nkwa's been busy." Vaughn chuckled. "You'll like this, sir. Mama's been cooking for us here for years, and this is one of her specialties. She calls it Chicken Nyembwe." He heaped a plate with the golden meat and held it out to Adam. "If we have the fuel, we may not stop on the way back 'cause you're going to be hot as hell in those suits. We'll want to get you on that plane and into quarantine as fast as we can. Better eat what you can now."

The chicken was delicious, smoked with something that gave it a subtle hint of apple and flavored with garlic, onions, and a sweet sauce.

"Cooked in palm butter," Robertson said, holding up a strip of the chicken on a fork. "Not only tastes great but will keep you regular."

"Not what I'm going to need in a bio suit," Adam grunted, but finished his plate.

As the men ate, none of the fliers asked about the mission or their passenger. Adam questioned them about flying Black Hawks and about how the men survived in the oppressive heat of the jungle.

"You stay inside, fly with the doors open, and rotate out as soon as you can," Taggart said. "We're in the dry season now, but there's always cloud cover. Every day's an eighty-eighty. Eighty degrees and eighty percent humidity. It's good duty, but you never get used to the heat."

They lifted off again exactly at 11:30 p.m., climbed to five thousand feet until approaching the border with the Republic of Congo, then dropped to two hundred feet above the jungle canopy. Vaughn followed the Likouala River until it turned sharply south, then headed over a black carpet of treetops toward the confluence of the Congo and Ruki Rivers.

Adam's intercom crackled to life. "We're about thirty minutes out," Vaughn said. "Better give your boy a call."

Adam pulled the satellite phone from a pocket of his cargo pants and hit "Preset," then "3."

The nervous voice answered immediately.

"Andrew, you doing OK?"

"Yeah. Is it time?"

"About twenty-five minutes. Do you remember what you're supposed to do?"

"Yes. I have everything ready."

"Good. As soon as I disconnect, get things going. Remember, I'll be in a white biohazard suit, so don't let that scare you. And we need to get you into one before we can put you on the helicopter. Strip down to your shorts, and don't try to hurry too fast when we're putting it on, or you'll get tangled up in the thing. Just let me get it ready for you, and step into it. I'll zip you in and help you with the mask and goggles. You got it?"

"Got it," the boy said. "Have you found my mom and dad?"

"Not yet. But we have lots of people looking. We'll get you together with them as soon as we can."

"I don't like leaving here without them knowing where I've gone."

"Did you write the note?"

"Yeah. But it really doesn't tell them anything. Just that some people came to rescue me and will contact them."

"Until we can get you together, that's all they'll want to know. Now, you ready to get going?"

"I'm ready."

"Then go," Adam said, and disconnected.

"I've got the coordinates in," Vaughn said over the intercom. "Our visual's the big metal warehouse right on the riverbank. Right?"

"Right," Adam said. "The clinic is a *U*-shaped building behind it, across the street and to the left. There's a fenced soccer field behind the clinic. The boy's house is on the other side of that field. A gate connects the house to the field. We want to land as close to that gate as we can. He should be waiting just on the other side of it and will come through when Frost calls him."

"We're ten minutes off the river," Vaughn said. "Better get suited up."

Adam had already spread both Tyvek bio suits on the floor of the passenger area and quickly stripped to his boxers. He wrestled the larger suit on and pulled a respirator and goggles over the hood that covered all but his face.

Vaughn signaled for him to hold a headphone to his ear. "River's coming up. We should be straight across from the warehouse. Everything looks pretty well blacked out. We shouldn't have any trouble picking up his signal."

"I hope we're the only ones," Adam muttered and stepped up between the pilots. Both had pulled masks over their own faces. "OK, Andrew," he said. "It's your play."

30

There had been days when Andrew knew his mother worried that he thought about nothing but "that infernal cube." It was true that he carried some version of it with him everywhere—the three-by-three-inch if he had his backpack, and a two-by-two if he just had pockets. When he had an idle moment, it was always in his hands, the faces twisting through a subconsciously understood sequence like an old woman knitting and talking without giving any thought to the needles in her hands or the "knit one, purl two" sequence of the pattern.

But he thought about lots of other things. The cube was simply a way of dissipating pent-up energy and of providing him with a bit of status among his classmates. Deo could bounce a soccer ball off his knee and, while it was still above his head, flip backward, kicking the ball into a goal behind him. Sese could run as fast as the gray fishing birds that skimmed along the river, and Pelo was the school's best dancer, leaping about wildly as his classmates beat out a rhythm on their desktops. But nothing drew a circle of mesmerized students as quickly as Andrew and his Rubik's Cubes. Though his mother didn't believe him, he knew when his friends had had enough, and the thing would go back into his pack.

But one of the cube's great values was that it helped him remember things. For Andrew, it was better than writing out a list. Learning solutions to the cube was a matter of memorizing algorithms: sets of rules that if exactly followed always produced the result he wanted. Never something else. With a three-by-three, the rules could be divided into five steps that were always the same and a series of sub-steps that varied depending on the alignment of the colored squares when he picked up the cube. Andrew had developed his own system for matching other information he had to remember to the steps. The man who said his name was Adam had given him five things to do before the pickup. Andrew had assigned each to a step in the cube solution. He had already completed the first step, the one he called White Cross.

If he were working the cube, he would first make the moves needed to form a white cross on the top surface. As a memory cue, White Cross reminded him that he needed to find what disinfectants his parents had around the place. He knew he still had a jug of chlorine bleach, one of the choices Adam mentioned. And with a little additional searching through cupboards, he had found a bottle of Lysol. Adam had specifically suggested he find some phenol, and the Lysol bottle said it contained phenol.

Step two, what Andrew called White Corners, was a series of moves that brought white squares to each of the top corners, creating a solid white top. It reminded him that he needed to divide his remaining clean water into three portions, making sure he had enough in the drinking-water portion to keep him for a few more days if the pickup didn't go as planned. He had taken care of White Corners last night.

This morning he had moved to Middle Layer. In a puzzle solution, he would have turned the white face to the bottom and started through a series of steps that moved one of the other colors into the middle layer. His substitute action in Middle Layer involved putting his mother's big kettle containing a third of the water on the kerosene stove, adding a cup of bleach and a cup of Lysol, and letting it come to a boil. He added a pair of his undershorts and a bath towel for five minutes, fished them out with a long-handled wooden spoon, and dropped in his flip-flops. He wrung out the shorts and towel and draped them over a wooden drying rack his mother had purchased in the market. When the flip-flops had boiled for five minutes, he looped the spoon under the straps, carefully placed them upright on the floor beside the sink, and when the water cooled sufficiently, poured it down the drain.

Top Face, the moves needed to make the new upper layer a solid color, hadn't begun until Adam called from the helicopter, telling him he was half an hour away. The third portion of water was beside him on the floor in the kettle, heated as warm as his body could stand it. He had already stripped off his clothes. As soon as he put down the phone, he replaced it with a bar of soap and started to scrub.

"What has your mother told you about washing hands?" Adam had asked during an earlier call.

"Sing through the ABC song while I do it," he said with a flush of embarrassment. "That's supposed to take the right amount of time."

"Just right," Adam had said. "But in this case, you need to scrub every area of your body, including your hair, for that amount of time. If you can't rinse off all the soap, don't worry about it. After you've washed your face, put one of the masks you have back on. Once you've washed all but your feet, towel off with the sterilized towel and put your shorts on. Nothing else. Then lean with one hand against something and wash your feet. When one is clean, step right onto the flip-flop. Not the floor. Then do the other foot the same way. Once you have them on, wash your hands again and stand there until we call to say we're there. Don't touch anything." That's where Andrew was now. Standing in the kitchen in his shorts and mask, not touching anything.

He heard the distant rotors of the approaching helicopter and moved into Top Layer, the final set of steps that completed the puzzle. Carrying the towel and phone, he opened the door onto the back step with a corner of the towel and crossed the strip of bare dirt to the gate that opened onto the soccer field. The thumping of the blades grew louder. He could feel the downdraft and hear it throwing things against the other side of the fence. Then his phone rang.

"Now!" the voice said at the other end.

156

Andrew swung open the gate and squinted through the dust at the dark shadow of the idling aircraft. A tall figure in a white suit jumped from the open side door and hurried toward him in a crouch, carrying a white bundle. When he reached Andrew, he reached out and squeezed his shoulder. without speaking, the suited figure turned him around and unfolded a smaller version of the protective gear. Holding it open at Andrew's side, the man lifted one of the boy's legs, leaving the flip-flip on the ground, and inserted it into one leg of the suit. Shifting Andrew's weight onto the suited leg, he did the same with the other foot. The man wriggled the suit up Andrew's back and helped him find the arms, zipped the front up to his neck, and led him under the slowly rotating blades to the side of the copter. At the door, his mask was stripped off and a hood pulled up over his head. The man fitted a new mask and goggles snuggly over his face, then turned and hoisted himself up into a sitting position on the aircraft's floor. He pulled Andrew up after him and climbed to his feet, lifting Andrew into the aircraft.

"We're good!" he heard the man shout through his mask as he slid the door shut. The huge blades immediately sped into a dizzying whir. The craft rocked slightly, then was in the air, turning almost immediately in the direction of the river.

"You doing OK?" the man shouted at Andrew, helping him into a seat and pulling a shoulder harness down over his suit.

Though Adam had described everything that would happen on Top Layer, the speed with which things had moved since he passed through the gate onto the soccer field left Andrew feeling two steps behind. All he could do was nod numbly.

"I think we've got company," a voice yelled from the front. "Hang on!"

31

The waitress had just delivered Janet's smoked-salmon omelet with sliced tomatoes and bacon when she noticed the man step into the hotel's breakfast room, glance about, and stand studying her from the arched entrance. She spread her napkin and poked about at the omelet without looking up but sensed that he was making his way through the tables toward her.

"*God morgen*," he said brightly.

"Good morning," she said, looking up without being inviting.

"Ah. You speak English. Please forgive the intrusion, but I saw that you were eating alone. I will be as well, unless you agree to let me join you. I always find a little company and conversation makes a better start to my day." His English was well spoken but with a heavy, East European accent.

She paused long enough to let him know this might not be her preference, but said, "You are welcome to join me. But I won't be eating long and have an early appointment."

"Thank you," he said, pulling out a chair and waving to a waitress. "I will not keep you. My name is Sava." He sat without offering his hand, smiling across at her as he unfolded his own napkin.

"Anna," she said with a slight nod and smile. "What brings you to Ålesund?"

The waitress had arrived. He ordered his "usual." "I have a summer home here where I like to spend as much time as possible," he said.

Janet sipped at her dark coffee. "But you choose to come here for breakfast?"

Sava laughed a little longer than seemed necessary. He looked to be in his mid-thirties, perhaps forty, with a strong, stocky build, square face, and strong jaw. His brown hair and brows were thick but neat, giving him the appearance of Janet's vision of an East European party boss. If this was the womanizer, he must have some hidden gifts that attracted the girls of Ålesund.

"I stay here at the hotel," Sava said when the laugh had worked its way out of his system. "The house is an old, ancestral place and is being redone. The grounds are beautiful, and I enjoy walking there. But it is still not a comfortable place to spend the night." The waitress arrived with an open-faced sandwich of salmon and sliced egg and a side plate of assorted cheeses. "And you? You sound American or Canadian. What brings *you* to Ålesund?"

"American. I'm visiting my great-aunt, who lives out on Giske Island."

"You speak Norwegian, then?"

"Regrettably, no. My grandfather refused to let his children speak it after he moved to the States, and my father didn't speak a word. In fact, we've hardly been in touch. I've come back to try to reestablish some connection."

"And who is your great-aunt?"

"Kari Eikram. She's now in her nineties." If Janet wasn't mistaken, Sava's rugged face seemed to tighten.

"I believe I know of the woman," he said. "I have met her granddaughter. I believe my own grandfather, who first acquired the house, mentioned her as something of a force in the community when he was here."

"You're obviously not Norwegian, either."

"No. Serbian. My grandfather came here after the war to get away from what was happening in Yugoslavia. My father kept the place, but not in good condition. I am restoring it."

"And is it here in the city? I understand the city burned almost completely at one time."

"That was well before my grandfather came. Nineteen-o-four. And the home is over on Ellingsøya Island across the fjord. I would be happy to show it to you sometime if you are staying for a while."

Sofi was right, Janet thought. The man was a player.

"Perhaps sometime." She had finished most of her omelet and took a quick last sip of coffee. "But if you'll excuse me, I really must be getting out to visit Aunt Kari. I promised I would help her get ready this morning."

Sava stood and nodded pleasantly. "I hope we see each other again."

"If you're staying here, I suspect we will," Janet said, and left the breakfast room without looking back.

32

Adam was pulling the belts of his own harness tight over his shoulders when he heard Vaughn's warning and felt the chopper nose down as it sprinted toward the river.

"Congolese gunship," Vaughn said through the intercom. "Mi-8."

Adam snapped the harnesses into place. "Can we outrun him?"

"No. But we can out maneuver him. He'll be pretty loaded down, and that's a pig of a ship." As he spoke, tracer fire from the gunship's machine guns ripped past the window to Adam's left.

"Shit!" Vaughn exclaimed and pulled the nose up into a steep climb. "He'll have us on his radar, so we need to get into a position where it isn't painting us. Are you buckled in?" They were over the river with the shoreline of the Republic of Congo immediately in front of them.

"We're cinched in tight. Will he follow us into the Republic?"

"The countries don't like each other much," Vaughn said, pulling the Black Hawk over into a modified loop that left Adam and Andrew hanging sideways in their harnesses. "But there's no one up in this part of the country to see him. He might feel like he can follow."

Adam knew the pilot was maneuvering to get above and behind the gunship, where he could keep it in his own sights and where armament that didn't have guidance systems couldn't target him.

"He's turning back," Frost said sharply. "Or he's trying to get us to turn and follow him. He may have someone else coming to intercept."

"My guess is he thinks we'll keep going west, and he can slip in behind," Vaughn said, pulling the nose again into a steep climb. "I'm going to get up into the overcast and make a run for it. By the time he gets turned, he may have trouble picking us up if we're well above him."

Frost followed the gunship on radar as it continued east across the river. "Must not want to engage in hostile territory," he said, and for five minutes they flew in silence, the pilots' attention pinned to their instruments and the green radar screen. In the seat beside Adam, the boy sat stone still, his gloved hands tightly clenching the straps of his harness. Adam began to tell him that it looked like they were home free when Frost's voice crackled again through the intercom.

"Bogey at six o'clock. Closing fast . . . This is no chopper, and he's painting us."

"Activate the CIRCM," Vaughn ordered. "On auto. And get your night eyes on. We're going back to the treetops." The Black Hawk rolled hard onto its left side and dove toward the canopy below. Adam heard Andrew grunt involuntarily. The boy's hands gripped the tubing that formed the frame of his seat as if it were a life preserver.

"Incoming!" Frost said, his voice steady but urgent.

"Guess we'll see if this new system works," Vaughn muttered, pulling the chopper out of the dive. The night was pitch-black, and the Black Hawk flew without lights, the terrain-following radar in the nose displaying a ghostly gray-green image of the jungle immediately below. Vaughn banked hard right, and the crew flew visually, scanning the canopy around them through night-vision goggles. Adam could see nothing through the windscreen.

A sharp explosion behind them rocked the chopper and lit the jungle for an instant, then was gone. Vaughn whipped the chopper back to the left, staying just over the treetops.

"*He's fired again,*" Frost barked. "Coming in fast!"

Vaughn kept the chopper in a tight turn for several more seconds, then again pulled up hard. There was another explosion, this time to the aircraft's right, buffeting the Black Hawk and squeezing a sharp squeal out of Andrew. Vaughn suddenly pulled the Black Hawk back over and dove again for the trees. They leveled again and waited, Adam's headphones completely silent.

"He's turning away," Frost announced, keeping the intercom live as if he might need to correct himself at any moment. "You must have lost him."

"I doubt it," Vaughn said. "My guess is he thought he could fire on us when we were still close to the river. Could claim he initiated the action from his side of the border. We're too far in for that story now."

"Hell of a job," Adam said into the intercom. "What detonated those missiles? I didn't see you do anything."

"A missile-warning system is standard on this thing," Vaughn said. "And in the exercises we've been doing with the Gabonese, we've been testing a new system called CIRCM—Common Infrared Countermeasures. It's designed for missiles shoulder-fired from the ground and screws up the guidance system. The missile detonates when it hits something else. They've had systems like it on Chinooks for a while now, but that equipment's too heavy for Black Hawks. This is a scaled-down test model."

Adam chuckled. "Seems to work."

"Good news for us," Vaughn said. "As far as I know, this was its first combat test. And with an air-to-air firing. The guys at Northrop are going to pee their pants when they hear about this."

"The guys at Northrop can't know," Adam reminded. "This mission didn't happen."

"Ah—roger that," Vaughn muttered. "Damn shame."

Adam looked again at his passenger. "You doing all right, Andrew?"

The boy didn't turn to look at him. "I think I'm going to be sick," he mumbled.

Adam leaned over and pulled away the mask. "We're going to be flying pretty steady from here on. Take some deep breaths, and think about something you really love to do. But if you need to throw up, lean over toward the door."

The boy sucked in several breaths and leaned back against the webbing, eyes closed behind the wide goggles. His hands came again to his lap and began to twist and turn as if trying to mold a ball of jelly. After ten or fifteen seconds he paused, wrinkled his forehead, and began again.

Strange kid, Adam thought. *I wonder what's going on in that head.*

33

Breakfast, it appeared, was when Sava Gavran chose to try to work his magic on a potential conquest. Janet had asked Sofi about the city's nightlife and had the impression it was pretty low-key. Quiet bars and restaurants, a few with live music, but no real pickup hotspots. No natural places for the man to troll for partners. The second time Sava had approached Sofi, she had been at the desk at the travel agency where she worked on Brunholmgata. He'd spotted her through the window and wandered in.

"At first, he just asked me to make flight reservations, then began to suggest dinner or a visit to his place on Ellingsøya," she told Janet. "He was never overly aggressive and tried to be charming—but he was persistent. I had to be very direct to get him to stop asking. After that, he didn't come in anymore."

On the morning after their first encounter, Janet saw him again enter the breakfast room and look about until he saw her. He said something to the hostess, nodding toward her, and came immediately to her table.

"Good morning, Anna. I told the girl that I would like to join you again. I hope you don't mind."

Janet's look was acceptant but not warm. "I haven't ordered yet. And there's no need for both of us to eat alone."

"How is your great-aunt? Is Kari well?"

"She has lost her sight, but her mind has remained sharp. I'm surprised she's chosen to stay out there. When I visit, she seems desperate for company."

"That's a lonely spot, Giske Island," Sava said. "I would think she would worry about living there alone."

Janet chuckled lightly. "She's managed for forty years and seems to think nothing is going to happen now that hasn't happened already. And if it does, she's pretty circumspect about it. Says she's already older than she ever planned to be."

The Serb smiled thinly. "I hope I can have such an attitude—and the time to demonstrate it!"

They ordered, both having the smoked-salmon omelet. Until the food came, Janet fielded questions about her imaginary past and how she had the resources for an indefinite stay.

"I practiced law for a large firm that specialized in product liability. Are you familiar with what we call tort law?"

"Generally. Yes. When a person sues another for some kind of personal injury."

Janet nodded. "Well, when that second party is a company, some of those settlements are extremely large. The legal profession has been very successful at fighting off limitations to tort settlements. I was the beneficiary of several of those large settlements, and that money—and a crisis of conscience—freed me to travel."

"Conscience about the settlements?"

Janet frowned and chased a slice of tomato around her plate with a fork. "Let's just say that I became concerned we were far more interested in big settlements than in seeing that justice was served for our clients. When there were several plaintiffs, we often made more than any of our clients singly. And we put some pretty decent companies out of business."

She looked up and smiled grimly. "But enough about me. Tell me about your old home. I think I've seen it on the hilltop across the fjord—or at least a bit of it through the trees."

"Better yet, would you like to visit it? I would be most honored to give you a tour."

Janet thought for a moment, then nodded with a slight shrug. "Yes. I think I might enjoy that. I don't want to impose on your time . . ."

"Oh. No imposition. Are you free this morning?"

Janet feigned mild surprise. "Well, yes . . . Kari's granddaughter is taking her to visit her doctor this morning, and it sounds like that can be quite a lengthy process. I could go this morning."

"In the foyer in an hour?"

"Why not?" she said, showing a bit more certainty. "I was hoping for something interesting to do today."

"Dress to walk. The grounds are lovely, and they are very much a part of the home's charm."

She pushed away from the table. "This is very kind of you. I'll see you in an hour."

* * *

The gray-stone manor on the hilltop east of the village of Hoffland looked strangely out of place among the clean stucco and wood-sided homes of the island. As Sava walked her through the spacious home, Janet thought it appeared to be in mothballs rather than under repair. The furnishings on the main floor were mostly under dustcovers. The few visible pieces dated to the years when the home was constructed and showed little sign of use. Though the interior had been beautifully finished in Norwegian spruce, Sava seemed uninterested in displaying its finer points and was much more concerned about her appreciation for its size.

"This is certainly the largest home on the islands," he boasted as they walked without pausing from room to room. Their footsteps echoed ominously in the dim, hollow spaces. Janet's only reassurance that she hadn't been lured here for an assault was their meeting with an ancient caretaker at the door when they arrived.

"We'll be walking through the house and gardens, Gier," Sava had said to the old man who looked Janet over quickly with an appraising, but unsurprised, eye.

"I'm doing some trimming and will be here if needed," he had said in Norwegian-inflected English, and shuffled toward a partially pruned boxwood hedge. Unless the gardener was complicit, it would be hard for her guide to emerge from the house without her.

"Part of the upper floor is where I stay when I choose to sleep at the house," Sava was saying as she brought her attention back to the tour. He guided her back to the center of the main floor and up a wide staircase. The upper hallway ran the length of the house, dividing it front and back. It was sectioned by doors that separated a narrow balcony overlooking the main entrance hallway from rooms at either end. Sava led her into the portion to the left, pushing open the first side door that faced the front of the manor.

"I have a sitting room here with a splendid view of the fjord. This is where I spend my time when I stay here," he said with a note of pride. The curtains were pulled back on a wide dormer window that looked down over the front gardens and a panoramic view back toward the city. The furnishings were still central European and contemporary to the house, but dusted and polished to give the space a comfortable, airy feel.

"Very nice," Janet murmured. "I can see how you could enjoy being here."

"Here . . . and in here," he said, guiding her to a set of French doors that separated the sitting room from a spacious master bedroom.

"There is something especially exciting about spending a night in this house," her host murmured, his voice flowing like thick honey. "The people in Hoffland say it is haunted. Though I don't really believe in such things, I find that fear and arousal are so close to the same sensations. Don't you agree?"

Janet had stopped in the doorway and felt his hand on the small of her back. She resisted pulling away or glancing over at him.

"I've tried to avoid situations that combined the two," she said dryly. "So, I'm afraid I couldn't offer an opinion."

"Perhaps sometime we can broaden your experience," Sava said lightly, adding slight pressure to his touch. "You shouldn't be spending all of your time caring for your aunt."

"It's a little early in our getting to know each other to be broadening our experience," she said evenly. "And I believe you wanted to show me the gardens."

As he led her back toward the stairs, she looked inquiringly at the door that led into the other half of the upper floor.

"Nothing back there but closed, stuffy rooms," he said matter-of-factly. "Someday, I may get to them."

The gardens that surrounded most of the house were as impressive as Sava had promised: less floral than the pictures in Janet's head of formal English gardens, with a more limited variety of cold-hardy plants. But the lawns were thick and lush, the trees and evergreen shrubs that lined the graveled walks expertly pruned into balls, cones, and spirals. An occasional bed of bluebells, Hesperus, daisies, and a tall, thin-stemmed plant with delicate star-shaped purple flowers brought touches of color to the rich green and served as centerpieces where walkways converged.

"This really is lovely," Janet said as they followed a hedge-bordered walk along one side of the house and turned across its back. "Would you mind taking a picture? Or better yet, I have a selfie stick. Let's get one of both of us with the gardens and house in the background."

Sava hesitated, then shrugged and led her to a circle in the walks where one of the flowerbeds added color, the house clearly visible through the manicured trees. He pulled her in closer than was necessary with his hand on her hip, keeping it there while she snapped three poses and clicked back through them to review the shots. She didn't object and held up the best of the photos.

"Pretty good!" she said. "I want to be able to describe the place to Aunt Kari. When I told her I had met you at breakfast, she said she'd always wanted to see this house and gardens."

The pressure on her hip released. "It's too bad she wasn't able to come when she had her sight," Sava said without conviction.

Thirty feet ahead, a branch of the heavy stone wall that surrounded the property extended through the trees from their left to meet the rear of the house. It was covered in heavy ivy with a thick plank door arching through it directly in front of them. The passage was fastened by rusted hinges, a heavy slide bar, and a tarnished brass ward lock. To their left, closer to where the walls branched, she could see what appeared to be steps descending below the inner wall.

"And what's in there?" Janet asked with a mischievous smile, pointing to the gate in front of them. "It looks like the entrance to some secret garden like in the books I read as a girl."

Sava chuckled. "Nothing so mysterious—or interesting. There's just a large concrete pad behind that door that holds an emergency generator and tanks with our supply of heating oil. There's a large gate for vehicles on the other side, and I don't think this door has been used for fifty or sixty years."

"And the steps down there?"

Sava followed her gaze with a furrowed frown. She sensed she may be asking too many questions.

"I hardly even remember anymore," he said. "There was once a furnace in the back that dropped ash through a grate into a collection area. I believe there is a small hatch down those stairs that was used to clean out the ashes."

Janet looked back along the length of the stone enclosure. It was a good fifty feet to where it met the barrier that surrounded the property. Quite a concrete pad!

"This really has been lovely, Sava," she said. "But I think I'd better be getting back to town. I want to see how Kari's visit with the doctor went."

They walked back to the circular drive that fronted the house and to Sava's Audi. The drive into Ålesund was friendly, but Sava couldn't resist another invitation to his bedroom.

"My offer to experience a night in the haunted house remains open," he said as he helped her from the car.

"Perhaps some night when I really want to be frightened," she said. "But thank you for a very pleasant morning."

She went directly to her room, where she opened her tablet on the small desk and logged into Google Earth. Within seconds, she was hovering above Ellingsøya Island on the Norwegian coast. The hilltop manor and its grounds appeared as a large green square near the island's center. With a few clicks, she zoomed down on the walled compound, centering her cursor on the gray concrete patch that extended from the rear of the house to the back wall of the compound. At first glance, it was exactly as he had described it.

34

Dreu had remained on the plane in Ålesund long enough to be confident that Janet was safely on her way into the city, then stepped into the cockpit.

"Back to Newcastle as soon as you can file a flight plan and get clearance," she instructed. She needed to be where she could better monitor the aftermath of the Rothbury explosion, but able to return to Norway within a few hours if their new agent needed immediate backup.

The British investigation of the explosion at the Northumberland farmhouse was predictably thorough but led in all the right directions. Forensic evidence indicated that four people had been huddled around the explosive when it detonated. One had been identified as the owner and longtime IRA sympathizer Patrick Flynn. Several of Flynn's Irish mates were certain he had been accompanied to England by a female friend, an American, who had recently developed a relationship with the Irishman.

News sources in both Great Britain and the United States had somehow been leaked information that the woman may have been a US federal agent, on loan to England's National Crime Agency to keep an eye on renewed IRA activity centered in Dublin. Britain's *Daily Mirror* had acquired a photograph of the American woman that it displayed beside one of Flynn. Either the paper had managed to get its hands on an early, drab passport photo of Janet, or Nita had worked her magic and replaced Janet's FBI file picture with one from her college-era driver's license. Should Oslo's *Aftenposten* publish the photo, no one would connect it with the new Anna Eikram.

Media sources in England also announced that a number of Flynn's compatriots had been arrested on suspicion of carrying out the bombing at Thiepval Barracks. Only thirty xFold Dragon drones had been purchased in Ireland during the previous six months. One had been traced to the brother of Conor Walsh, a close Flynn associate. From the window of her adjoining row house, one of Walsh's neighbors in the Dublin suburb of Ballymun had seen Conor unfold the black drone in his small, enclosed back garden. It appeared that Patrick Flynn's revolutionary cell had fallen on hard times.

Dreu created a mini command center at the Premier Inn at the Newcastle Airport, where she kept a steady flow of encrypted messages flowing among Nita, herself, their new asset in Norway, and Adam, when he bothered to take the time to let her know what he was doing. She knew Nita had arranged for a Black Hawk crew with the Eighty-Second Airborne to fly him into Mbandaka to bring out Andrew Martin. The rescue had been a success, and Adam and the boy were safely back in Libreville. Three brief messages. Three bits of reassurance.

Janet had been more communicative. Messages arrived every few hours, describing Sava Gavran and his house on Ellingsøya Island, detailing her plan to let him think he was coaxing her into a relationship, and keeping her posted on Kari Eikram's condition. Janet had been to the Gavran home the day before and suspected that if a laboratory of some kind existed, it was beneath a concrete pad at the rear of the manor.

The area is completely walled, Janet's message said, *and is exceptionally large for the uses he says they make of it. I dropped down on it using Google Earth and, just as he described, there is a standby generator and a large tank for heating oil. These two items and what looks like a satellite antenna of some kind. Television or Wi-Fi. On a pad that must measure thirty by fifty feet.*

Dreu had smiled as she read. The woman was shrewd, observant, and gutsy—just as Nita had guessed she would be. The rest of her note affirmed the wisdom of the choice.

I was able to get down low enough on Google to see a lot of the detail, and several things struck me as strange. The fuel-oil tank is large—probably the equivalent of 1,000 gallons. Maybe 5,000 liters. Why would he need a tank that size if he's just keeping the pipes from freezing in the winter when no one is there? Same with the generator. It looks like it could be in the 16 to 20 kw range. That's a lot of backup power. I asked around about power outages. Although Ellingsøya has aboveground cabling and occasionally loses power to ice and snow, the outages are rare and short. I can't see any reason to have that much backup unless you're using a lot of energy you don't want showing up on a bill.

Dreu sent a quick note to Nita on her secure line requesting a check on the Ellingsøya home's energy use, then returned to Janet's message.

Please see if you can get a close-up of that pad. I believe I could see several vents coming through the surface, but the resolution wasn't good. If there are, I need to get into the place again to see what's under that slab.

Another note to Nita. "*Get us some sharp satellite images of a concrete pad behind the hilltop house about a half mile east of the village of Hoffland on Ellingsøya Island, Norway. There's only one hilltop house—made of gray stone and surrounded by a walled garden.*

At the end of Janet's message was an attached photograph—her standing in a formal garden with the house in the background and a smiling, dark-haired man pressed tightly against her. The picture was labeled *Sava Gavran*.

Dreu again turned to her phone, this time entering Adam's number. *I'm planning to meet you at Ramstein,* she wrote. *And here's a selfie of Janet with our Serbian friend.*

35

Once the Black Hawk touched down in Libreville, it was immediately guided into a remote hangar. Three clearly nervous US military police and an army nurse met Adam and his charge and ushered them into a side room. There, they were unceremoniously hosed down and ordered to strip off the white suits.

"Please—through that door," the nurse instructed. "You'll find showers where we would like you to scrub thoroughly with soap and water as hot as you can stand. There are clean shorts, T-shirts, and bio suits for both of you. When you've suited up again, we think you'll be safe with just the hoods and cloth masks. We want to get you back in the air as quickly as possible, so please use the facilities while you're in there. Any questions?"

Adam shook his head and Andrew just stood, looking nervous and confused. Adam took the boy's gloved hand and led him into what looked like a gym locker room: showers at one end, toilet stalls at the other, and lockers and benches in between. Two white hazard suits lay on the benches with green towels and a pair of boxer shorts and shirts for each.

The shower heads extended from both sides of a central wall. and Adam deposited Andrew on the side closest to the benches, turning on the water and adjusting the temperature until tolerably hot.

"I'll shower on the other side," he instructed. "Scrub every part of you as well as you can, then do it again. Hair, ears, between your toes. Everywhere. When you're through, turn the water off, and go get dried. Figure out which suit is yours and get into your underwear. I'll be just on the other side of the wall."

When he heard the water stop and Andrew pad his way to the

pile of clothes, Adam wrapped a towel around his waist and joined the boy at the benches. While they had been washing, someone had placed a tray of sandwiches and fruit just inside the door. He sent Andrew to eat while he dressed.

Thirty minutes later, they were strapped side by side into two reclining seats in one of the agency's Embraer Legacy 650 jets, lifting off for the first leg of their flight to Ramstein Air Base in Germany. The Embraer had a thirty-eight-hundred-mile range, requiring a refueling stop in Dakar, Senegal. But Adam, Andrew, and the two accompanying nurses would not be leaving the plane until it was securely tucked away in a hangar at Ramstein. There, they would secretly be transported to a quarantine unit at the US Army's Landstuhl Regional Medical Center.

Andrew had his seat fully reclined and had aimlessly been spinning the rows of the one Rubik's Cube they had decontaminated and allowed him to keep. The fidgeting had stopped, and Adam thought the boy had dropped off to sleep— something he needed to do himself. But first, he needed to catch up with Dreu.

He activated his phone, selected the secure decryption app, and opened his mail. Only one message from Newcastle, a summary of an article in the *Times* of London about the Rothbury explosion, and a catch-up on Janet's progress in Ålesund. *And here's a selfie of Janet with our Serbian friend*, the message ended.

Adam clicked open the attachment. Janet's auburn hair had been trimmed above her ears, and he was surprised at the change it made in her appearance. The man beside her wasn't any taller but was twice as wide, with rugged, square features and . . .

Andrew had pushed himself up abruptly beside him and had torn away his blue surgeon's mask. "That's him!" he sputtered, spilling the cube onto the floor. "That's the man who was passing out the baby formula!"

Adam held the phone over for the boy to examine more clearly.

"Are you sure, Andrew? This man is way up in northern Europe."

"That's him," the boy said. "There aren't that many white people around Mbandaka, and I looked at him pretty close. I know that's the man."

Adam looked again at the picture. Sava Gavran looked strong enough to reach out and crush Janet's neck with a single squeeze.

"Well," he muttered. "This may be a little more of a test for you than we anticipated."

36

To Janet, the most impressive thing about the high-resolution aerial photographs of the concrete pad behind the Ellingsøya manor was that Dreu had been able to get them to her in twenty-four hours. She couldn't fathom how the shots could have been taken, processed, shipped to some secure courier, and delivered into her hands at Kari Eikram's cottage in a single day. But Janet was quickly learning to accept that the resources of the unit were as good as Adam had described. She thought it best to accept the results and not ask questions.

The photos confirmed what she had already suspected. Vents in the surface of the pad indicated that something lay beneath. There was no indication of access to the area below from inside the walled enclosure. Beyond the outer wall, the property for half a kilometer around was owned by the estate and covered with thick pine and birch forest. It was possible that access to whatever lay beneath the pad was through a bunker entrance somewhere in those woods. She would begin there, but her gut told her that the way into the underground rooms was from somewhere inside the house.

A cut in the trees where power lines crossed the island backed the hilltop property. Janet parked her rented Nissan Leaf on a gravel siding along the Ellingsøya coastal road and followed a well-worn path past an old barn up into the treeless swath. She judged from one of the photographs that the stone wall at the rear of the house was only a few hundred feet into the woods from the power lines as they crossed the crest of the hill. At the summit, where she could see the fjord on either side, she left the path and struggled through heavy underbrush that had grown beneath the towering power poles. When she reached the woods, the ground cover thinned, smothered by the shadows of thick pines. The ground beneath was bare other than a heavy blanket of brown needles.

She had been right about the wall. It was one hundred thirty paces from the edge of the cut. A clear swath of earth twenty feet wide ran beside the stone barrier. Remaining far enough under the cover of the forest that she could not be seen, she walked its length, looking for entrances and surveillance equipment. There was no evidence of either.

From the rise of the house beyond the wall, Janet was able to judge where the enclosed pad ran to the back of the enclosure. She moved to her right, beyond where she thought the perpendicular wall with the garden gate might intersect the barrier in front of her, then walked ten paces farther into the trees. Using the compass on her phone, she hiked parallel to the wall until certain she had passed the other end of the concrete pad but found no underground tunnel. She moved another ten paces toward the power lines and repeated her search, trekking parallel again and again until back at the path. No bunker access from the woods behind the house.

Back at the Nissan, she drove another kilometer along the coastal road to Sperre Industries, a collection of three long, concrete buildings that manufactured marine compressors and cooling equipment. In the parking lot, she found an open spot among the cars in the row nearest the highway.

No access to the area under the pad from outside the wall, she typed into an encrypted message to Dreu. *Sava out of town this weekend. Will see what I can find inside.*

The response was almost immediate. *Use great care. New confirmation that research at house is biological rather than chemical. May be the threat you warned the Bureau about.*

37

Though most of Oslo's whores had moved to Karl Johans Gate after the 2009 law making soliciting sex illegal, Sava preferred to find his women closer to the harbor on Skippergata or along the north end of Ekeberg Park. More of the sex workers there were foreign women, many from Nigeria, who were in the country illegally and worked for pimps who were just as illegal. Neither would call the police if things got a little rough. Plus, he liked black women, the feel of their smooth, ebony skin, full lips, and strong, round asses. So far, he had picked up five, and there hadn't been a single report of their disappearances in the national media. As far as the country was concerned, these women didn't exist.

He found a woman he liked walking away from the harbor a block from the Clarion Hotel and made a turn around the block to see if he could identify her pimp. No one was parked or lurking nearby who looked like a likely suspect. The man might be a few blocks away or monitoring her from a hotel lobby, but Sava should be able to get the woman into his car and out of town without being followed. He was driving a black Volvo XC60 with stolen plates. He would find a place in open country to switch them during the drive to Ålesund.

The woman's trace of a blue halter top barely covered her full, firm breasts. Her long, shapely legs and full hips, wrapped in white spandex like a cured ham, swayed in a way that made Sava ache.

"What a shame to waste such a thing of beauty," he murmured and slid the car up to the curb, rolling down the window. The woman stopped, glanced quickly up and down Skippergata in both directions, then stepped to the window, leaning in to reveal most of what had been covered by the halter.

"Are you looking for some fun company?" she asked in soft

African English.

"I'm looking for someone for the entire night," Sava said.

"I do not think so," she said, looking back toward the Clarion. "That would mean giving up a lot of work. There is a convention in the city."

"How would two thousand kroner sound to you? You will not make that much, even if you take on the whole convention."

She glanced back again toward the hotel, then pulled open the door.

"How about a sample first?" Sava said, holding out a two-hundred-kroner note. "This will be in addition to the two thousand."

The woman smiled broadly. "You want some right here? You know, I can't be arrested, but you can."

"These windows are tinted. No one will see us. Just a quick sample before we finalize our arrangement." Sava released his seat belt and wrestled his pants down over his hips.

"Oh," she said, whisking the bill from his hand with long fingers. "You are already happy to see Essie." She knelt on the seat and leaned forward over the center console, grasping him with both hands and lowering her head onto his exposed lap. He pushed her down hard with his left arm and, with his right, reached behind the passenger seat and lifted a syringe from the seat pocket. As she rocked forward, he thrust the needle deep into her raised buttocks and emptied the sedative, at the same time forcing her forward under the dash to prevent a crippling bite.

The woman yelped and tried to struggle upward, but he held her firmly for the few seconds it took the drug to do its work. When she was completely unconscious, he pushed her up into a loose sitting position, drew his pants back up over his hips, and strapped her into the passenger belt. Checking his mirrors and the area in front of him along the street and seeing nothing unusual, he eased the Volvo away from the curb and started the eight-hour journey that would be Essie's last.

Sava pulled the Volvo into the looped drive in front of the stone manor a few minutes after 2:30 a.m. Essie had been conscious for the final five hours of the drive but was now tied at her wrists and ankles.

"Don't make a fuss, and don't be worried," Sava had assured her when she awoke. "I just didn't want you getting upset and difficult when I took you too far from the city. I want you to stay with me for a few days. I will pay you very well. Then, I will put you on the train, and you will be back in Oslo."

Essie had ridden in silence for another half hour, then asked to use her phone. "I am OK with going with you, but I need to let my friend know. If I don't come home, she will have people looking for me."

"Your phone is in a garbage bin in the city," Sava told her. "I'll give you enough to buy a new one when you go back."

The woman was again silent, and he could see the agitation growing as she became still and intense. "You are the man who has been taking the Nigerian women," she said finally. "And they have not been coming back."

"I don't know anything about other women," Sava said. "You are my first black woman. I wanted to have some time with you."

"When Amenza disappeared, she went with a man in a new black car. Amenza did not come back."

"I don't know anything about Amenza," Sava said, realizing that the woman who called herself Ama had been Amenza.

At the front door of the manor, Sava remained in the car with a silenced Ruger 9 mm pointed at Essie until Geir appeared with his lamp.

"If you shout," he warned the woman, "I will have to hurt you badly. And shouting won't help. This man works for me and won't care if you get hurt." He stepped out to meet the caretaker.

"It's just me," he called to Gier. "I have a friend for the night, but we will be leaving early. You can go back to bed."

The old man frowned disapprovingly but shuffled back toward his cottage, his light swaying unsteadily in front of him.

Sava walked to Essie's side of the car and loosened her feet. "We're going inside and straight through the entryway to the first door on the right. When you reach it, open it and go down the stairs. I will be right behind you with the gun."

As the clutter of the basement became clear to Essie, she began to mumble what Sava took to be prayers. He stood her in a corner beside a back wall covered with shelving, the gun centered on her blue halter, and slid a stool to a spot between the base of the staircase and the rear wall.

"Stay very still," he ordered as he climbed awkwardly onto the stool. He pushed firmly upward on the section of beam that released the false wall and stood as the shelves slid away. Squatting on the stool top, he lowered himself carefully back to the floor.

"Do not get too worried now," he said. "This is just my little playroom. After we have had our fun, I will send you back to Oslo." He spun the combination into the exposed metal door and waved Essie into the stainless-steel prep room, closing the door behind them.

"You are going to kill me," she whispered. "What is this place?"

"It's been here a long time." He opened a second door and pushed her through into a small observation room. "This is the room," he said, waving with the Ruger through the window wall, "where we will have some fun. You will stay in here until I send you back. It has food and a shower and a nice bed. Take off your clothes, and we will have sex now. We can spend the day here again tomorrow. The next day, you will go back to Oslo."

Essie stared through the glass wall at the cot with its thin mattress and single sheet as Sava began to remove his clothes. "Do people come to watch?" she asked, appearing to accept that her captor simply might be some crazed exhibitionist.

"No. This was an old laboratory. It is very quiet down here. I like to use this room . . ."

Movement on a row of monitors that stretched across the top of the window wall caught Sava's eye. It was coming from an infrared camera that covered the cluttered basement. A shadowy figure had slipped from behind a stack of old plastic chairs beside the staircase and was looking up at the ceiling beam that triggered the moveable wall. He started toward the door to the clean room as the figure moved quickly to the stairs, then thought better of it. Essie had removed her top and was nervously stripping off the spandex tights. His own trousers were at his ankles. The intruder would be out of the house and into the woods before he could get back into the basement. And he knew he could find her when he needed to.

"That old woman will know that you are here, Anna Eikram," he muttered. "I may as well take care of you both at the same time."

38

He met her again at breakfast, looking surprisingly alert for a man Janet knew had spent the night driving the black woman up from Oslo and doing whatever he had done to her after their close encounter in the basement. The few hours of sleep she had managed had come in spurts, interrupted by pangs of conscience during which she wrestled with herself about choosing not to call in the authorities.

When Sava had told her he would be out of town for a few days, she had picked up a pair of dark, flexible climbing pants; two pairs of Evolv climbing shoes; a tight black long-sleeved pullover; and a small, flat backpack from a sporting-goods shop near the hotel. Dressed in her new gear, she had gone back through the woods the same way she had approached the house when looking for an outside entrance to what she knew must lie beneath the pad.

During her tour of the gardens, she had studied the security system, noting that aside from the one at the main gate, cameras around the grounds were all inside the walls, watching the paths and drives. The graveled walks had hooded illumination that at night cast light down, leaving the tops of the walls in deep shadow. And she had seen when touring the house that upstairs rooms had early twentieth-century sash windows with twist latches. The windows in both Sava's sitting room and bedroom had been open, and she guessed the latches would move freely.

The summer night had provided no more than hazy dusk as she scaled the wall along the back of the property and found the branch that framed the side of the concrete pad. For nearly five minutes, she sat at the junction of the two walls, listening for dogs or armed guards. When none appeared, she wondered if she might be completely wrong about the Serb and his reason for being in

Ålesund. He might simply be a man who loved to seduce women and found the remote manor a perfect pleasure palace. Or the owner may simply believe that his secret was well enough hidden that standard security was sufficient.

No lights showed at the back of the house. She balanced her way along the top of the inner wall until she was over the stairs that appeared to descend below the cement pad, the ones Sava had said were used to empty an old furnace. Lying along the stone cap, Janet was able to lean far enough to see that at the bottom, there was nothing but a bricked surface with a small arched cast-iron hatch a few feet across. Just what he had described.

She rose and tight-roped her way to the side of the building without notice. The stonework masonry was inset, giving her comfortable finger and toe grips, and she easily scaled to a rear window in the upper corner bedroom. Bracing herself in the window frame, she drew a flexible jimmy from the flat backpack and slid the latch aside on the upper half of the window. Trapping a breath, she slowly eased the pane downward. No sirens shattered the hush of the surrounding forest. If there were entry alarms, they had been installed only on the lower floor. She crouched on the sill and threw a leg through the opening, found a foothold on the inner sill, and twisted her body into the room.

She was in a bedroom similar to the one Sava had taken her to, but with sheets thrown across most of the furniture and a dusty spread on the double bed. Avoiding a covered side table that stood below the window, she hopped silently onto the thick carpet and quickly crossed to the door. During her house tour, she had seen motion sensors on the lower floor, but nothing in the upper hallway or on the stairs. To get to the door she guessed went to the basement, she would have to navigate a six-foot stretch of hallway when she reached the lower corridor without activating a sensor above the front entrance.

As she recalled the sensor and the layout of the lower floor, she knew she had two things working in her favor. The alarm was an inexpensive ultrasonic unit mounted at the end of the hall opposite the stairs she would be descending. The staircase to the upper floor climbed at a right angle to the hallway, disappearing immediately behind the sidewall. So any movement on the steps would not be a problem. Her area of exposure would be the three paces from the moment she stepped into the hall until through the door into the cellar.

Like many things about this assignment, Janet was about to try something for the first time with no real confidence it would work. She had seen it done—on *MythBusters*, if she remembered correctly—and she knew it was reckless to hinge her life on this maiden attempt. But she had no better plan.

Near the bottom of the stairs, she fished a twin-size bedsheet from her pack and looped one end over a folding wooden meter stick she had purchased at a homewares store on Apotekergata, a short walk from the hotel. The measuring stick was designed to hold firmly when fully extended. She slowly inched the suspended sheet out into the hallway at head height so that its length fell to the floor. The alarm remained silent.

Carefully, she slid out behind the sheet and stood motionless, gripping the drape above her head. Still, no alarm. She eased silently forward, each step as slow as she could manage while maintaining her balance. The door to the basement opened inward, and once beside it, she pressed the edge of her cover tightly against the wall and quietly turned the knob. Again, the Serb seemed unconcerned about keeping the basement locked. The door swung silently inward. With dream-like care, Janet slid sideways into the stairwell, drawing the sheet after her and closing the door.

The area beneath the house was where unused furniture, appliances, and yard ornaments went to die. Three generations of Gavrans must have kept everything, packing it into the basement when it no longer served a useful purpose. The area in front of the wall she knew must separate the clutter from whatever lay beneath the concrete pad was more open, confirming her belief that a section must somehow move to allow access. With a broad-beamed penlight between her teeth, she began at one end of the wall and systematically worked her way along it, pulling, pushing, lifting, and probing each piece of shelving. She carefully moved aside dusty bottles, sprinkler heads, ceramic bowls, and boxes of assorted hardware, examining and probing the back wall for anything that might serve as a latch. She was two-thirds of the way along the wall with nothing to show for an hour of searching when she heard footsteps in the hallway at the head of the stairs.

With the flashlight off, the room collapsed into pitch-black. She stood with eyes trapped shut, hoping they would adjust enough to move without tripping over something if she heard the steps approach the door above. When she opened them, there was still only inky darkness. Above her, the door swung inward.

"The light switch is on the wall to your right," she heard Sava say. With light from the hallway, she could see the legs of a black woman feel tentatively for the upper step. Before the basement burst into full light, Janet sprung back along the side of the staircase and dropped behind a stack of chest-high plastic chairs. As a single bulb cast pale light across the musty room and footsteps descended toward her, she squatted on her seat with her back against the wall, peering through an inch-wide gap that separated the stack from the staircase. The light was on the other side of the stairs, leaving her hiding place in half shadow.

The woman was mumbling under her breath as she descended into the basement. At the bottom, Sava pushed her to the side, and Janet could see most of both of them. Sava held a gun. The woman was clearly a prostitute, dressed in poured-on white spandex and a skimpy blue top. The Serb turned directly toward Janet's cover, and she resisted the urge to press more tightly behind the stack of furniture.

Sava grabbed the back of a high stool that stood only inches from the plastic chairs and slid it toward the shelf-covered wall. With the gun centered on the woman's chest, he climbed onto the stool and pushed upward on a wooden beam that seemed to support the ceiling. A section of wall beside him slid outward and swung to the side. Behind it, Janet could see a heavy metal door with a round combination lock.

"Do not get too worried now," Sava said to the woman, climbing back to the floor. "This is just my little playroom. After we have had our fun, I will send you back to Oslo." Sava was forced to crouch sideways with the gun on the woman as he entered the combination. From her hiding place, Janet could see the top of the dial: *12, 36* . . . The woman looked toward the stairs, and Sava inched menacingly toward her, shielding most of the dial. The third number was blocked from Janet's view, but she could see *60* at the nine o'clock position. He shifted farther toward the woman as he entered the final number, hiding the entire dial. The door swung inward, and he waved the woman through with the pistol, closing the door behind them. The section of shelving automatically slid quietly back into place.

Janet closed her eyes and ran the combination through her memory until certain she would remember it: *12, 36, 60* at nine o'clock, and *X*. With no more than a hundred tries, she should be able to find the final digit. Sava had closed the hall door above when he'd come down the stairs and extinguished the cellar light when he'd entered the hidden chamber. The basement was again smothered in darkness. Janet sat for a moment until convinced the Serb was not immediately coming back, then moved to the stool and inspected the overhead timber with her penlight. It was the fourth beam in from the wall to her right.

Quietly, she climbed the stairs and entered the hallway, not worrying about the alarm. Sava would have turned it off when he entered the house. In the second-floor bedroom, she slipped back through the window, lifted the upper pane, and slid the latch back into place with the jimmy. Ten minutes later, she was through the woods and down the path beside the power lines to where she had hidden the Nissan.

In her previous life, she would be calling the police. But she had no idea what the rooms under the concrete slab contained. She needed to know before its existence became public. She could now get into the house and through the basement wall. She was certain of that. The question that plagued her was how quickly she needed to return to the house to save the woman.

* * *

Sava now approached her breakfast table with a satisfied smile that immediately made Janet uneasy.

"I'm glad to find you," he said lightly. "What have you done to keep yourself busy while I ahve been away?"

"You've only been gone for a day," Janet said dryly. "That's not a lot of time to fill. And I certainly have plenty to do."

"And how is your great-aunt? She is well?"

"Very well, thank you. Sofi and I will be taking her shopping later this morning. It will be the first time she's been out for a number of months. I think she's quite excited about it."

"She must be very pleased to have you here." He slid uninvited into the chair opposite. "I was hoping you could join me for dinner this evening. Are you free?"

Janet wiped at her lips with a napkin and studied the eyes that seemed to have become much more direct and penetrating. "What did you have in mind?"

"I thought perhaps dinner at Nomaden. And then I have a little surprise for you. Something I think you will enjoy."

Could he know? Had she left some trace in the house that showed she had been back inside? He might be planning another

190

trip to the basement with her as his victim. She smiled pleasantly.

"Not back to your fancy bedroom again, I hope. I don't think I'm quite ready for that."

He laughed, and she thought she could see his eyes harden. "No, no. Not until you are ready. There is just an extraordinary view I would like to show you. It does not get very dark this time of year, but it is still spectacular."

She nodded her agreement. "It sounds fun. What time for dinner?"

"I will meet you in the hotel lobby at seven?"

"I'll be waiting."

He pushed away from the table, bowed slightly, and was gone.

Back in her room, Janet slipped out of the gray-and-pink pullover she had planned for her outing with Kari Eikram. She pulled a long-sleeved denim shirt from the closet that fell to midthigh and placed it on the bed, returning to open the small safe that was bolted to the wall below a closet shelf. She had not worn the Glock, a compact model 19, since she went undercover in Ireland. It felt weighty on her hip. But the shirt covered it well. She stood in front of the mirror, turning from side to side to ensure there were no obvious bulges.

After their first meeting in the breakfast room, Sava hadn't again mentioned Kari Eikram until this morning. It had been as if he didn't wish to think of the woman or acknowledge that she existed. Suddenly, he wanted to know how she was. As she checked her light makeup, Janet wondered if it might already be too late to help the prostitute. But her greater concern was to survive the night herself, and to protect others she had grown to see as close to being family.

39

The three stood within a few feet of one another, separated by a glass partition that protected the visitor from those in quarantine. Adam and Andrew were in rooms of their own, special isolation cells with full-glass walls that could be curtained when they wanted privacy. Dreu sat in a long corridor that reminded her of a visiting room at a prison, with wall-length windows that looked in on each of three isolation units. From a folding chair, she visited with the two patients through wireless headsets that allowed her to speak to Adam, Andrew, or both over discreet channels. The patients were on similar chairs, within touching distance if glass hadn't separated them. Adam leaned toward her with elbows on knees. Andrew absently spun a Rubik's Cube, his eyes on the woman on the other side of the glass.

"Andrew, this is my friend Dreu," Adam introduced, though he couldn't see the boy. "She helped with your rescue by coordinating all the things that . . . that needed to be coordinated."

Andrew nodded without taking his eyes off Dreu. "Nice-looking friend," he said.

Dreu laughed and shifted in her chair to face the boy. "The doctors say you're both looking very good. No sign of illness. And Andrew, Adam tells me you did a pretty amazing job of being ready for the rescue and keeping your cool during the ride out."

He lowered his eyes to the cube. "I was pretty scared. Sometimes that helicopter was flying right on its side. And they were shooting at us!"

"I would have been terrified," she said. "You handled it much better than I would have." She drew a set of photographs from a file folder. "We could still use some help from you, if you're willing. Would you mind looking at these pictures and telling me if you recognize any of them?" She held the six photographs up one at a time for the boy to examine. When she lifted the fourth, Andrew's mouth tightened, and he again nodded.

"That's the same guy. That's the man who was passing out the baby formula." Dreu had selected photos based on similar complexions, features, and builds, worried that they might be too similar to be fair to her witness. She hadn't presented them in any order and had to turn the picture to see Andrew's pick. The photo was a close-up of Sava Gavran standing beside a parked automobile.

"You're certain, Andrew?"

"Yup. Certain. I have a pretty good memory."

"Thank you. Now I need to talk to Adam for a few minutes privately. Would that be OK?"

"Sure." He stood and slid his chair across the room to a small desk where a computer displayed a video game featuring a boy in what looked like a green Robin Hood outfit.

Rather than switch to Adam's channel, Dreu pulled a phone from her pocket and held it up to catch his attention. He reached behind him on the chair and lifted a matching unit. "Let's see if passing through the sanitizing process ruined this thing," he said and switched off the intercom.

She selected the only number on her menu and went to the text function. *Is this working?* she wrote.

He quickly typed: *Seems to be.*

I received a message from Nita. Two senior CIA officers have been assigned to negotiate purchase of the package for the US. It looks like the sale will be next week.

Are they trying to find the seller? he entered.

She believes so. But they are well behind us. They weren't able to trace the message from Andrew's mother to the CDC back to the boy before we pulled him out. If they're trying to stop the sale, they won't be able to do it in time.

Adam looked quickly up from the message, then typed: *Do you think they'll want to stop it? Or would they prefer to own it?*

Nita and I discussed this. Her question was, "Why do bidders still want to buy when they have samples of the Mbandaka strain?" What do you think?

Adam frowned thoughtfully. *They must be convinced there's been a lot of development since then. Something that makes it even more lethal and will be hard to duplicate in the short run. And maybe not all in this pool have the capability.*

Dreu nodded grimly. *Should we just bring them* . . . She paused, then inserted. *The CIA* . . . *in and let them either destroy or acquire the virus?*

How would you feel if they decided to acquire rather than destroy?

I wouldn't like it. This is a strain that doesn't need to be held by anyone.

Adam smiled cynically when he read her entry. *You think all these bidders who have the capability won't be scrambling to duplicate, now they know it's been done? Even if it's destroyed, in five years, someone will figure out how they did this.*

Maybe. But maybe in five years, we'll be more civilized.

The cynicism spread across his entire face. *Yeah. Right!*

So, what do we tell our person on site? No time to delay.

Find and destroy. No delay, Adam typed.

Agreed. I'll contact her now.

A door at the far end of the visitors' area opened. An aide nodded in at Dreu, whose face brightened. She tapped at her headset. Adam set the phone aside and again pressed the On button on the receiver for the intercom.

"Andrew?" Dreu was saying. "Are you still connected to me?"

The boy was guiding the Robin Hood figure through a jungle of some kind, sword raised above his head. He remained concentrated on the game until a good place came to pause, then looked over at her.

"Yes. I can hear you."

Dreu waved him back to the window. "I have a surprise for you." She nodded to the aide who stepped aside. A thin, bearded man in loose khaki pants and shirt stepped into the doorway.

"*Dad!*" Andrew shrieked, loud enough that all could hear him through the heavy glass. "*Dad!*" The boy dashed to the other end of his window and pressed against the glass until he seemed to melt into it. The man knelt across from him and glued himself to the other side, tears streaming down the separating pane.

Dreu stepped over to Andrew's father and handed him the headset. "I was about to leave," she said and turned back to Adam.

"His mother?" Adam mouthed through the glass.

She shook her head slightly. "I love you," she mouthed back and stepped around the kneeling father to see if she still had time to keep the world from making a grave mistake.

40

Blindness had pushed much of Kari Eikram's world back into memory, and age had progressively shifted that memory farther into her past. Talking to the woman she called Anna about the hilltop house on Ellingsøya again knitted those memories to the present, and Kari looked forward to Anna's visits with a relish that bordered on obsession. Blindness removes many of the cues that define time, eliminating the visual differences between day and night, cloudy or sunny, windy or calm. Hearing becomes the guiding sense, sharpening awareness of when birds wake and sleep, what the waves sound like as the wind shifts from off the sea to down from the hills, and how cold changes the sound of footsteps on the path. Anna had a way of adding color and dimension to what Kari was hearing. Their meetings reanimated her world, and the old woman awoke each morning anticipating Anna's visits.

What little Kari knew of Anna's reason for being in Ålesund brought an additional tingle of excitement to her aching bones and otherwise dreary days. The young American seemed to trust her and, when Sofi wasn't part of the discussion, told her about her meetings with the Serbian and about her visit to the stone manor above Hoffland. Anna had described the house in detail—the period furnishings on the lower floor draped with dustcovers, the lavish bedroom above with its oversize bed, the closed section that had seemed intentionally ignored, and the gardens that ended at a mysterious wall with a vine-covered door. While she waited for Anna's daily visits, Kari now imagined her way through the house and gardens, visualizing what lay in the other half of the upper hallway and behind the ancient door in the stone wall. She marveled that Anna could describe the surface of the pad in such detail, using images taken from space by a satellite.

Oh, to be young again—to be the girl who had carried messages for the *Hjemmefronten*. She would go with her new American niece, and they would find a way into the underground lair—discover what this *utlending* was up to, and what he was hiding in those closed upper rooms.

She was beginning her mental search of the second floor when she heard Anna's Nissan brake on the gravel beyond the gate, heard footsteps coming up the path, and caught the first few snatches of conversation. Sofi's was describing a new nail spa she had tried that wasn't far from Anna's hotel. Kari sighed deeply. She had no interest in going to the shops today, but Anna and Sofi had insisted that she needed to get out. If it would make them feel better, she would go.

When the two came together, the first few minutes were always the worst. Both fussed over her as if they were surprised to find her still sitting upright and breathing. "Are you feeling well today? Were you able to wash yourself when you got up? Have you eaten anything this morning?" Today was worse than usual with the added, "Let me straighten that sweater for you. I need to run a brush through your hair." She was allowing Sofi to re-button her sweater when she reached for her granddaughter's arm and squeezed her to silence.

"Someone is coming," she said urgently. It was not the sound of another visitor that created the alarm, but the effort by the approaching person to hide any sound. Sofi stood and pulled away in confusion, but Kari heard and felt Anna step quickly behind her—behind the high back of the overstuffed chair that faced the door. Then she heard the slight creak of hinges and felt the movement of air against her cheek.

"What are you doing here?" It was Sofi, now standing a step to her left.

"How nice to find the three of you together," a deep male voice said. "And to finally meet you, Kari Eikram."

Kari heard a quick intake of breath from Sofi. "*Bestemor*, he has a gun!"

"So, this must be Sava Gavran," Kari said as calmly as she could manage.

"Is this woman really your grandniece, old woman? Or are you still putting your nose into things that are none of your business?"

"This woman is my niece," she said firmly. "Why are you in my house—and with a gun?"

"Because this woman—your niece—was in *my* home and somehow managed to enter and leave without setting off any alarms. And while she was there, I'm afraid she saw too much." She heard him step farther into the room and push the door closed. "Who are you really, Anna Eikram, that you could appear and disappear in my home without turning off or triggering the alarm?"

Anna spoke from behind her. "Who and what I am has nothing to do with these ladies. Let's go outside, and I will explain why I was in the house."

"And you expect me to believe that they don't know enough to be a problem?"

"I don't have any idea what this is all about," Sofi sputtered. "Anna, what is he talking about?"

"She's here because I asked her here," Kari said. "But Sofi knows nothing about this. Let her leave."

"I can't let any of you leave," Sava said. "This woman, whoever she is, has killed you all."

"If you shoot us here, you'll be caught," Anna said. "Someone will have seen your car come down the lane. It won't be hard to trace."

"The car can't be traced to me," Sava said with enough certainty that she believed him. "How do you think I drive those women from Olso without someone catching me? And I parked it this morning at a turnoff along the coast a kilometer from here. It's an empty coastline between here and there. You shouldn't have picked such an isolated place to live, old woman." He raised the Ruger toward Kari.

"I'm one of the bidders for the package," Anna said quickly. "We were just trying to get to the product before it went onto the market. Let's go outside, and we can negotiate something."

Sava snickered. "Too late for that," he said, and the blackness that surrounded Kari suddenly exploded.

41

Janet knew instantly when she heard Kari's warning that Sava Gavran had come to the house. She had circled around the chair and, in the same motion, drawn the Glock from her hip holster, holding it at her side. When Gavran stepped through the door with his hand in the pocket of a wool peacoat, she knew the man was armed.

She needed to get him out of the house without harming the other women—convince him that she and others knew about the virus and were willing to negotiate.

"I'm one of the bidders for the package," she said when it looked like he was about to act. "We were just trying to get to the product before it went on the market. Let's go outside, and we can negotiate something."

When she tried to recreate the scene later in her head, she didn't remember if he had answered at all. She just recalled seeing him lift the Ruger. She had thrown herself to the side, hoping to draw any fire, and triggering off two shots of her own as she fell. Gavran had also fired at least once. She vaguely remembered hearing glass shatter behind her. Then she was on her side on the floor with both arms extended toward their attacker, who had pitched backward toward the door. Sofi was screaming—high-pitched wailing that was suddenly the only sound in the room, muffled by hands pressed over her face. Then Kari spoke.

"What has happened? Anna, are you all right? I heard the man fall."

Janet eased up onto one knee, the Glock locked on the still figure in front of her. Her first shot had hit him in midchest. The second struck the left shoulder as he was thrown backward. She glanced over at Kari, who sat stone still, her vacant eyes staring straight ahead and hands clutched rigidly to the arms of her chair.

"Quiet!" Janet snapped at Sofi. "We're all OK. Check your grandmother to be sure she wasn't injured."

The young Norwegian woman continued to stare at her with hand over her mouth, then turned to the body on the floor.

"We need to call the police," she mumbled through her fingers.

From the moment Sava Gavran had walked into the house, Janet had been working through the options if she were able to bring him down. Contacting the police had fallen off the list immediately. She really had no idea if the virus was in the house. Gavran might be using the manor only as a pen for his sex slaves. But if it *was* in the house, there may also be records showing who had been approached for bids and who had responded. Those needed to stay out of the hands of local authorities. The ideal resolution would be for Sava, an occasional and unpopular visitor to Ålesund, to just disappear. Leave town and never return. Step one of that solution lay on the floor in front of her.

"No police," she said. "We're far enough from the next house that no one will have heard the shots. We'll leave the car where he parked it. If it can't be traced, the local police will just have an unsolved car theft. If they trace it to him, nothing ties it to this home." Janet slid around on her knees to face her adopted aunt.

"Kari, we need some things. I know you have heavy trash bags, but we need cleaning gloves. And some pairs of old shoes or boots? I think both of us can fit into yours."

"I have those things," the old woman said.

"And more than anything, we need to know where to put this body that it won't be found."

The old woman appeared also to have been thinking through solutions. "I know the right place," she said. "We'll clean things up here and wait until night. You two wanted to take me out. I am going with you on this one."

"Good. We'll need your directions," Janet said, knowing that

Sofi could guide her to any spot on the islands. But she felt that Kari Eikram needed to be part of ending what her suspicions had started. She turned to the younger Norwegian woman. "Sofi, you'd better call your husband and tell him you need to stay the night—that Kari isn't feeling well. We won't want to be moving the body until early morning. Let's get gloves on. And nothing—and I mean nothing—related to Sava Gavran gets touched with bare hands. Stay out of the blood with these shoes. Where are the gloves?"

"Under the sink. And there is also something you need to get from the shelf of the armoire in my bedroom," the old member of the *Hjemmefronten* added.

* * *

"When we helped Bud escape the Gestapo," Kari explained as they skirted the village in the Nissan, headed toward the Godoy Tunnel, "we first moved him over to Godoy Island to a hideaway the *Hjemmefronten* used." She was seated in the back of the Leaf with Sava Gavran's body propped beside her in two heavy black trash bags, tightly wrapped in duct tape. Janet and Sofi had spent the afternoon with the corpse on a sheet of plastic that Kari had used to cover a cold frame when she was still able to garden. They had mopped the floor of the cottage and cleaned up shards of glass and china from the small cabinet that Sava's bullet had shattered. They decided to leave his Ruger in his hand. If the body were found, the gun might be traced to crimes that would link his death to other criminal activity. The bullet holes in Kari's walls would take longer to repair. But if they were careful, there would be plenty of time for that.

As they worked, Janet had shared part of the truth with Sofi. She told the Norwegian woman that she was an American agent sent to investigate Kari Eikram's concerns that something evil was taking place in the house on Ellingsøya.

"Why was an American agent sent here?" Sofi wanted to know. "Why not the local police?"

Her grandmother answered for Janet. "You know I have been to the police many times with my suspicions," she said. "And they ignore me. Our messages to my friend Bud weren't taken so lightly. Anna was sent to investigate. As you can see, there was reason to be concerned."

"But the police would take it seriously now," Sofi argued. "They can get in and check the house."

"You need to trust me on this," Janet had insisted. "If we don't handle this right, the consequences could be catastrophic."

Kari had inserted herself back into the conversation, her voice stronger and more insistent than Janet had ever heard it. "We need to do what Anna asks, Sofi. This is very important."

Her granddaughter had complied. She had helped Janet wrap the body and wrestle it into the car where it now kept the old woman company in the rear seat.

"When they built the Alnes Tunnel, we thought they might discover the hideaway," Kari said as if nothing were out of the ordinary. Blindness, Janet thought, could be a real advantage when seated next to a bagged-up corpse. The old woman's slow, aged voice sounded as if they were out for a Sunday drive.

"You will see that the tunnel to Alnes comes out only a few meters from the barn. While the tunnel was being built, the workmen used it as a storage place. But no one ever bothered to look under the floor . . . Oh! I hear that we're going down into the Godoy Tunnel!" She sat silently, listening to the echoing rhythm of the car moving through the passage beneath the fjord. "I don't hear anyone passing us," she said.

"We haven't seen another car since we left the house," Janet muttered as they emerged onto Godoy Island. "It's kind of eerie. It looks like early evening outside, and everything's quiet as a . . . well, as a graveyard."

Sofi spoke for the first time since leaving the cottage. "Visitors forget that in the winter, there may be only five hours of daylight and in summer, no complete darkness. Everyone here sets a regular schedule for living that stays the same, light or dark. It's now two forty-five in the morning. About the quietest time of night. I would be surprised if we pass anyone." She pointed right as they approached an intersection. "There. Turn there."

The road passed through cultivated fields, past prosperous houses in white, red, and yellow, their bright colors muted in the nautical dusk.

"It looks like there's money here," Janet said. "Do these farms do that well?"

"Most of these people drive to the city each day," Sofi said. "Only a few farm these fields."

They entered another tunnel. Kari grasped the back of Sofi's seat and pulled herself forward. "As soon as we leave this tunnel, it will be just to the left. Tell me if there is a red barn. Or it was once red." She listened intently until the sound widened around her. "There! On the left! Just against the rocks!"

The barn was there as she said, and it was still red.

"There's a gate," Janet muttered.

"It won't be locked. Sofi can open it. There will be room for the car behind the barn."

Janet pulled quickly to the side, and Sofi jumped from the car. A steel rod lifted from a short piece of pipe in the ground to release the gate. Janet quickly steered the Nissan onto the gravel drive. As Kari had remembered, the drive continued past the side of the barn and along its back.

"When were you here last?" Janet wondered.

"I brought her here ten years ago when the tunnel was built," Sofi said, climbing out and stooping beside the driver's window. "She could see then and walked around the construction site. The workmen finally had to tell her to leave."

"Well, Kari, I hope you're right about this place beneath the rocks." Janet took the short hook that had been secreted in the back of Kari Eikram's wardrobe from the console between the seats and slid from the Nissan to join Sofi. The first traffic of the night sounded deep in the tunnel, and the two women pressed tightly against the side of the automobile as the car passed their hiding place without slowing.

"There is nothing about this that makes me feel good," Sofi said, shaking her blonde head.

"We're alive," Janet muttered. "That should be worth something. At least we can hear anyone coming a few seconds before they exit the tunnel. Now, stay here while I see if I can get into the barn."

The building's door faced the tunnel entrance and, for a few seconds, Janet would be fully exposed. Listening intently for the sound of approaching traffic, she slid around the side of the rough wooden building. The door was fastened only with a piece of board that twisted to keep it from swinging inward. She lifted the brace and quickly slipped inside. The interior was dark enough to require her flashlight and smelled of cement dust and old rubber. She pulled the light from her pocket and flashed it about the open space. A dozen worn tractor tires leaned in three rows against the wall to her right, and the back-left corner was stacked with empty pallets. That was the corner that held Kari's hatch to the passage under the rocks. She moved to the wall to her left.

"Sofi, come on in," she called.

Five seconds later, the young Norwegian woman was standing beside her with a larger black flashlight in one hand. Janet directed her own beam at the pallets.

"It should be under there. Help me lift those aside, and let's have a look."

It took only a moment to move the seven pallets. The barn floor was laid out in squares about four feet to a side. Though covered with a thick layer of dust and wood chips, the area beneath the pallets looked no different from the rest of the planking. If Kari was right—and the passage hadn't been discovered and filled when the tunnel was built—the back-corner section should lift toward the rear wall.

Janet dropped to her knees and examined the seam between the last two flooring sections with her light. A short space about two inches long on the side of one of the blocks was wide enough to accept the flat end of the wardrobe hook. She scraped away the dirt that had filled it and worked the metal tip into the slot. The tool resembled a miniature ice hook, with a stout wooden handle and shorter, flattened point. The tip slipped easily down into the slot and back under the board. Janet pulled on it sharply. The square of aged wood creaked upward on rusted hinges. Sofi stepped up beside her to squint into the shallow passage that ran into the hillside from the corner of the building.

"That's hardly big enough to crawl through," she muttered. "And there can't be any top on that tunnel."

Janet knelt and stooped into the opening, looking along the passage. "Those big boulders come right up against the corner of the barn. Kari said this passage goes to a space in the middle of them that's covered on top by more big rocks. If the Gestapo discovered the barn and someone was hiding here, they could drop through the floor and crawl back under the boulders."

"Do you think we can get the body through there? Sava was a pretty big man . . ."

"I'll go in and see how much room we have," Janet said. "Then one of us will have to crawl in first and pull while the other pushes."

Sofi squatted beside her. "I'd better go. If you got stuck in there, I'd be out here with a body in the back of the car and nowhere to hide it." Before Janet could object, the woman stepped into the pit and dropped onto her knees. With her light extended in front of her, she wriggled into the passage. A moment later, she called from what seemed to be just on the other side of the barn wall.

"There's lots of room in here—and it's not very far. We can get him in." Her light shown again in the tunnel, and Sofi scrambled after it back onto the barn floor. "You could almost stand up between the rocks, and a big one covers the top," she said. "Plenty of room."

Janet tilted her head toward the door and doused her light. "Time to get our man put away."

Back at the car, Kari was full of questions. "Did you find it? Was it still open? Can you get the body in there?"

"We'll fill you in when we're driving back," Janet assured her. They pulled the body from the seat while the old woman pushed feebly from the other side.

They had left the barn door ajar and dragged the wrapped corpse to the corner of the building, pausing long enough to catch their breath and listen for traffic. When certain the road was clear, they pulled their bundle to the door and hoisted it over the six-inch sill. At Janet's insistence, the women struggled to carry the corpse to the open square in the floor.

"I don't want any drag marks on these boards," she explained. "No one should come looking, but let's not give anyone reason to poke around if they happen to come in here."

"I think they'll smell something before long," Sofi said. "Nothing covers that space but big rocks that are piled above it."

"They'll assume it's some animal that's crawled in from outside and died," Janet said. "And even if they find it, the only person he's been seen with is me. And I'll be gone."

"You want to push or pull?" Sofi asked.

"You fit well before. Climb in, and I'll push him in to you. He'll be coming on his back."

Sofi scooted again into the opening. "Ready," she called from beneath the rocks. Janet stepped into the pit and pulled the wrapped body after her, forcing the head into the tunnel. Straddling the corpse, she grabbed its sides and forced it into the passage. On her third pull, the body moved several feet as Sofi was able to grab the wrapped shoulders. When the feet disappeared, Janet dropped to her stomach and slithered after them, pushing as her adopted cousin pulled from the other end. The rock chamber was four or five feet across and nearly as high, and they rolled the body under the edge of one of the larger boulders. Janet nodded and waited while Sofi slid back out, following at her heels.

They again stacked the pallets over the movable floor section. Janet broke a low limb from a fir behind the barn and roughly dusted the floor. With Sofi driving, they eased the car back through the farm gate and secured it behind them.

Back on Giske Island, they stoked a hot fire in Kari's stone fireplace and burned the shoes and gloves as well as they could. Janet scooped charred remains into another heavy plastic bag.

"I'll put these in a trash bin in the city," she said, kneeling beside Kari. "It's morning, but do you want us to help you to bed before we go? You haven't slept."

Kari shook her head, smiling distantly. "I'll sleep in the chair. And I have lots to think about. I haven't had this much excitement in years."

Janet's phone buzzed silently against her leg. She recognized the text as coming from Dreu.

Bidding begins today, it said. *Bidders to have their first offers in by 6:00 a.m. EDT.*

Producer is out of commission, she typed in reply. *Has been since 10:00 a.m. yesterday, my time.*

The reply was immediate. *Then there's another player. The bid message just went out an hour ago.*

42

The message to Dreu's phone came while she was exchanging texts with Adam through the glass of the quarantine station. He had just asked for her thoughts about how they should deal with Nita's note about the bid instructions. She held up her hand to signal a pause while she read the text from Janet, then typed a quick relay to Adam.

Janet says the Mbandaka distributer is out of the picture and has been since yesterday. So he couldn't have sent the bid information.

Adam frowned as he read the message. *Any sign of a partner at her end?*

Dreu exchanged several short messages with Janet, then shook her head. *She says no. But believes the house is still involved somehow. Plans to go back in tonight.*

I wonder if the place is a red herring?

She thinks she can get into the area under the pad. That should tell us.

Adam sat for a long moment before sending a reply. *I suspect this bidding process will move quickly. Possibly over three or four days. If the Mbandaka guy isn't our man, we don't have much time to find out who is.*

Dreu nodded as she read, then typed, *Any ideas about where I might start looking for other possibilities?*

Adam punched in a quick reply with his thumbs. *If she finds a computer inside, it may be our best tie to whoever's sending the bid orders. You should probably get up there.*

What did they tell you about your time in here? How many more days?

Two, if no symptoms. Same for Andrew. You need to find our new player before then if we're going to keep the product off the market.

Instead of responding, she stood and placed a hand against the glass. He pressed his to it. "Be careful," he mouthed.

* * *

The bid announcement had come in on Don Hendren's phone a few minutes after 3:00 a.m., Eastern Daylight Time. He hadn't been able to sleep and was absently thumbing through a copy of the *Atlantic* when the phone buzzed beside him on the lamp stand in his study. He read the brief message, pushed himself from his leather recliner, and quietly walked through the dark house to the master bedroom.

"Lynn," he whispered, leaning next to his sleeping wife's ear. "I need to run back out to Langley for a while. I'll probably be there the rest of the night."

She was on her side with her face to him and opened her eyes, looking up without lifting her head. She knew better than to ask if everything was all right. Things weren't all right on good days, and a midnight call didn't suggest that they were better. She nodded groggily and he kissed her cheek. "Be back when I can," he said.

He sent Jay Bedford a text from his car while still in the driveway. *Bid's due by 6:00 a.m. Headed to the office.* Bedford lived closer and would be waiting when he reached CIA headquarters.

Security at the gate gave his car a careful once-over. He had learned to appreciate the thoroughness and sat patiently while mirrors examined the underside of the vehicle and flashlights probed the trunk and backseat areas.

Bedford was waiting outside his office. "Do we want to submit right at six?" he asked as Don unlocked his door and flipped on the office lights.

"Let's see where it starts. The seller's promised to post the bids as they come in. We'll watch for half an hour, then jump in."

"This open three-day process drives me crazy," Bedford said, pulling a chair over beside Hendren. "I know we've guessed at where others might start, but we really have no idea."

Hendren nodded. "Pretty shrewd, really. But I'd guess everyone will lowball this first round to feel out the competition."

"I don't think of two million as lowball," Bedford muttered. "But that's just me."

For the next few hours, the men speculated about the bid pool and discussed strategy. They had walked through the sequence a dozen times before and had little to do but wait. Hendren tried unsuccessfully to concentrate on another project, finally abandoning it to sit and stare at the idle screen of his phone. Bedford sat slouched nervously in his chair, playing Free Cell on his own cell.

Five minutes after 6:00 a.m., the first bid passed through the encrypted channels to Hendren's screen. Boxer was opening with $1 million. Two minutes later, Bassett posted $5 million, followed immediately by Chow at $10 million.

"So much for two million seeming like a lot," Bedford muttered.

At 6:20 a.m., Bloodhound offered $20 million. Greyhound countered with $25 million.

"Why are people playing at all?" Bedford wondered. "Why not just sit this out until the third round?"

"Bidders are testing the field," Hendren suggested, "and seeing if they can drive out some competitors. Let's get in at thirty and see what happens." He typed in Bulldog's offer and hit "Send."

The bid appeared almost instantly. Two minutes later, Greyhound came back at $50 million.

"Want to counter?" Bedford asked.

"No. Let's just watch this for a while. I want to see what others do."

For the final thirty minutes, nothing changed. At exactly 7:00

a.m., a pulsing message informed them that bidding was closed. They had twenty-three hours to formulate their next bids.

"Hot damn!" Bedford swore. "This thing is going to go high!"

"I think we should lay out of the second round," Hendren suggested. "Each bid just drives up the price."

"Others are going to do the same. I'm not sure I see the value of a second round. Want to speculate again about who any of the players are?"

Don shook his head. "Not at these levels. Any of those we listed could bid at the numbers we're looking at right now. The seller may have been thinking that round two will go high enough to knock some of them out."

"Will a hundred million do it?"

"I'd be very surprised. The third round's going to be a free-for-all."

"Do you think we'll be able to go high enough, with what we've been authorized?"

Hendren stared intently at the figures on his phone screen, his chin propped on his fist. "The director wants this. He'll let us go higher than we've discussed, if push comes to shove."

"And if it's not high enough?"

Hendren shrugged. "The Agency will have to figure out where it went and go get it."

43

Janet let the alarm wake her at 6:00 p.m., took a quick shower, and placed calls to Kari and Sofi. Disposing of your first body can be traumatic, and she wanted to be certain neither was having second thoughts about contacting authorities.

Kari's quiet voice showed the same animation Janet had heard in it the night before. "If I were only sixty years younger," she said with a laugh. "You would not be dealing with this by yourself."

Sofi's "hello" was groggy. She had also slept all day. Not indicative of a guilty conscience or any misgivings. "Can we get together for dinner?" she wanted to know.

"Let's meet here tomorrow for breakfast," Janet suggested. "My evening's already pretty full."

By ten, she was hiking up the trail beneath the power lines on Ellingsøya Island. The night had clouded over, leaving a leaden sky that shut out what muted light the sun normally provided during its shallow dip below the horizon. Janet moved into the woods, finding the shadows deep enough to require her light.

Twenty minutes later, she had scaled the wall and was working her way up the stone face of the manor. The clasp on the window was in the position she had left it. No one appeared to have opened it since she'd passed through two nights earlier. In the upper hallway, she thought briefly about investigating the closed rooms but felt the urgency of getting to the woman she had seen pass through the basement wall ahead of Sava Gavran.

The sheet again disguised movement from the stairs to the basement door, and she moved with even-greater care. Someone had initiated a bid request twelve hours after she had shot Sava Gavran. If the message had come from this house, she was still in mortal danger.

Once on the lower staircase, she closed the door silently, gripped a penlight in her teeth, and folded the sheet back into her pack. The door had an inner latch, but she left it unlocked. Should she again be followed into the cellar, she wanted whoever came after her to find things just as he expected them to be.

The stool was back against the side of the staircase. With the yard-wide circle of her light playing across the ceiling, she counted four beams from the wall on the right and placed the stool beneath the one she had seen Gavran push upward to trigger the door. It required much less pressure than she expected and lifted as if on a light spring. The wall in front of her quietly slid outward.

Janet stepped to the floor, paused in the darkness of the basement with eyes closed, listening intently, then knelt in front of the combination dial. Right to 12. Left a full turn to 36. Right until 60 was at nine o'clock and 85 at the top. Now it was simply a matter of turning the dial to the right a notch at a time, checking the handle in each position. She patiently started through the rotation: *86, 87, 88 . . .* After ten attempts, she stopped and pressed the fingers of her right hand against her leg, stretching cramps out of her palm. Fifty-five positions later at *43*, the handle released and she was able to push the metal door inward.

The room she entered was black as pitch. She flashed her penlight around until able to locate switches to the right of the door. With a long, florescent above her illuminating the space, she found herself in what looked like a hospital scrub room: two sinks on the stainless-steel wall in front of her, showers to the left, and white hazmat suits in an open cabinet to her right. This was no man cave where the Serb took his playmates for sex. This was part of a laboratory—and one that dealt with potentially dangerous material.

Another metal door passed through the wall beside the sinks. She glanced around the sterile space for cabinets that might hold test tubes or scientific equipment. Seeing none, she moved across to the door. Pulling the Glock from her pack and dousing the flashlight, she eased the lever downward and opened the door away from her. A thin bar of light seeped through the opening.

Janet pushed the door open several feet, took a quick look around the frame into the dimly lit space to her right, and pulled back again into the darkness of the scrub room. The part of the new chamber she had seen was empty, illuminated by a long window in the opposite wall and by a row of monitors bracketed above the window. She eased the door fully open.

One of the displays above her showed the storage portion of the basement in infrared relief, explaining how Sava had known she was in the house during her first visit. Another gave a long, distorted view of the room in which she stood. With the Glock in her right hand, she dropped into a low crouch as she stepped sideways into the room, facing the half she hadn't been able to see. It was also empty, but a third monitor now showed her squatting with the extended weapon.

She rose slowly with the gun still at the ready, turning to examine the room beyond the window. Against the opposite wall, the African woman she had seen enter with Sava Gavran lay motionless on a metal cot with her back toward the window. A white thong stretched across her full hips, but she was otherwise naked. Janet moved to the window and watched the woman's back rise and fall with slow, even breaths. She thought fleetingly about tapping on the glass with the butt of the Glock, but decided against it. Another screen above her showed that a camera scanned the room where the woman lay. Janet couldn't see the camera and guessed the room might be wired for sound.

At the end of the observation room to Janet's right, another door opened through the polished steel wall. Beside it was a closed inset cabinet that looked like a breaker box. She tested the latch and found it unlocked, discovering inside a panel of switches and knobs and a central gauge, labeled in German.

As she had made her way through the basement into the

observation area, her sense had been that she was seeing only half of what must lie beneath the concrete pad and that an area of equal size must extend beyond the wall to her right. The door beside the cabinet opened in that direction. In the cell where the woman slept, another door entered from beyond that wall. If there was a production laboratory somewhere, that's where it must be.

She paused beside the cabinet and examined the panel. Nothing complicated. Two switches with knobs above them marked in increments from low to high. A large, circular temperature gauge that topped at 1,200 degrees C. A row of six black switches, also labeled in German. Silently, she eased the handle down on the steel door beside the panel and felt it release. She pushed it inward into a black void.

Though she had no good sense for why—possibly from the way what little sounds she made seemed to disappear into the space— the room in front of her gave the impression of being much larger. She reached left around the frame and fumbled for a switch, but found none. With the penlight in her left hand and Glock in the right, she stepped cautiously into what she could immediately see was a well-equipped laboratory with a bank of computers and monitors lining the far wall. As she cleared the door, a hand reached from the darkness to her right, pressing the cold muzzle of a handgun against her temple.

"Do not move," a male voice said calmly. "Not even a small bit. I can see much better than you can, so do not try anything. Three steps in front of you is a table. Move forward, and place your weapon on it. Then step back."

Janet's first thought was to pitch backward into the observation room and try to take down her assailant when he came around the door. But the door had partially closed behind her, and she realized immediately that she may not be able to clear it quickly enough. Time to use her head instead of her Glock. She eased forward and lowered it to the top of the metal table.

"Now . . . move back into the other room," the voice said. "Very slowly."

As she backed into the room that held the video monitors, the man followed. The voice materialized into an older, thinner version of the Serb she had pushed beneath the boulders on Godoya Island. He was as pale as death, the result, Janet guessed, of days spent in this underground lab and nights closed away in the mysterious upper wing of the house. But his gray eyes were cold and clear as ice, and his hand held the weapon without a tremor. Reports of his ill health had been greatly exaggerated.

"Where is Sava?" he asked, waving her toward the window wall with the barrel of the gun. Like his son's, his English was clear, with the heavy accent of Eastern Europe.

"I have no idea," she said.

"He left yesterday morning to get rid of you and that meddlesome old woman. Now you have returned, and he has not."

"I haven't seen Sava. And I haven't been to see Kari Eikram for the last two days. But if he has done anything to her . . ."

"What?" he said, smiling cynically. "You will break into my house and threaten me?"

"There are already others on their way to this house," Janet lied. "If you are wise, you will let his woman and me go, and get out of here yourself."

"There are no others on their way. You don't want anyone else to know what you are looking for, or you would have called the authorities after your last visit."

"I'm here because of your son's uncontrollable need to abuse women. Unless you're a part of it . . ." She nodded at the woman who was still curled on the metal cot. "Unless both of you are abducting these women, you don't have anything to worry about. And the authorities are going to arrest Sava whether you keep us here or not."

"The Norwegian police brought in an American to investigate

Sava's abuse of women? One who knows how to enter my home without setting off the alarm and can open a combination lock? I don't believe so."

"I work for the American FBI," Janet said, holding the man's glare. "I actually *am* Kari's great-niece, and Sava has been harassing my cousin Sofi. I went with her to the police here. When they learned about my background, they asked for my help. Unofficially, of course. Everyone seemed pretty certain Sava would hit on me. He did, brought me here, and showed me enough that I suspected something was under the back pad."

The man's eyes flitted nervously with the first sign of uncertainty. He stood silently for a moment, the weapon still centered on Janet's chest.

"No," he said finally. "The connection with Kari Eikram is no accident. She has always been suspicious of this place. And I am willing to risk that even if she knows you have come here, no one else knows how to find or get into the laboratory." He looked beyond her at the African woman. "And you have solved one of my problems. I have two tests to run and little time. And until now, I had only one subject. Please—lie down on your stomach with feet away from me."

She didn't move. He took a step closer, extending the gun, the cynical smile again creasing his lips. "I can get by with a single test, and if I shoot you, no one will hear it down here. I assure you, I can dispose of your body without ever leaving this place. Your chances of surviving the test are much greater than surviving a bullet."

She thought of charging the man, but he had maintained a distance that would allow him to get off at least one shot before she could reach him—one more than she could risk. She lowered herself slowly onto her stomach. Beyond the glass, the African woman continued to sleep.

"You must be Josif Gavran," she said. "You're Sava's father.

Don't make things worse for yourself, Josif."

"Now—hands behind you," he ordered. She felt plastic restraints slipped about her wrists.

"You just happened to have those with you?" she muttered.

"You are right about Sava. He likes to enjoy himself with our test subject before our experiments. They are not always as cooperative as he would like. He will be quite pleased to find you here. I know he found you very enticing. Now, you can get up, and we will go back through the laboratory into the isolation room."

The plastic straps cut into her wrists, and she twisted uncomfortably as she knelt up and pushed back onto her feet.

"I will remove those when we get under way," he said as he directed her through the door into the laboratory. Without turning on any lights, he ushered her a few steps to her left to a second door with a small, shadowed window that she recognized as one-way glass. With the barrel of the gun in the small of her back, he reached around her and pushed the door open. "Now, please go inside. I will be with you both in a few minutes."

The door opening disturbed the sleeping black woman. She sat up with a start, began to speak, but fell silent as Janet stepped into the room. The steel door clicked shut, and the two women faced each other.

"Do you speak English?" Janet asked, quickly taking in details of the room that hadn't been apparent from the observation area. The woman nodded but remained silent.

The wall-length window was also mirrored from the inside, preventing test subjects from seeing anyone looking in. Vents and nozzle heads punctuated the ceiling, and a shallow trough ran the length of the floor along the wall opposite the window, ending in a foot-long drain. Her immediate thought was that the room had been designed by the Nazis to test gases and that she would soon see Zyklon-B pellets drop from the overhead vents or hear the ominous hiss of carbon monoxide. But for the moment, there was absolute silence.

A small steel table stood a few feet from the wall opposite the door, and a toilet in the corner showed the room's one bit of humanity. It was hidden from those looking in through the glass. Beside it was a small sink. Otherwise, the room was bare.

"Who are you?" the African woman asked, turning to sit on the edge of the cot.

"I'm going to try to get us out of here," Janet said. "What's your name?"

"I am Essie."

"Where are you from, Essie?"

"I have been living in Oslo. That is where he found me. But I am from Nigeria."

"What has happened to you since you got here, Essie?"

"The man who brought me here, we had sex. Then he left for a long time and came back later for more sex. He said he would take me back to Oslo, but he took my clothes, and I have not seen him."

"Has the older man been in to be with you?"

"I have not seen any older man."

"Have you had anything to eat?"

She shook her head. "I had water from the sink, but no food."

"Has anything come through these vents?" Janet nodded up toward the ceiling.

"No. Not that I know of. I have just been sleeping and waiting. What are they going to do with us?"

As if on cue, the door opened. Josif Gavran entered the chamber, carrying a tray in his right hand that held two syringes. His left hand held the gun.

"Both of you—kneel on the floor by the bed, and lean over it. If you cooperate, this will be harmless and will only take a few minutes. Then I will bring you some food. If you resist, I will shoot you."

Essie looked up at Janet with terrified eyes, and Janet knew they were running out of time. "What's in the shots?" she demanded. "I might be better off with a bullet in the head."

"We are testing antiviral drugs," Josif said, again waving the barrel of the pistol to get Essie to kneel over the cot. "They may make you feel sick, but the drugs will not harm you."

"And what are they supposed to protect us against?"

The man with the gray, pale face pointed the weapon at her knees. "Do you want me to give this to you with a shattered knee, or will you cooperate?"

Again, she decided that buying time was her best option, and she knelt beside Essie. With the gun to their backs, Josif Gavran injected serum into each of the women's hips.

"Now—stay where you are. I will be back in a moment with food. If either of you has moved, I will shoot you. One is enough for the experiment." With the women kneeling across the cot, he left the room and was back almost immediately, carrying another tray that he placed on the metal table. He moved behind the women, and Janet felt her plastic restraints release.

"You will both be here for several days," he said. "There is enough food for both of you. I have important work to do and won't be back until tomorrow." She heard him back toward the door and the sharp metallic snap of a bolt sliding into place as it closed behind him.

From the moment she had entered the room, Janet knew she was in a death chamber. And she knew that her captor had no intention of letting either of them out. As she had knelt over the cot with arms bound tightly behind her, expecting to feel one of the needles, she ordered the pieces of the puzzle until certain she could see at least most of the picture.

Sava had been no more than the workhorse, delivering the virus to the Congo, finding subjects for test runs, and serving as muscle if anyone came too close to the operation. Josif Gavran had always been the scientist, mutating and testing the virus and managing the bidding. Though neither man had probably thought of it in these terms, Josif had positioned his son to be dispensable. The younger Gavran was the visible piece of the operation while his father remained secreted away in the closed-off rooms of the mansion or in the concrete bunker that was the laboratory.

What remained uncertain was how she and Essie fit into the grand design. She had feared initially that they were to be given a new strain of the virus, knowing that its designers had promised a much more deadly variety than what had been demonstrated in Mbandaka. But when the old man mentioned antiviral drugs, the whole thing fell into place for her. The Gavrans were testing their new strain against the current antiviral drugs to be able to assure bidders that nothing existed that could slow or stop an endemic spread of the disease. She and Essie were the final pair of guinea pigs.

It struck her that the antiviral serum wouldn't be immediately effective—that it must take some time for the women to develop antibodies. But their captor didn't have time. The bidding was already under way. If Josif was really about to abandon them for a day, she suspected he would infect them before he left. He seemed wary enough of the American woman that she doubted he would leave her there unbound without first infecting her. She had little time. If she and Essie were to survive the next few days in this death chamber, she needed to find a solution in the next five minutes. She had part of it planned before the door clicked shut behind their executioner.

At the sound of the bolt, Janet was on her feet, pulling off her black polyester pullover and the cotton T-shirt beneath it as she went to the table to see what Gavran had left with the tray. She had hoped for a knife—even a dull plastic blade—but found something much more useful. She bit into the hem of her T-shirt in the center of the front and ripped a tear up into the neckline. As Essie watched in confusion, Janet turned the shirt to the back, bit into the bottom center, and tore the shirt in half, handing one piece to the Nigerian.

"Pull the armhole down over your head. You don't want to be sitting in here completely uncovered."

The tray on the table contained a loaf of dark bread, thick slices of white cheese, two plastic cups, and a divided plastic fruit tray, neatly wrapped by the shop owner who had prepared it in flexible plastic wrap. Janet bit at the shoulder seams of her pullover until able to tear the arms off, slipped the armless body back over her head, and pulled her half of the T-shirt after it. She then turned her attention to carefully unwrapping the fruit. If Gavran looked in, she wanted it to appear that the two were concerned about the black woman's modesty and were desperate for something to eat. And both did need to get something into them if they were to go another few days without food. She handed the African a slice of cheese and two pieces of apple. Before tearing off a chunk of the bread, she carefully tore the plastic wrap into two long strips, each about eight inches wide, and laid them on the tray beside her shirtsleeves.

At the sink, she filled the plastic cups. "Is the water good?" she asked.

"I think it is good," Essie said. Janet carried both back to the table, lifted the bread and cheese from the platter, placed them on the tabletop beside the fruit tray, and laid the platter across the top of the full cups.

"Eat what you can. It may be a few . . ." The whisper of a puff of air coming through a vent above the door stopped her in midsentence. "Essie, pull the shirt up over your mouth and nose," she ordered, demonstrating how she meant the cloth of her T-shirt to be doubled over and pulled to surround her lower face. "Now . . ." She tossed one of the sleeves to the woman and showed her how to tie it around her face over the cotton mask. She lifted a strip of the plastic wrap and pulled it tightly across her eyes and forehead, lapping it down over the cloth sleeve and sticking the plastic to itself on the back of her head.

"You do the same!" She handed Essie the other strip of wrap. The African seemed to sense what was happening and obeyed quickly and without question.

"He may come in and pull these off us," Essie said through her heavy mask.

"He can't come in now with whatever he sprayed into the room. If he comes in wearing one of those suits, we need to jump him as soon as he's through the door and pull off his mask."

A speaker crackled in the ceiling above them. "Very good effort, ladies. It will add to the value of my experiment. But the virus now has an aerosol lifespan of two or three days. When you uncover that water, it will become contaminated. And the virus is only eight one-hundredths of a micron in size. Not even a good surgical mask will provide guaranteed protection. The plastic wrap, perhaps. But not the masks you have made from your shirts. I'll be leaving you now until tomorrow. I have work to complete."

The speaker fell silent. Janet thought she heard the faint click of the door beyond the glass window. She turned to Essie, whose wide dark eyes stared back at her through a layer of plastic.

"I had just started to eat the cheese," the woman said, her voice muffled by the layers of cloth. "Is it safe to finish this piece?"

"Anything that's out in the air is dangerous," Janet said. "We need to touch as little as possible until we figure out how to get out of here."

44

As Hendren had anticipated, there was no bidding during the first forty-five minutes of the second round. As minutes ticked toward the closing, another flashing alert appeared across the bottom of his phone display.

If there is no bidding in this round, I will assume there are no higher bids than the fifty million offered by Greyhound. I will award the bid to Greyhound when time expires today.

"Sly SOB," Bedford muttered. "Looks like we're going to have to get back in."

"Let's give it another ten minutes," Hendren said. "If no one comes in, we'll bid sixty."

As he was preparing at 6:50 a.m. to enter a $60-million offer from Bulldog, Bassett jumped in at the same number, followed three minutes later by Bloodhound at $70 million.

"At least two still in play," Bedford said. "Do you want to trump them today?"

Hendren shook his head. "That should keep the third round alive. Let's save our powder until tomorrow."

"Do you think most of the others are out?"

"My guess would be no. We didn't bid. I suspect others were playing the same way we did. But we know there are at least two others in the game."

"Damn clever, this whole thing. And pretty diabolical."

"I agree. But what are you thinking?"

"Well, the bigs," Bedford said, ". . . us, Russia, and China—all have biological weapons like this that we know we won't use unless someone uses them against us. Producing them is one of those international agreements we all violate in secret and know everyone else does. We all want this one mainly so ISIS or some other bunch of crazies doesn't get it. We all believe those SOBs might use it. And with this blind bidding, if we don't get it, we won't know that ISIS didn't—and neither will anyone else."

"Except the winner," Hendren corrected.

"Exactly. So none of the others can feel safe unless they get the bid. I think the third round will go high."

"Even though it's lost its caliphate, ISIS is estimated to be worth a couple of billion dollars. They can go high with the rest of us." Hendren turned back to the phone screen as time expired. "I think tomorrow will start slow like today. All the action will be in the final minutes. We'll have to stay right on top of things."

* * *

When Dreu knocked at Kari Eikram's door, the old woman answered, "Anna, is that you?" Dreu pushed the door open to find the old woman wrapped in blankets in her overstuffed chair, staring expectantly at her with vacant eyes.

"No. It's me, Dreu—who came to see you with Adam to tell you about Bud's passing."

"You're here to help Anna, aren't you? Is she in trouble?"

"She sent a note saying she was going back to the house. We think there's still significant danger. Has she come back yet?"

"No. I think she was going during the night, but she didn't tell me much about it. Just that she believed the laboratory was out there under a concrete pad."

"And she said in her message that Sava Gavran was out of the picture and had been for some time. Can you tell me what happened?"

"I'll leave that to Anna," Kari said, a satisfied smile folding her wrinkled face. "This is her operation."

"How long has she been gone? You say she went during the night."

Kari lowered her blank eyes and furrowed her brow. "I think she believed that Sava might have some woman locked up in there, so she would have gone as soon as she thought it was safe. If I were going in, I'd have gone about twenty-two hundred. I think I just heard the clock striking seven, so she's probably been there nine or ten hours."

"Way too long," Dreu murmured. "I need to get out there. Can you direct me?"

The old woman stared in her direction for several seconds. "Is this the kind of thing you do?" she asked finally.

Dreu wondered if the woman couldn't see a little, after all. Her uncertainty must show on her face, and the old woman must have heard it in her voice.

"Well, not normally. No. But why do you ask?"

The old woman's smile had an embarrassed curl to it. "When I felt Anna's face, I could tell she was what you would call a woman of action. Yours was the face of a woman who spends a lot of time keeping your skin in perfect condition."

Now the embarrassment was Dreu's, and she couldn't stifle a self-conscious laugh. "You see very well with those fingers. But each of us does what she needs to do. Every now and then I have to get my makeup smeared a little. Where will I find Anna?"

* * *

Fifteen minutes later, Dreu turned up the long, curved drive from the Ellingsøya highway. A sturdy black wrought-iron gate with an ornate *G* in its center blocked passage through a high stone wall into the grounds surrounding the home. She could go over the wall, as she knew Janet had done. But if there was any security, she would be stopped within minutes and end up in an Ålesund court with no good story. Instead, she pulled up beside a speaker on a black metal post and pushed the call button. After an impatient moment, the box squealed, a surveillance camera mounted on top of a gate post whirred in her direction, and a rusty voice said, *"Hvem er det?"*

"I'm here to see Mr. Gavran," Dreu said in English.

"He is not here. What do you want?" the voice demanded.

"A friend of mine came here with Mr. Gavran and called to ask that I come join her. She said you would let me meet her at the house."

"There is no one here. If someone came with Mr. Gavran, she left with him."

"I don't see how that's possible. She only called about thirty minutes ago. I came directly from Ålesund."

There was silence at the other end. Then, "I will go check the house. You wait, please."

"May I come to the house while you check? I'm certain she's there . . ."

"No. You wait there. I will call if I find someone." The call box went dead.

Dreu looked up into the camera, wondering if she was still being watched. It was a wireless Micro Digitech, and she knew her image was being recorded into memory somewhere in the house.

After five minutes, the speaker again crackled to life. "No one is at the house," the voice muttered. "Your friend must have gone with Mr. Gavran."

Nothing to be gained by arguing. Whoever was behind the aged voice had control of the gate.

"Thank you for checking," she said, and backed the car into a three-point turn. When out of sight of the gate camera, she pulled onto a wide spot beside the drive. Janet was in the house—she was certain of that. And Sava Gavran wasn't. Either someone else was holding her, or she'd been injured trying to get into the area beneath the pad. Dreu pulled a tablet computer from the case on the seat beside her. If she couldn't get into the house as Janet had, she would have to go over the walls the way she knew best.

45

Janet's first inclination was to attack the window. The room offered nothing in the way of a battering tool, and her fists and elbows didn't even make the glass vibrate. She realized that as long as water came into the room through the faucet, it would not be contaminated, so she lifted the tray from the glasses, emptied their contents, and set them again upside down on the table beneath where the tray had been. Gripping the tray in both hands, she smashed it against the glass, feeling the plastic shatter as the window remained unmarked. Her next thought was the table, but it was too heavy for the two of them to lift and force against the glass.

"I think that pane must be an inch thick," she muttered to Essie through her mask. "It doesn't even scratch when I hit it."

Essie said nothing.

Janet thought back on her surprise encounter with Josif Gavran as she stepped into the laboratory. One comment by the old scientist gave her hope. "I can dispose of your body without even leaving this place," he had said. If he had indeed sprayed an aerosol containing the virus into the chamber, she guessed the knobs and switches in the observation room gave him a way to sterilize the cell after it was used—and probably dispose of its contaminated contents without having to remove them. How might that be done?

The overhead nozzles suggested steam or disinfectant. But where would a body go? She paced the length of the room examining the polished concrete floor while Essie watched silently from the cot through her plastic visor. The surface was without seams—nothing that would indicate a hinged section that could be released. And the legs of the cot, though not attached to the floor, were hooked to it with . . .

Janet dropped to her knees beside Essie's bare legs. The bed was attached to the back wall on its underside with a long, piano-type hinge and rested on the floor on two metal legs about two and a half feet long. Each stainless-steel leg had been manufactured in a *U* shape, with pins welded at six-inch intervals across the open side of the *U* for strength. A flat metal hook secured the bottom pin to the floor—and appeared to be retractable into a slot in the concrete surface. At each end of the bed, a quarter-circle bracket attached the frame to the wall.

Janet climbed back to her feet and knelt on the cot beside Essie, facing the wall. While the floor had not shown seams, the shiny steel of the back wall did—a tight line that started at the ends of the cot and defined a rectangle slightly smaller than the bedframe. She twisted back into a sitting position and reexamined the room, looking for a lever to use against the floor hooks. Their steel cell had been carefully designed to provide nothing.

"What are you thinking?" Essie asked in a muffled whisper through her mask.

Janet leaned forward and pointed to one of the hooked pins. "I think this bed releases and folds backward into the wall—sort of like a Murphy bed, if you know what that is."

"I do not know this Murphy bed," Essie said.

Janet stood, pointing to the seams in the wall behind them. "I think the bed folds back, and that section of wall opens up."

The African stood and turned beside her. "Why would it do that?"

No need to add to the woman's fear, Janet decided. "I think they can spray this room to sanitize it, and it lets them get the bed up out of the way. There might be some way out behind that wall. If I could find something to pry back these hooks that hold the legs . . ."

Essie stepped back from the cot, then walked to the door and turned back to look at it from the end of the room. "The legs are weak," she said. "You don't need to pry the hooks off. Just kick the legs backward. I think they will bend."

Janet chuckled despite herself. Sometimes the most obvious . . . But she was wearing a pair of Evolv climbing shoes with a soft heel and sole. She retrieved the block of thick cheese from the table and laid it against the front of the leg. Positioning herself at the end of the cot facing the glass wall, she drove her heel into the cheese pad and felt the leg pop from beneath the hook. Another blow at the second leg, and the cot was free.

"Now," she muttered, "there's probably something that makes this bed tilt back and forth. Let's hope that whatever it is, we're stronger than it is. Help me lift this up . . ."

With Essie at her shoulder, they grasped the bottom of the cot frame and strained upward. For a few painful seconds, the bed refused to move. Then, behind the wall, Janet heard the reluctant whir of a motor beginning to turn. Slowly, the bed edged upward, and the seam in the wall separated. A sharp, pungent smell poured through the gap, filling their cell and choking the women through their masks.

Essie shook off the smell and dropped to her knees, twisting her shoulder under the frame and grunting loudly as she strained to push the cot high enough to get her feet beneath her. At what appeared to be a midpoint, the motor refused to give more ground, and the women hesitantly relaxed their pressure. The bed held at a forty-five-degree angle to the wall, with an equal gap in the stainless surface. Janet threw her own shoulder under the frame and braced her legs.

"Pull that table over here, and push it tight under that end," she instructed. The African woman cautiously released her brace on the frame. She edged away, watching the cot as she reached back and pulled the heavy metal table until it was jammed tightly against the underside of the cot. Janet slowly released her pressure on the frame, then gingerly climbed onto the tabletop. Grasping the edge of the open wall with one hand, she leaned into the gap and peered over the lip of the opening. Light from the cell cast deep shadows into the space beyond and she pulled back, stretched toward the ceiling to gasp a deep breath, then leaned back into the gap.

"There's a steep slide just inside the wall," she called to Essie. "It ends at a metal grate that's maybe four feet wide and twice as long." She straightened and drew another breath. "I need to get down in there."

Essie shook her head. "If this closes up, you are trapped. I can't lift it again by myself."

Janet was thinking of the steps in the garden that descended to the arched iron door. If she was picturing the underground complex correctly, that hatch should be on the left end of the pit below— probably under the grate.

"We're trapped in here, anyway," she said. "The door to the room is steel and bolted from the outside. We can't break that window. But there may be a way out down there. If I can find it, I can get help and get you out."

Essie's face showed nothing but fear. "If they catch you, they will kill us both."

"They've put a deadly disease in here with us, Essie. If we don't get out, we're going to die."

The African looked up at her helplessly but finally nodded. "You go," she said. "Can you climb back out if there is no other way?"

Janet thought, then carefully pulled the sleeveless shirt up over her masked head.

"You keep this. If I can't find a way out, you can hold it over the edge and pull me back."

While Essie again braced the outer edge of the cot, Janet stepped into the *V* created by the bed and wall, threw an arm over the section that extended into the darkness, and pulled herself up along its edge. She twisted inward onto her stomach and slid backward until hooked by her elbows. Slowly, she eased downward until hanging by her fingertips. Closing her eyes and tightening her jaw against a jarring landing, she dropped into the pit.

The slide was immediately below her feet, and she pitched forward against it, slipping on her chest until her feet lodged against the grating. She lowered herself into a crouch and turned slowly, letting her eyes adjust to the dim light that came from the cell above. As she began to see detail, she realized that the grate was in two long sections that lay on steel cross bracing. A few inches beneath it, two long metal tubes, each fitted with what she knew were nozzle jets, stretched the length of the pit. She had dropped into a gas furnace.

She knelt forward onto the grate and peered through it. The area beneath the jets was piled deep with ash that tapered off as it got closer to a charred brick wall. She could make out the outline of the arched hatchway rising above a layer of gray dust.

"There may be a way out!" she shouted back at Essie. "I just need to get below this grate."

She wedged her knees against the bite of the iron and grasped the half of the grillework in front of her, pulling upward. It released easily but took every ounce of her strength to lift. When it was hip high, she hoisted it with a quick jerk up to her chest, surging the weight upward like a lifter throwing herself under a barbell. The grate bit into her knees, and she twisted her hips sideways, inching her body around and under the raised section until she could lower her legs between the gas jets. Bare metal bit into her back as she slid downward into the space below the grating, pushing the iron grid upward and forcing it against the far wall. The powdery ash covered her legs to midcalf. She shuffled her feet, lifting a thin cloud of light powder that coated her mask, leaving a chalky taste on her lips and tongue.

"I'm through!" she called to Essie. "Is everything OK up there?"

"OK here!" Essie shouted. "Can you get out?"

"I don't know. Hang on. I should know in a few minutes." She dropped onto her elbows and knees beneath the grate and jets and crawled through the ash to the door, pushing aside the powder that covered its bottom edge. The hatch was hinged, fastened on the right by a two-inch metal strip that twisted with an outer handle across the inside of the frame. She forced the knuckle of the index finger of her right hand against its bottom and strained upward. The latch didn't budge.

Janet rocked backward onto her haunches, leaning beneath the grillework that pressed down onto her back. "I need something . . . ," she murmured, casting her thoughts about the space around her. There was pressure against her right ankle, and she fished down into the ash, pulling up what she recognized as a section of tibia, including a portion of the ball. The rounded end was broken in half, giving her the flat edge she needed.

As she eased herself forward again toward the hatch, Essie screamed down into the pit. "The bed is moving! It's closing up, and I can't stop it! The table is sliding back!"

Janet twisted onto her side and looked upward. Before she could turn back and get her hands against the iron door, she was plunged into complete darkness. As she fumbled forward for the wall, the jets above her hissed loudly, and the strong, garlic-tinted odor of gas filled the chamber. She dragged her hand frantically across the rough iron, feeling for the latch as the fuel flashed into flame with a breath-draining *whoosh*.

46

It took Dreu less than two minutes to locate the log-in site for the surveillance system that monitored movement around the Gavran estate. She knew Micro Digitech well and, before joining Adam, had done security work for companies that used the Internet-protocol-based technology. One of its features, and an inherent weakness, was that it allowed users to remotely access both cameras and video files—and provided the same access to anyone with the skills to hack the network. One of her first recommendations to management was that they replace their video surveillance with something more sophisticated and preferably not Internet-based.

There were three fairly simple ways to enter a Digitech network. The most basic was to unhook the USB feed on one of the cameras and connect it directly to a notebook. But she wasn't willing to chance driving back to the gate, climbing onto the wall, and tinkering with the camera. Instead, she accessed a file on her server in Scottsdale that held all preset usernames and passwords Micro Digitech used when it installed new systems. It wasn't uncommon for clients, particularly with something like camera surveillance, to leave log-in information at the preset access codes. Within ten seconds, she knew Gavran had reset his password and username. A greater challenge, but only because it took a little more time.

Using a Trojanized version of the client server PuTTY, Dreu created a fake server for the network and instructed the system to install and register a new camera. As the Digitech software initialized the added device, system credentialing information—including the authentic server's address, port numbers, usernames, and passwords—were fed to the fake server, where they appeared in a corner display. The username was HofflandHaus, and Gavran had done a good job of creating a secure, but memorable password: *42EllingSoya#3Josif.*

With the tablet propped on her lap and the car idling in case she needed to make a quick exit, Dreu returned to the system's log-in site and entered the credential information. Her screen immediately displayed four menu options: *Gärten; Innenraum; Labor;* and *Verbrennungsanlage.* It surprised her that the choices were not in Serbian, but she realized using German spared the need for a Cyrillic keyboard or conversion software. And though she didn't recognize the final choice, *Verbrennungsanlage,* thank God for German influence on English! She selected *Labor.*

Feeds from seven cameras filled her screen, but only one showed activity. At the bottom right, in the only lighted room among those displayed, a partially naked black woman stood with her back to the camera, leaning over what looked like a single bedframe that had tilted back into the wall. A black and white cloth of some kind covered her lower face, and it appeared that her eyes and nose were wrapped in clear plastic. A distant voice echoed from the dark space beyond. Dreu eased up the volume.

"I'm through!" the voice called. "Is everything OK up there?"

"OK here!" the black woman shouted back in African-accented English. "Can you get out?"

"I don't know. Hang on. I should know in a few minutes." Though distant and echoing, the voice was clearly Janet's.

Dreu scanned the screens projected by the other six cameras. Two showed infrared images of what looked like a storage room for old household items. One was of a clean room of some kind. Showers, sinks, and an open cabinet holding white hazmat suits. Another appeared to be an observation room that looked in on the one that held the women, and two cameras scanned the dark spaces of a large open laboratory. A circled microphone with a diagonal slash bar indicated muted speakers in each room. Dreu clicked the mic for the occupied chamber. Before she could speak, movement caught her eye on one of the screens showing the darkened storage room. As she watched, unwilling to reveal herself without knowing where sound would be transmitted, a bent figure slid a stool across the cluttered floor, climbed onto it, and pushed at something overhead, out of view of the camera. A section of shelving a few feet in front of him slid inward and to the side. The man knelt in front of a metal door and quickly turned a combination into a large wheel lock. The door released, and on another of the displays, the man hunched forward into the clean room. He passed immediately through and walked into view in the observation chamber, where he paused for a moment, leaning toward a long, glass wall. As quickly as his stooped body allowed, he turned to a cabinet in the wall that the camera showed to be beside a second door, opened the metal case, and flipped up one of a row of black switches.

"The bed is moving!" the black woman in the next room screamed. "It's closing up, and I can't stop it!" As Dreu watched in horror, the metal bed forced aside a square table that had been propped beneath its end and gradually closed. The African woman threw her shoulder beneath the front edge and struggled to fight back, but couldn't counter the pressure.

The man at the switch box snapped up two switches on a larger display, twisting knobs that sat above each. Dreu clicked the camera to zoom and swooped the lens down onto the knobs and a large central dial. Below the display was that same word: *Verbrennungsanlage.*

Dreu split her screen and clicked back to her web browser. Her fingers flew across the keyboard.

What is Verbrennungsanlage?

The answer was immediate. *German: Incinerator.*

She clicked back to the menu screen for the Micro Digitech system and tapped the cursor on *Verbrennungsanlage.* A panel with two slide bars, a large temperature gauge, and a red button labeled *außer Kraft setzen* appeared. Both slides showed that whatever they measured was in the "Full-on" position. The needle on the temperature gauge was sliding rapidly upward toward 70 degrees Celsius. Without using the cursor pad, Dreu jabbed her finger onto the touchscreen, depressing the red button.

* * *

Don Hendren slammed his fist onto the oak desktop with enough force that he blanked the screen on his phone and toppled a Styrofoam cup of lukewarm coffee onto its side. "Damn, damn, damn, damn, damn!" he sputtered, snatching two tissues from a box beside the spill and slapping them onto the puddle, splattering his shirt front. Jay Bedford walked to the table beneath the heavily shaded window and retrieved a stack of paper towels. Without comment, he surrounded the brown liquid and closed in on it, dropping the soaked towels into the wastebasket.

"Where did Chow come from?" Hendren fumed. "They sat out in the second round and then, *Bam!*"

The third round had again been silent through the first thirty minutes. At 6:30 a.m., Hendren had opened for Bulldog at $100 million to see who was still in play.

There was no action until 6:45 a.m., when Bloodhound again came in at $150 million.

"They're trying to thin the field," Bedford had said. "Just like we are. How do you want to play this?"

"We prepare at two hundred million and drop it in at the last minute, if no one else has raised," Hendren replied, tapping in the offer. "They've been timing this to the exact second, so I think we can play it close."

The screen had continued to display *Bloodhound—$150 million*. With ten seconds showing on the timer, Hendren punched "Send." The screen had blanked for a fraction of a second, then displayed Bulldog at $200 million. As the pair had turned to each other to bump fists, the screen again blanked and as the final second ticked away flashed *Chow—$270 million.*

"They guessed someone would come in late above two hundred and laid out a number that would be safe," Hendren fumed. "Chow had that two-seventy ready and risked waiting till the last two seconds."

"You think it's ISIS?"

Hendren shook his head. "My guess is Russia, but we can't take that chance."

Bedford nodded. "I doubt the seller even knows. He'll have the money sent to that numbered account somewhere—part now, part on delivery—and arrange a blind exchange. And from what we're hearing from the chief, we don't seem a bit closer to knowing who this is."

Hendren grunted his agreement. "We need to be ready to jump back in if the buyer doesn't come through with the full payment."

Bedford was doubtful. "They've been promised exclusive rights. The buyer will lose that if he doesn't pay in full. And we're assuming the seller will honor the deal."

"For two hundred seventy million? I think so." Hendren picked up the tipped cup and tossed it into the wastebasket after the soaked towels. "We'd better make the long walk upstairs. The director's going to be one pissed son of a bitch."

"He approved us at two hundred," Bedford reminded him. "We all agreed that should do the job."

Hendren cast him a sour glance. "Yeah. I'll bet that's just what he'll say."

47

Dreu watched the black woman claw desperately at the closed section of wall and weighed her options. Adam had returned the secure phone after each of their exchanges, concerned that he was being too carefully watched and had too little control of his surroundings. No way to talk this through. It was time to either storm the gates or call in Norwegian authorities. But as well-hidden as Janet had described the lab facilities as being, the women's captor could simply refuse to cooperate and let them die beneath that pad.

She turned to the video display of the holding cell and selected another icon, a small representation of an old hard disk. A drop-down menu invited her to review recorded images, working backward in ten-minute intervals. She selected the last ten minutes. The segment began with Janet climbing over the edge of the tilted bed into the back chamber. For the next ninety seconds, there was silence with the black woman standing nervously, leaning against the raised edge of the frame. Then, Janet's voice. "There may be a way out! I just need to get below this grate . . ."

Another moment of silence, and the video reached the point where Dreu had begun to see the action as it occurred.

"I'm through!" Dreu heard Janet say again. "Is everything OK up there?"

"OK here!" the black woman shouted. "Can you get out?"

"I don't know. Hang on. I should know in a few minutes."

There may have been a way out—and Janet may have had enough time to use it. Dreu closed her eyes and tried to envision the house plan, what she had seen of the basement and underground rooms from the video feed, and how they might lie under the rear pad. If the incinerator was farthest from the main building . . . She had seen the satellite footage of the pad and no signs of any break in that surface larger than a vent. So outside access to the furnace area would have to . . .

Snatching a small, shoulder-strap handbag from the seat beside her and turning off the ignition, Dreu jumped from the car and sprinted back up the road to the gate. At the wall, she turned to her left and ran along the cleared strip that separated the barrier from the surrounding forest. After a hundred yards, she turned right as the wall turned, jogging another hundred to where the wall turned again across the back. Midway down the rear section, she paused, stepped away from the wall until she could see the top of the roof, then backtracked for twenty paces. Throwing the long strap of her bag over her neck and shoulder, Dreu began to scale the gray stone.

* * *

When the jets kicked on overhead and the chamber burst into flame above her, Janet instinctively yanked the plastic from her eyes and pulled the cloth wrap from her face. They would melt and burn before her skin did. The flame provided enough light to see the latch clearly, and she gasped a breath of the little remaining oxygen in the chamber and pounded downward on the metal latch with the piece of bone. It refused to budge. Above her, the flames sucked the air upward in a deafening roar. Sweat poured from her body, burning her eyes and sticking as gray paste to her skin. She felt that at any moment her hair would ignite and pulled her hands back across it, bracing her elbows against the bricks of the floor and tucking her head downward. She thought for a moment of Michael Bond, of how he wasn't even aware that she was no longer Janet McIntire, and of how she had always dreaded the thought of burning to death. Her shoes began to scorch the bottoms of her feet, and she wondered if it might minimize the pain to just stand up into the flames. Then, she was suddenly plunged again into blackness.

242

Janet's first thought was that she had passed out—slipped into some semiconscious state where she was still aware, but light and sound and pain had disappeared. But the pasty taste remained on her lips, and her feet still burned. For some reason, the flames had gone out. She needed to escape before the chamber again filled with fire.

She reached for the iron door and latch, running her fingers over the hot metal strip. Feeling told her what her eyes had not seen before—that the latch rested *down* against a slight lip. From the outside, the handle was pushed downward to open the hatch. From the inside, the latch had to be forced *up*. Scooting forward, Janet again braced her elbows and thrust the length of bone up against the flat bar. It scraped upward. Again, she hammered at it from below. This time, it popped free, and the hatch edged outward. Cool air tumbled through the gap onto her wrists, and she thrust forward with the bone, forcing the door farther open. Pulling her knees up beneath her, she dove headfirst through the arched opening.

The stones beneath her were wonderfully damp and the air thick with the smell of moss and wet earth. She pushed onto her knees and looked up the stone steps that had been her initial clue that the hatch existed. For the first time, it occurred to her that she might carry the virus, that whatever she touched or breathed on might become contaminated. But she had to get back into the house and free Essie. And Josif Gavran must still be in there. He had seen her enter the furnace, closed it after her, and ignited the flame.

Janet stood unsteadily and stripped off her shoes and tight black pants, tossing them back through the hatchway into the furnace pit. Any of the pathogen that had been on her mask and plastic visor was still in there, and the airborne virus would have been consumed by the flames. What remained may be in her hair and on the skin of her upper body. As soon as she freed Essie, they could use the showers in the prep room. She still might escape this plague.

A shadow fell across her from the top of the stairway, and she instinctively turned flat against the damp bricks as she looked up. The man Sava had called Gier stood above her, a shotgun cradled in the crook of his elbow. His weathered face was sad but determined.

"You shouldn't have come poking around here," he said flatly. "I don't like what the Gavrans have been doing, but I am too much a part of it to escape it now."

Janet turned back into the center of the stairwell. "You can go to the police, Gier. Tell them what you know. They will go light on you if you help them stop these men."

He shook his head grimly. "I knew all about the rooms down there and helped young Sava burn the bodies, just as I was trying to burn you. I'm too old to go to prison."

"You won't need to go to prison," Janet insisted. "Go with me and . . ." She took a cautious step toward him.

"You've got the sickness," he said, raising the shotgun. "Josif said when he left that I can't let you out of there. I'm very sorry, but you can't come up the stairs." The barrel swung upward, centering on her chest, and the air cracked loudly. *Bam!* Sharp and crisp. Not with the full-throated boom of a heavy-gauge shotgun— a boom she would not have heard if the weapon had discharged into her body. As Janet watched in puzzled surprise, the old man lurched forward with a startled gasp, the gun clattering down the stone steps as he tumbled after it.

48

Beyond the wall, Dreu had been able to hear the faint scratching of footsteps on gravel. They were to her left and moving farther in that direction, some distance into the grounds. She cautiously reached an arm over the cement cap of the wall and pulled herself upward until she could see into the grounds, feet and legs trembling as her toes gripped at the space between the rough stones.

The man was moving along a center path at a fast shuffle, his aged body bent slightly forward and eyes down, arms cradling a pump-action shotgun. As he reached a wall that connected the one surrounding the property to the back of the house, he swung left. If he were to look up and scan the area about him, he would see her, and she ducked her head below the cap. After a few seconds, the scraping on the gravel stopped. She heard him speak with a rolling Norwegian accent.

Dreu pulled again upward until she could see the man staring down into a stairwell that descended below the base of the interior wall, thirty yards away. She heard Janet's voice reply from below, muffled and unclear. Somehow, she had managed to escape the space beneath the pad.

The old man shook his head. "I knew all about the rooms down there and helped young Sava burn the bodies, just as I was trying to burn you," he said. "I'm too old to go to prison."

Dreu found a higher toehold and pulled herself upward until she could throw a leg onto the top and roll onto her stomach, stretching along the cap. Her left hand fished into her carry bag for the Bersa .380 that Adam had insisted she learn to fire before he would allow her to go into the field again. She had proven to have a natural eye, but hated the thought of ever having to use the thing. As she watched the man at the stairwell begin to lift the shotgun, she knew this was the time. She stretched with the weapon extended at arm's length, braced in both hands.

"I'm very sorry," he was saying, "but you can't come up the stairs." She fired once, and the man pitched forward into the stairwell.

Dreu dropped her chin onto her extended arms, her eyes glued on the empty stairs. She had just shot a man—killed him, she hoped—and she felt nothing but fear and emptiness. As she watched, a dust-covered head peered tentatively over the edge of the stairwell, looked about quickly, and disappeared. Dreu raised her head and tried to steady the Bersa. The gray head and shoulders emerged again aboveground—a slender female form wearing only a blackened bra and panties. One cautious step at a time, Janet climbed from the stairwell. For the first few seconds, her eyes stayed low, searching the trees and manicured bushes for the shooter. She looked up first at the windows of the house, then at the wall. Her eyes met Dreu's, and she fell to her knees on the gravel.

Dreu swung down the inside of the wall, lowered herself as far as her arms allowed, and dropped heavily to the ground. She cut across a carefully clipped section of lawn and was midway to Janet when the woman raised her arms.

"Don't come any closer," she called. "They exposed me to the virus. I might be contaminated."

Dreu stopped fifteen paces from the soot-covered woman. "We need to get you to a hospital as quickly as we can. Were those hazmat suits I saw in the house?"

Janet struggled stiffly to her feet. "There are three. My guess is that the front door will be open, and I can take you to them. You walk ahead. I'll give directions until you're suited up. One of the other suits needs to go to a woman inside." Words tumbled from Janet as she emptied a dammed-up river of thought. "Let me close this hatch, and let's get moving. You stay ahead until we get into the room with the suits and get them on. There are computers down there that may tell us who's been contacted about this sale and where Josif Gavran's gone."

Dreu had started toward the front of the house but stopped at the mention of a second Gavran.

"Oh, yes," Janet called after her. "Sava's father's been doing most of the work on this thing and living upstairs. I'm pretty sure he's the brains behind the operation and suspect he's taken off with the merchandise. You need to see if you can track him. But once we open the door to the room we were being held in, that whole area will be contaminated. You need to be protected."

Dreu walked as far ahead of Janet as communication allowed, found the front door unlocked, and was guided into the basement and to the shelf wall. Janet stopped midway down the basement stairs and sat on a step, directing Dreu through manipulating the overhead beam and dialing the combination into the steel door.

"When you get in there, suit up and come let me know," Janet called from the stairway. "I don't want to get any closer than necessary—especially if you aren't covered."

Inside the first chamber, Dreu pulled on the largest of the suits, including the hood and full-face mask. Instead of the heavier gloves, she found a pair in latex on the shelf above the suits. Back at the door, she waved Janet into the room.

"There are masks and goggles in here on the shelf," she said. "Get showered, and get them on. Where's the other woman?"

Janet waived her to silence, stripped off her ash-covered underwear, and turned the shower full-on. While Dreu stood impatiently with one of the suits draped over her arm, Janet scrubbed and scrubbed again before toweling herself dry. When the suit, mask, and goggles were in place, she led Dreu through a second door into the observation room. The African woman sat hunched forward on the cot, elbows on knees, and head hanging, her face still covered with the torn shirts and plastic wrap.

"Come with me," Janet instructed and passed through another

door, groping along the wall until she found a bank of light switches. When the room illuminated, Dreu found herself in a well-equipped laboratory. Four stainless-steel tables covered with racks of glass tubes and flasks, sophisticated instrumentation, and bottles of chemicals filled most of the space. On the opposite side, three computers and a row of screens stretched along the wall.

"I'm going to get Essie, and we'll get her showered and suited up," Janet said, walking to the door that entered the contaminated chamber. "Why don't you get to work on those computers and see what you can find?"

As she wound her way between tables, Dreu heard the woman called Essie shriek in delight as she recognized Janet in the open doorway. The door closed behind them, and Dreu was alone with the computers. She selected the one with notes scattered about it and a worn desk chair tucked beneath the keyboard. Its user had left in haste, and a notepad beside the computer gave Dreu her first clue that she was at the right place. Scribbled across the center of the pad were two eye-catching sums: *$200 million*, followed by *Bulldog*; and *$270 million*, followed by the word *Chow*. A large star was scribbled beside *Chow*.

Dreu turned on the machine and waited for it to run through its booting sequence. It happened rapidly, and she knew she had fast service and good connection. Behind her, she heard Janet and Essie leave the contamination chamber and move back through the observation area into the prep room, closing off each section as they passed through it.

When the log-in screen appeared, Dreu again entered *HofflandHaus* as the username and sat for a moment, then pushed back and made her way across the laboratory to the prep room. Essie had showered and donned the suit. Janet was again scrubbing beneath a stream of hot water with her suit still on.

"Janet, what was Gavran's father's name?" she shouted over the noise of the showers and muffling of her hood. Janet twisted off the steaming flow and shook water from her mask.

"What?" she shouted back.

"Senior Gavran. What was his first name?"

"Josif," Janet said.

"I thought so," Dreu muttered.

Back at the computer, she typed in *42EllingSoya#1Josif* and hit enter. The computer immediately jumped to a task screen. Dreu shook her head.

"Foolish man!" He had selected a strong password, but like many who have trouble remembering a complex sequence, the man used slight variations of the same symbols as different access codes. She opened the file explorer, scanned the list, and swept the cursor down to a Word entry titled *Bids*. The document opened to a list of seven dog names with three columns of financial entries beside each. Beside Bulldog and Chow in the final column, the dollar figures matched the scratching on the pad beside her. Chow was the top bidder at $270 million.

She exited the Word document and ran her eye over the icons on the desktop, immediately recognizing an e-mail encryption app that drew incoming and outgoing messages from the primary mail servers and encoded or decoded as needed. The app was again password protected.

"Let me guess," she murmured, entering *HofflandHaus* as the username. The Gavrans' primary security strategy was to keep the basement laboratory secret. If no one found their underground station, additional security needs were minimal. She counted on Josif continuing to be careless and entered *42EllingSoya#2Josif* as the password. The username remained in place, but a message indicated the password did not match. Dreu substituted a *4* for the second *2* in the password, and the program opened. Dreu shook her head in disbelief.

Five of the last mail exchanges were incoming and had arrived earlier in the day, each from a different nondescript address. She opened the first and found the message brief, but revealing: *Greyhound $170 million.* The last round of bidding had occurred that morning. Five buyers had been in play. The last two messages were outgoing. The first had been sent to seven addresses, including the final five bidders. It was equally brief. *Chow has taken the bid at $270 million.* The last message had gone only to one address.

Dreu knew she was intentionally saving the most recent message to add an element of suspense for her own benefit. If Josif Gavran had permanently left the house with the virus, he would have provided Chow with instructions for the exchange in his final instruction to the buyer. With a quickened pulse, she opened the Serbian scientist's final text. It was considerably longer. She found a pencil in the clutter around the computer, tore the page from the notepad that showed the two highest bids, and wrote out the message. Before shutting down the computer, she sorted through the remaining files, opened those that looked useful, and copied another page of notes.

"Unbelievable!" she muttered, moving to a final folder that managed the surveillance system. Systematically, she worked her way backward through the files, deleting all recorded footage for the past week. Moving into "Settings," she ordered the computer to reset all programs and preset apps to defaults, deleting all content. A skilled technician could reconstruct much of what had been on the machine, but it would take time. And the technician may not be as fortunate as she had been in discovering passwords to enter the bid files.

Dreu found a large manila envelope in a file drawer and filled it with the notepad, pencil, and other scraps that lay scattered around the desk. She carried it back through to the prep room where both of the other women were now encased in clean protective suits.

"You're going to have to let me lock you back in that cell and stay put until I get rescuers to you," she told Janet. "They'll then have to pass you through a decontamination-and-quarantine process. I'll leave this suit at the top of the basement steps. But it needs to appear that Gavran had it on and left the two of you in the room. In about half an hour, the local police will get a message from Josif telling them two women are being held under his house and that he has killed his caretaker who tried to stop him. It will tell them how to get into these rooms and that the area might be infected with a lethal virus." She looked questioningly at Essie. "Janet will tell you a bit about this. Can you help us with whatever story she gives you?"

"You get me safely out of here, and I will tell the police you came from the moon, and they will believe it!" the woman said.

"What did you learn from the computers?" Janet asked.

"Somebody called Chow won the bid. There's no clue as to who that is. But I know where the money's going, and I know when and where Josif plans to deliver the package."

Janet smiled grimly. "So I get to stay here while you have all the fun. Are you going to tell me when and where?"

Dreu glanced at Essie. "Best you don't know," she said, and pushed through the steel door into the dark basement while Janet initiated the decontamination sequence on the holding cell.

49

Adam was waiting in the arrival terminal in Frankfurt when Dreu cleared the secure area. He greeted her as she had hoped he would—like a sailor who had been at sea for a couple of months too long. She let him thoroughly embarrass the older German couples waiting nearby, then pried herself loose long enough to check on Andrew.

"The boy was negative, too?"

"Nothing with either of us. I knew my exposure was minimal, and Andrew did a good enough job of keeping people away." He picked up her carry-on and took her hand, steering her toward the exit. "From what information we've been able to get out of Mbandaka, his mother was buried in a mass grave by some army cleanup detachment. It's been pretty hard on the little guy. But his dad's been wonderful about helping him deal with it." When they were clear of the terminal and other ears, he turned to business.

"How's Janet?"

Dreu let his hand drop and combed her fingers through her black hair, keeping her eyes away from his.

"I had to leave her and the woman the Gavrans were holding in the basement of the house. It was the only way her story would hold up. The Norwegian police should have reached her by now, and I suspect she'll be in quarantine for a week. I hope she fares as well as you did."

"Are you certain you weren't exposed?"

"Quite certain. I was suited all the time I was in the basement, never got close to either woman, and didn't enter the contaminated room. I carried a few papers out but burned most on the way to the hotel. As soon as I got to the room, I showered and got rid of the clothes."

"So the Norwegian police will be putting out an APB for this Josif Gavran. And they'll assume he's headed back to Serbia. We need to get to him before they do."

Dreu nodded. "We have the advantage of knowing exactly where he'll be and when. And no one's seen this man for twenty years."

"If he passes through Serbian customs, they'll have a photo."

"*Passed* through," Dreu corrected. "My guess is he's already in the country."

"If we're going to get to him in time, we need to leave for Bucharest this afternoon. I have us booked on an Avalon river cruise, but instead of going with the group to Silistra to board the ship, a driver will take us up to Vidin to catch one that's three days upriver." They had reached the car, and he slipped her case into the backseat and patted her rear as he held the door for her. "So we'll get two very private days of cruising with a nice comfortable stateroom before we have to be in Belgrade."

She waited until he had come around and climbed into the driver's seat. "How are you planning to get your parcel onto the boat?"

"You remember our friends with the Heavy Airlift Squadron at Pápa in Hungary? The parcel's being flown from Ramstein to Pápa and will be coming downriver on a cruise ship from Budapest. It should be in port in Belgrade the night we get there. Someone will deliver it to our ship."

"What does the cruise line know about what we're doing?"

"Not a thing," he said. "As far as the captain and crew know, we are a couple of tourists who were willing to pay for an empty stateroom and pick up the ship at Vidin. We'll just choose to spend that day touring on our own in Belgrade and be back on board when the ship pulls out in the evening. We're booked all the way to Vienna."

"Sounds lovely," she said, again taking his hand. "Was Nita able to get the information I needed?"

"The American bidder was Bulldog."

"We didn't get it!" she said with some amazement.

"Nope. And no one but the buyer knows who did."

"Well, at least we won't be making a hit on our own people."

Adam shook his head. "Not unless they've been brought in by the Norwegians and are able to stumble upon Josif Gavran in Belgrade. We should get to him and the buyer first."

"I'm thinking we may want to give them Gavran," Dreu said. "After the deal's over. I'd rather they have him than someone else."

Adam thought for a moment, then nodded. "Good thought. But not until we have the package. We've got a few hours before we need to be back here. I'll send them a note when we get to the room. But first . . . now that we're both decontaminated . . ." He grinned at her invitingly and leaned across for another of those desperately missed kisses.

* * *

Jay Bedford was hunched over Hendren's desk, studying a printout that showed daily tracking of movements of large quantities of cash among foreign banks when a symbol flashed in the corner of Don's screen, notifying them of the arrival of a coded message. Hendren pushed aside the bank statements and opened the mail file, glancing quizzically over at his partner. It appeared to be from the same sender who had been managing the virus bidding.

"What the hell is this?" he muttered, tapping the message open.

The content showed immediately that it wasn't from the seller.

Virus to be transferred to Chow in Belgrade on Thursday at 11:00 a.m. Vendor is Serb named Josif Gavran. Identity of Chow unknown. Research Gavran, and you will learn much. Josif Gavran is currently wanted by the Norwegian police. Find that story, and you will know even more. Be in Belgrade by Thursday at the

Jugoslaija Hotel on Bulevar Nikole Tesle. At 10:30 a.m., call the number below. We will guide you to Gavran.

Hendren looked up at his colleague. "*What* the hell is *this*? If this Gavran's the vendor, someone's taken over his mail server and knows who Bulldog is."

"Or is inviting all of the other bidders to this party in Belgrade," Bedford suggested. "Let's see what we can learn about Gavran, and we might know which. And we'd better start making plans to get to Belgrade by Thursday. I don't think the director will want our station people there to handle this."

Hendren shook his head grimly. "I don't like it. Feels like we're being played. Could we be getting set up to look like the vendor?"

"We've got to assume that even if someone's figured out who Bulldog is, they haven't put our faces to it. We go, see what goes down, and if it looks like a setup, we walk away."

"Two very American-looking men just melting into the background," Hendren sniffed.

Bedford scowled. "We don't show up in pinstripes. And there'll be hundreds of American men wandering around Belgrade this time of year. It's a huge tourist destination."

"Probably not at the Jugoslaija Hotel," Hendren argued. "It sounds like a place that caters to locals. It wasn't picked randomly."

"We don't need to stay at the Jugoslaija," his partner reminded him. "Or even go inside. We're just close enough at ten thirty that if we need to get somewhere else within a prescribed amount of time, we can make it."

"Sounds like a setup," Hendren muttered again.

50

Chief of Police Tor Meling sat stiffly in his starched blue uniform shirt and navy pants with a white surgical mask stretched tightly across his pale face. He was in his early sixties, had short-cropped graying hair, and a face that had once been described as ruggedly handsome but was now beginning to sag around the jowls. Though he worked out daily, the paunch above his belt seemed impossible to firm away. He was beginning to count the years until he would be eligible for his national pension. Four years and seven months, give or take a few days. But for the first time in as many years, he was having the kind of day that restored some of the early glamour and excitement to police work.

Meling sat in a small cubical facing a white-robed woman through a glass partition in Ålesund's *Helse Sunnmøre* isolation wing. He guessed the woman to be in her early thirties, but chose not to thumb through the folder in front of him to confirm her age. She was a pretty woman with short auburn hair, expressive green eyes, and full lips that, by the way they bowed into a slight smile or frown, seemed to anticipate every question.

He had interviewed the other hostage, a Nigerian immigrant, who had admitted to being involved in prostitution in Oslo. She was undoubtedly illegal and had little to say. Her captor, she said, had picked her up on the street near the harbor, drugged her with an injection of some kind, and driven her to the house on Ellingsøya Island. She and the man she called Sava had engaged in sex several times, and she had been left in the steel room in the basement until the second woman arrived. Then an older man had come. He had taken their clothes, thrown them down a chute in the wall, and again injected them with something. That was all she knew. But the American woman—the great-niece of the fabled Kari Eikram—had a much more elaborate tale.

"So, you visited the house with Mr. Gavran once before, just to be shown the place, but did not go into the basement. Do I understand that correctly?" he asked.

"That's right. We toured part of the house and most of the grounds, but didn't go into the basement."

"Why did you return?" Meling asked.

"My aunt Kari—perhaps you know her—seemed convinced that something sinister was going on out there. A continuation of experiments that had been conducted there during the war."

Meling knew better than to ask why Kari hadn't come to the police with her concern. The old woman from Giske Island had been by to see him on several occasions. Meling and two other officers had been to the manor and confronted Sava Gavran, informing him that people in the village were convinced that the house was being used as a laboratory. Gavran had willingly shown them around the estate, dismissing the concerns with a toss of his head. "There's still bad feelings from the war," he'd said. "But you are free to look wherever you wish." Meling and his men had walked through the entire house, including the basement. They had found nothing.

"And you thought you could discover what was being done?" he now asked the American woman.

"I only planned to look around enough to let her know she had no reason to be concerned, or to find something that might get you interested again in the place. Aunt Kari can be very insistent, as you know."

"Hmmm," Meling agreed. "And Mr. Gavran found you nosing around."

"Actually, an old caretaker caught me. He was giving me a warning that I only half understood when Sava found us both. The next thing I knew, he had taken me into the basement and opened that door in the back wall. Essie was already in there in one of the rooms."

"Were you sexually assaulted?"

"No. And I think you know that. Your doctors looked me over pretty carefully when I arrived here."

"Why then did he keep you?"

"I think he may have planned to assault me, but was hesitant at first because he knew I was Kari's niece. He was worried she might know where I had gone and would direct the police back to the house. My guess is that he was waiting to see if I was missed before he did anything to me."

Meling scratched a few notes on a black-leather-covered pad. "The other woman—Essie—said he didn't come back. That another older man came instead."

"Yes. And he gave us shots of some kind. Said we were his final test subjects before he knew if his virus would work. Then he locked us both in the room where you found us."

"She also said you had her cover her face with your shirt, and her eyes with some plastic wrap."

"I guessed he was going to squirt something in through those vents in the ceiling."

"And why did you suspect that?"

Anna Eikram cocked her head slightly to one side. "You've seen that room. And you know who built it. I would think anyone would immediately suspect it was an execution chamber of some kind."

Meling looked thoughtfully at his notes for a moment. "I am curious," he said, "as to why he then had you put the suits on—if he was testing something on both of you that he blew into the room . . ."

Anna nodded as if she had wondered the same thing. "We were in there for about an hour before he brought the suits in—maybe more. My guess is that after he decided we were exposed, he wanted us isolated from each other. Wanted to be certain we had caught the virus from the air and not from touching an infected person. Plus, he said he had given us different vaccines. That's all I've been able to work out."

"Hmmm," Meling mused again. "He came in wearing the third suit?"

"Yes."

"Which he left at the top of the basement steps."

Anna shrugged, her green eyes seeming to tease. "I don't know what happened to it."

Meling stroked his cleanly shaven chin. "After going to all this trouble, why would this older man, who called himself Josif Gavran, contact us with a very detailed description of where you were and how to get to you?"

Anna arched her brows, then leaned toward him in her chair, eyes locking on his. "It may not have been this Josif Gavran," she suggested. "The caretaker seemed upset about what was happening there. He may have sent the message."

Meling shook his head. "I don't think so. We found old Gier dead at the bottom of some stairs on the grounds. And the message from Gavran admitted to shooting him."

The woman's eyes widened, and she again leaned back in her chair. After a moment, she said, "That *is* puzzling. I guess the message to you could have come from Sava. He didn't come back after leaving us."

"You seem convinced it wasn't the older man who contacted us. May I ask why?"

"When he left, he didn't appear at all concerned about letting us die. I doubt he had a crisis of conscience."

"Did he give you any idea where he might be going?"

"None. But my impression was that he wasn't coming back. That he was through with us."

"And wasn't coming back to see how his tests worked out?"

"I believe he thought he knew how they would turn out. And knew things were getting a little hot for him if he stayed at the house. Have you learned what he was working on?"

Meling shook his head. "An emergency-response team from Oslo is at the house now. They are having to move very carefully since we don't know exactly what we are dealing with or how widespread any contamination might be. It may be several days."

Anna nodded thoughtfully. "How long do you expect they will keep us locked up here?"

Meling had asked the doctors the same thing before he came in to question the women. "They won't have an answer to that until they know what the pathogen is. I'm afraid it may be some time."

"And what are you doing to find this Josif Gavran?" Anna asked.

"We've sent out bulletins through Europol and Interpol. But your descriptions were quite general. We found photos of the man from his days in Germany, but they are forty years old. We are only guessing at what he might look like now."

Anna smiled at him through the glass. "I have confidence that you will get him," she said. "And my guess is that it will be soon."

Meling rose to leave, then turned again to Anna Eikram. "One last thing. The ERT team found a large incinerator behind and beneath the room you were in. Some of the grating had been moved, and several pieces of your clothing were among the ashes. How do you suppose they got there?"

The woman answered without having to give the question thought. "Before he came in with the suits, we tried to cover our faces with torn clothing," she said. "He took them from us before we put on the suits and cast them into a chute behind the bed."

"And you didn't think to mention this to us?"

"Is it important in some way?"

"Only your clothing was found among the ashes. The other woman—Essie—did mention it, but none of her clothing was found."

"She had practically nothing on when I was left with her."

"There was ash found outside of the door that was used to empty the furnace—near where the old caretaker was found. And ash was tracked from there back to the house."

"I can't help you with that," Anna said. "As you saw when you rescued us, we were sealed inside the room. Perhaps whoever contacted you took something from the ashes and carried it to the house before leaving."

"Yes . . . Yes, you were closed in the room . . . ," Meling said. "It's a most interesting puzzle."

51

Adam wore the eyepatch and pulled his hair into a short ponytail during the two-day cruise from Vidin in Bulgaria to the Serbian capital of Belgrade. He and Dreu had flown into Bucharest in Romania, been driven to the river, and ferried across the Danube to Vidin early enough to be included in the ship's morning tours of the Bulgarian countryside. They had joined a group going inland to the famous rock formations at Belogradchik, sitting in the back of the coach with four retired Australian couples who felt a need to entertain the bus crowd with enthusiastic renditions of "Waltzing Matilda" and the Kookaburra song.

When back onboard, they chose a different table for each meal, danced until the vocalist gave up in the early hours of morning, and moved comfortably from one group of passengers to another as the ship churned upstream through the Danube's fabled Iron Gate. By the time the cruise docked in Belgrade, had any of those aboard been asked when the couple joined the tour, they would have sworn that the lanky American with the eyepatch and his beautiful raven-haired wife had been with them from the beginning.

At the Serbian port, Dreu and Adam opted out of the city bus tour and waited until most of the passengers had gone ashore. They dressed casually in the dark pants and shirts popular with Europeans. Adam slipped the package that had been waiting for him into a light backpack. Once away from the dock, he removed the eyepatch, pulled his hair up under a nondescript gray ball cap, and fixed a dark mustache that turned down around the corners of his mouth above his upper lip. He looked critically at Dreu through dark wraparound Oakleys.

"I'm not sure what we can do to make you look plain," he laughed, looking her over critically. "I wish there was a way for me to take care of this myself. But your part's as critical as mine." She had pulled her own hair up under a floppy, wide-brimmed hat and donned a pair of oversize sunglasses, but it gave her a sultry *Vogue* cover look that didn't exactly blend. He stopped at a street vendor's kiosk and bought another ball cap with *Belgrade* emblazoned across the front.

"Let's try this," he suggested. Although her face and figure were still head-turners, she now looked more like a very pretty tourist than someone people would think they should recognize.

They took a cab to Republic Square, then caught a trolley up Ulica Uzun Mirkova past Studentski Park to the entrance to the Kalemegdan Fortress. The medieval citadel covered a sweeping ridgetop where the Danube met the Sava River, the fortress encircling all of what had been Belgrade during the fourth and fifth centuries, but now filling only a corner of the sprawling city.

They crossed a dry moat filled with a display of rusting tanks and artillery pieces and passed through a high-arched gateway in the stone walls. A white clock tower rose above the battlement.

"Ten fifteen," Adam noted. "We're probably ten minutes from the statue. We need to split up. Keep moving toward the river, then bear left. You'll see it."

"There's no admission fee to this place?" Dreu wondered as they approached a second gate.

"A lot of the space is public park," Adam said. "No admission. No guards. Everyone's welcome. That's probably why Gavran picked it."

"See you at the statue," she said, and slipped off into the crowd of couples strolling hand in hand, ragged lines of tourists ambling behind their guides, and families carrying picnic baskets.

Adam moved upward through two more tiers of battlements until in the upper level of the park. To his left, the Victor Monument rose above the treetops, perched on a paved terrace above the confluence of the two rivers. According to what Dreu had retrieved from the laboratory computer, at 11:00 a.m. Josif Gavran would be waiting on the low seat formed by the base of the Victor column. He would be wearing a red-tartan flat cap and red windbreaker with a camera lying beside him on the seat.

Adam glanced back toward the last of the tiered battlement gates at a small building that housed restrooms. A cart sat beside it stacked with orange cones and cleaning supplies. Nita, as always, was a step ahead of them.

He turned along a shaded walk toward the monument, studying the crowd for a face that might belong to Chow. It was like looking for a cowboy at a rodeo. The park attracted people of every size, nationality, and ethnicity, some in small groups, others strolling in pairs, and many walking alone. And Chow, whoever he or she was, would send someone who blended.

On the edge of the terrace, two wrought-iron benches faced the monument, providing a view down onto the rivers. Otherwise, the plaza was clear of places to sit. Most visitors leaned against a waist-high lattice-wire fence that ran along the edge of the embankment. Beyond the fence, the hillside dropped steeply for fifty feet to a road that traced the riverbank.

Adam pulled off his backpack and sat on one of the benches beside a matronly woman in a brown headscarf with the bag propped on his lap. He nodded pleasantly to the woman, who didn't look at him directly but scooted a few inches farther away. Adam returned his attention to the sightseers. It was just after 10:30 a.m., and there was no sign of Josif Gavran. Adam settled in to wait.

Fifteen minutes before the time Gavran had given in his instructions to Chow, Dreu wandered across the terrace, dogged at every step by a young man in ragged jeans and a surplus army jacket. She was doing her best to ignore him, but her pursuer was obviously a man who couldn't recognize a brush-off when it was slapping him in the face. Adam suspected Dreu had told the kid she was meeting someone who would arrive at any minute, and he rose from the bench, swinging the backpack over one shoulder. In the periphery of his vision, a red spot caught his attention. He turned away from it, moving casually to a waste bin where he crumpled an imaginary wrapper in his hand and dropped it into the basket. When he turned again to the monument, Josif Gavran was seated at its base, fiddling with a digital camera.

Dreu had also seen Gavran enter the plaza and stood beside the guardrail fence with her admirer chattering amicably at her expressionless face. As Adam watched, she turned on the pest with a fury in her eyes that stunned the man to silence. She spoke for a few seconds, waved in the direction of the main gate, and held the man with a withering gaze while he slunk awkwardly away across the terrace. Adam feared that she would look over at him and give him a "what a jerk that kid was" look. But she merely stared down at the white pavers for a moment, shook her head in disbelief, and moved down the fence to a point where she could better see their target.

Adam recognized the buyer as soon as the person wandered onto the terrace.

"*Damn!*" he muttered under his breath. Since Dreu had contacted him with the description of the meet, he had spent a good portion of the time imagining whom he would send on such a high-stakes errand. The person who now ambled toward the base of the Victor was just what he had feared: no more than seventeen or eighteen, slightly built, East European in appearance, dressed exactly like the hundreds of teens scattered about the park—and female. He couldn't resist a glance at his partner, who had also ID'ed the contact. Her face showed the same resigned displeasure.

"*Damn!*" he muttered again as the girl stopped, as if noticing Gavran for the first time. She had a large geometrically patterned bag draped loosely over one shoulder and almost bounced over to where the man sat. Though her back was to Adam, he knew exactly what she was saying.

"You look like you need someone to take your picture with the statue and the rivers. Would you like me to?"

Gavran was saying, "I don't give my camera to anyone. You will run off with it."

"Here. I will leave my bag with you," was her scripted reply. "See? It has some valuable items in it. I won't leave them with you just to keep your old camera."

Gavran opened the large purse and looked into it, the hand holding his Nikon momentarily disappearing into the bag. "OK," he said, withdrawing the hand with an identical Nikon. "I'll keep the purse right here behind me. You take the picture."

The girl flounced to the edge of the terrace to within twenty feet of Adam, turned, focused elaborately, and snapped three shots. Adam glanced casually over and was relieved to see that when close, her features looked older. Early- to mid-twenties. She stood for a moment and checked the images in the camera's window, then marched proudly back to the old man.

"There you go," she said, handing him the Nikon and sweeping up her bag. "You need to learn to trust people."

She exited the terrace on the side opposite her entry, moving nonchalantly and nodding pleasantly at others as she passed. Adam took a parallel path, moving ahead, then cutting across on a diagonal intercept. As they met, he returned her smile and swung up beside her, grasping her left arm in his right hand. A small plate with short barbs was centered in his palm. She started involuntarily, but he knew she wouldn't scream.

"I have an injector in the palm of my hand," he said quietly in what he hoped was a convincing Slavic accent. "If I squeeze your arm, within a minute you will drop into a faint. So do what I tell you, or I will drop you where you are, take the camera, and be gone. By the time you wake, I will be in Moscow."

The woman allowed him to guide her toward the restrooms where yellow cones now warned off patrons, and plastic chains with a cleaning sign in Cyrillic directed the needy to other facilities.

"Duck under the chains," he instructed. "We are going into the women's toilet." He followed her inside, keeping a firm grip on her as he closed and locked the outer door and checked each stall. The room was empty.

Adam lowered his backpack to the floor, reached in with the hand that wasn't restraining his captive, and pulled out a silenced Glock. Slowly, he released the arm and stepped between the woman and the door. She turned, glaring first at the man who had intercepted her, then at the weapon.

"What are you going to do?" she demanded.

"Put your bag on the floor," he instructed. "Then reach into my pack and take out the vest. It's going to be a little large for you, but buckle it in front and pull the straps tight."

She stood for a moment without moving, apparently deciding that Adam wouldn't hesitate to shoot her. She lowered her bag and reached into the pack at her feet. As she drew the vest out, her eyes widened.

"This is an explosive vest!" she stuttered, holding the bound strips of C-4 at arm's length. "You are going to explode me!"

"This is what we're going to do," Adam said calmly. "You put on the vest. It has a GPS tracker in it that I can watch on my phone. If you move before fifteen minutes have passed, I will blow you up. I am going to take the camera and leave. Do you have a phone with a timer?"

The woman nodded dumbly.

"Then we will set it for fifteen minutes. Once the time has passed, you can leave this building and find someone to help you. A good explosives expert will be able to disarm it. You can tell them any story you want about how you ended up in the thing."

The woman's eyes flashed, and her mouth flattened into a tight line. "I won't put it on," she said angrily.

"Then I will shoot you right here, put it on you, and when I am outside the gates, blow you up. If you want to live, put it on."

Again, she glared at the barrel that pointed at her forehead and into the eyes of the man who held the weapon. Defiantly, she slipped her arms through the looped straps, snapped the buckles across her chest, and tightened the straps.

Adam took the camera from her purse and handed her the bag. "Get out your phone," he ordered. "And turn with your back to me while you set the timer. I need to adjust the vest."

While she found the phone and searched her icons for the clock feature, he snapped open a flap on the back of the Nikon. Four small clear vials, carefully wrapped in a foam sheath, filled the back of the camera. He gingerly lifted them out and tucked them into a pocket in the explosive vest between the woman's shoulder blades. He dropped the empty Nikon into his backpack.

"Turn," he ordered. When she again faced him, he pulled a phone from his own pocket. "Start your timer. I'll be watching for movement on my phone. If you so much as take a step before the time is up, I blow the vest. And the snaps are locked and wired. You won't be able to get it off without detonating it."

When she didn't answer, he leaned closer to her small face. "Am I clear?"

"If I could, I would explode the vest now," the woman snarled at him.

"You can leave the toilet early if you wish, and hope to kill me when I blow you up. But then, there will be no chance of recovering the camera. This way, perhaps the police will be able to find me, and you can get it back."

"Whatever is in the camera will be gone," she snapped.

"That's a risk you'll have to take. But it's your only chance of recovering it. Now watch your clock. Fifteen minutes, and you can move."

Adam slipped from the women's room and ducked back under

the orange chain. He stood outside for a moment, watching the crowd. When it seemed to thin, he moved to the edge of the clear area around the restrooms and shouted, "A bomb! The woman in the toilets has a bomb!"

In a dozen languages, the warning spread across the park like a grass fire as visitors hurried toward exits through the high stone walls.

"It's a bomb!" they shouted. "Someone has a bomb!"

52

Hendren stood outside the Stambol Gate with a phone pressed to his ear. To passersby, he appeared to be a typical American tourist: cargo shorts and imprinted T-shirt, white legs, and a burr haircut that hadn't changed since he left the navy. At the CIA, he was an analyst, not an operative, and blending into a foreign crowd had not been part of his training.

Hendren had been on the phone with the woman off and on since he and Bedford left the sidewalk opposite the Jugoslaija Hotel. She had first directed them to the Stambol Gate of the Belgrade Fortress and instructed one to stand beside the stone causeway on the outside of the arched entry. The other, she directed, should skirt the battlements to the Sava river side.

"There is a second exit from the base of the Victor Monument—a tunnel that goes down to a path along the river," she said. "Put one of your men just outside that tunnel."

As Bedford worked his way around to a position below the monument, Hendren made a half-hearted attempt to get the woman to identify herself. "Who are you, and how are you involved in this exchange?"

The woman sounded American, which was especially troubling. As far as he knew, within the American-security community only he, Bedford, and the director had known about the bid award.

She ignored the questions and continued with her instructions.

"The man you want will be coming through one of the gates sometime in the next twenty minutes. I will call as he approaches and identify him to you. Are you in communication with each other?"

"Of course."

"Have you done your homework?"

Bedford had searched the name Josif Gavran and learned that the man had worked for the Hoechst Company in Marburg at the time of the first Ebola-type outbreak in Germany and Belgrade. He had also discovered that the man had left the company to start his own firm. Hendren had followed up with Norwegian police and knew they were seeking Josif and Sava Gavran in connection with discovery of an underground laboratory near the city of Ålesund. Half a dozen women had been kidnapped and used as experimental test subjects for a yet-to-be identified virus.

"We did our homework. How did you know all this?"

"I'll call you back," the woman said. "Stay put."

After a ten-minute break, the phone buzzed again.

"Are you still in place?"

"We're here."

"The man you want is exiting through the tunnel below the monument. He's wearing a red-plaid flat cap and a light-red jacket. A Nikon camera is hanging around his neck. That's all the help you'll get from me."

"*Wait!*" Hendren shouted, loudly enough that people nearby turned to look his way. "Does he have the virus with him?"

"No. The exchange has been made."

"Where is it? We have to get to it . . ."

From beyond the Stambol Gate, he heard the sound of a man shouting, a cry that was picked up by the crowd that suddenly came surging through the archway.

"Bomb!" someone shouted in English. "Someone has a bomb!"

"Can you see our man?" Hendren asked Bedford through his other phone.

"Got him," Bedford said. "He's just coming through . . ."

An ear-splitting explosion boomed against the inner walls of the fortress and thundered through the archway over the heads of the hysterical crowd. Hendren ducked involuntarily.

'No need to worry about the virus," Hendren heard the woman

say. "You just heard it vaporize."

* * *

Within seconds, the area around the small stone building that housed the restrooms had emptied, and Adam had scattered with the crowd. Rather than running toward the closer Stambol exit, he backtracked to the Victor monument where he knew a second path descended under the wall to a route out of the fortress. The bomb alert had reached the terrace and overlooks along the battlement above the river. Patrons hurried for the exits, carrying children, trotting in a worried crouch, and scanning the area around them to ensure no one was approaching who looked like a suicide bomber.

A woman with an infant in her arms tried to herd two small children ahead of her, frantically pushing the smaller of the pair forward without stumbling over her. Adam jogged up beside the woman and scooped up the toddler.

"Let me help you," he said, and the woman gasped something that sounded grateful and hurried forward. As they descended into the underpass to shoulder height, he pressed the "Call" button on his phone and ducked below the rock face.

The vest had been designed primarily to implode, with a smaller incendiary charge beneath the rear pocket of the vest to ensure that anything in the pouch was vaporized. But the explosion was still deafening. He heard the rattle of stones clattering to the ground as the building collapsed.

"Keep moving! Keep moving!" he urged the woman's son, who had frozen in terror as the rush of the blast passed over them. The boy didn't understand the words but felt their urgency and ran ahead through the tunnel. They exited onto a wide gravel path that sloped downward toward the road that skirted the river. Beside the walkway, a middle-aged man in a Washington Nationals T-shirt had a firm grip on the arm of Josif Gavran, who still wore the red cap. Both had turned to stare up toward the top of the battlement that rose above them. Adam lifted the girl higher against his face as they hurried by, keeping her cradled against his chest until they reached the bottom of the walk.

"*Hvala! Hvala!*" the woman sobbed, gathering the children about her legs. He nodded and squeezed her arm. Before she could look fully into his face, he turned and walked into the crowd that milled along the bottom of the hill. He hurried along Pariska Street beside the river to the corner of the park, continuing straight for another quarter mile through faded shops and apartment buildings with graffiti scrawled across the peeling plaster. At a corner where a broad avenue crossed the Sava River over a bridge to his right, he stopped at a sidewalk café. Six tables filled a small island in the middle of a fuel station labeled NIS Petrol. Cars entering the station circled the island to a single pump where an attendant fueled the vehicles and served as waiter to anyone seated at the café.

The wall of the building in front of Adam displayed a four-story mural in reds, oranges, and grays of what he took to be some artist's whimsical vision of the Apocalypse. On the wall behind, a mouth four stories high displayed teeth painted to look like the battered tenements around him. The mouth was about to devour a sprig of broccoli.

Sirens sounded in the direction of the fortress.

When the attendant finished fueling a yellow Fiat, he hurried over, wiping his hands on a stained apron. Adam ordered two Cokes.

"My wife's shopping on Brankova Street," he said. "She'll be joining me in a minute. What's happening over on the hill?"

The young man, whose uniform beneath the apron looked more fuel station than sidewalk waiter, shook his head. "I heard a loud sound. Something is wrong, I think."

Adam nodded and sipped at the Coke. It wasn't as sweet as he remembered Coke to be.

He felt her hand on his shoulder before he heard her behind him. She slipped into a chair opposite and pulled the extra Coke across the table.

"I thought you might change your mind and keep the vials for us to dispose of ourselves, leaving the woman to the police," she said quietly.

He smiled cynically. "I'd be lying if I said it didn't cross my mind. But carrying them around would have been dangerous—and so would allowing the woman to talk to whatever group she represents. We needed no witnesses."

"I saw the surprise on your face . . ."

The cynical part of his smile disappeared. "I guess sexism enters into our business as well. If it had been a man, we wouldn't be having this conversation. Did you get pictures of her?"

"Several that were good enough to send to Nita. By tonight, we might know who Chow is. Did our friends from the Agency pick up Gavran?"

"One had him by the arm when I came out of the tunnel. The old man didn't look too surprised." Adam lifted his Coke. "Here's to a successful day. We need to get back to the ship to meet our returning tour—and I want to check on Janet."

"To a successful day," she said, and clinked his glass.

53

During their five days on the river until the ship reached Vienna, Dreu and Adam followed the news in every form they could receive it. The failed terrorist bombing in Belgrade was front page for two days until a devastating quake in Lima, Peru, and another mass shooting at a retreat center in California swept it from the headlines. Adam guessed that a man in a gray cap and wraparound sunglasses was on a "persons of interest" list with Interpol, identified through pictures taken by tourists near the monument at the time of the explosion. If the authorities had been lucky, they had come up with photos of him with the backpack, before and after the suicide bombing, with detailed analysis of changes in the appearance of the pack. But he remained confident that none of the pictures could be traced to the man with the eyepatch now lounging on the ship's sky deck.

There was no mention in the news of the arrest or extradition from Serbia of a Josif Gavran. Dreu began to wonder if the agents at the fortress had managed to hang onto the old man. A note to Nita relieved that concern and raised another. Gavran was in Washington, quietly being held by the CIA.

"They're trying to get him to tell them how to duplicate his experiments," Adam guessed. They were sitting together on the starboard side of the deck, admiring the picturesque blue and white tower of the Durnstein church rising at the water's edge on the Austrian shore.

Dreu sipped at a Bründlmayer Riesling. "Will they succeed?"

Adam shrugged. "I suspect the process takes years, even if you know the steps. They may not want to keep him under wraps that long, and he may not cooperate. And he may not have that many years left. Then again, if they offer him a deal of some kind, he might decide to give them what they want."

". . . in which case we've just postponed the inevitable," she said.

"It's the nature of the silent wars," Adam mused. "At least based on the ID we got from Nita on the woman, we kept this strain out of the hands of ISIS. She was Belgian and had joined them in Syria more than a year ago."

"Not a small victory," she agreed. "What did you hear from Janet?"

"She and the Nigerian woman are out of quarantine. Apparently, her masks worked. She feels like she needs to spend a few more days in the city to maintain her cover story with the police and stay close to Kari and Sofi Eikram while this investigation wraps up."

"Is her background solid enough to stand up to an investigation?"

"Nita is backfilling as we go and keeping Janet informed."

"She could probably use some moral support," Dreu said.

Adam stretched on the deck chair. "Then that's where we'll go. I'd like to celebrate this one with the person who started it."

* * *

Hendren and Bedford watched the interrogation through a one-way mirror while one of the professionals worked on Josif Gavran. It was clear that their colleague was also facing a professional.

The interrogator slid a photograph across the table in front of Gavran. "Tell me about this woman," he said evenly.

Gavran studied the picture long enough to make his answer credible. "I don't know this woman. She offered to take my picture."

"Did you give her anything?"

Gavran shook his head, frowning. "She didn't ask for anything. She was just being friendly."

"Some of the people who saw you said you spoke to her for a few moments and kept her bag beside you while she took the picture. Why did you want the bag?"

"I thought she might steal my camera. You hear about these things happening. So I made her leave the purse with me."

"And what did you leave in it?"

"As I said, she didn't ask for anything."

The interrogator changed his tack. "Why do you suppose the woman blew herself up?"

Gavran looked genuinely surprised. "I heard the explosion. I didn't know the woman was involved."

"She blew herself up with a suicide vest. She wasn't wearing it in that picture. Where do you think she got it?"

"I did not know she was the reason for the explosion. I know nothing about a vest."

The agent slid a set of photos across the table. "Do you recognize this man?" The pictures showed half a dozen angles of a man in a gray sweatshirt and dark pants, much of his face hidden by the low bill of a cap, contoured sunglasses, and a drooping mustache. One picture showed him standing only a few steps from the woman Gavran had just been asked about. She was holding a camera to her eye.

"I don't remember seeing this man," Gavran said.

"We believe he met the woman after she left you and gave her the vest. He may have taken the virus from her and used her suicide as a diversion."

"I don't know anything about this," the prisoner insisted.

"You know nothing about the laboratory under the home you own in Norway? Or about the experiments taking place there?"

"I know about the old laboratory. But I have not been to the house for years. My son goes there often, but I have chosen in my retirement to remain in Serbia."

"No one in Serbia remembers seeing you there for some time."

"I live alone in a cottage near Lestane. I choose to live by myself and don't go into the village."

"How do you get food and supplies?"

"My son gets them when he comes to visit."

"And where is your son, Sava?"

"I haven't seen him for weeks. He goes away sometimes for a long time. Then he will come back again."

"So, no one else sees you in Lestane?'

Josif Gavran sniffed. "Have people seen me in Norway?"

"Two women there identified you from a photo and said you told them you were Josif Gavran. They said you injected them with something."

The old man scoffed. "Where are these women? You have invented them. I have not been to the house in Ålesund for fifteen years."

The interrogator pulled the photos back across the table and tucked them into a folder. "I think we'll let you think about this for a few weeks and see if your memory improves."

"You have no reason to hold me," Josif Gavran said, hands folded in front of him on the table and eyes glaring at his captor.

"We have lots of reasons for holding you," the man said. "We just need a little more cooperation in understanding what they all are and what you can do to help us."

Gavran didn't move as the interrogator rose and started for the door.

"What are you going to do with me?" he asked before the man could leave.

"You like being by yourself and seeing no one," the agent said with a thin smile. "We're going to give you exactly what you enjoy."

54

The tiny sitting room in Kari Eikram's cottage on Giske Island held more visitors than its frail owner could ever remember for a single occasion. Sofi had carried two chairs from the kitchen and sat on one beside her grandmother, holding the woman's hand and gently massaging with a thumb the blue network of veins that patterned its back. The second chair held the woman who now laughingly referred to herself as Kari's "redheaded stepchild," though trying to explain the expression to the woman had been awkward.

"Haven't we treated you like our very own while you have been here?" Kari demanded in her thin voice.

"Of course, you have," Janet replied quickly. "I was thinking more of the fact that in the month since I joined the family, I've come closer to dying on more occasions than in all of the rest of my life, and you two have been in just as much danger."

"It is part of being an Eikram," Kari said with a satisfied smile. "And so is surviving. I am happy to know that we welcomed you as we should."

Dreu sat in the room's easy chair while Adam stood near the door, leaning back comfortably against the wall with arms folded. Kari's blank eyes moved about the room, following the conversation, the same smile creasing her wrinkled cheeks.

"So now the house is being taken down," she said, repeating Janet's report.

"No one was certain the place could be completely decontaminated," Janet said. "They sprayed the interior completely, tested everything in and around the house, but finally decided no one should live there again. So they're knocking it down and pushing it all into the basement. The plan is to continue testing for a year, then make the grounds a park."

"I'll have Sofi take me there," Kari said, turning her attention to Adam. "From what they are saying on the television, there was another man at the house—the father of Sava Gavran. Have they caught the man? I'm not certain I can feel safe until I know the police have him."

"I don't know if the police here will ever have him," Adam said. "But you can be very certain he won't be coming to bother you."

To the degree it was possible, the old woman's eyes seemed to twinkle. "He and his son both," she said, and as quickly as the light had come to her dead eyes, it disappeared. "I wish I could keep you all here. I would feel so much safer. And you have all made my days so much more exciting again. Like during the war—when Bud was with me." A tear slid into a crease that ran down the woman's cheek, and she quickly brushed it away with her free hand.

Dreu pushed from her chair and crossed the small room to kneel in front of the old woman, taking the hand.

"We can't stay, of course, but you're in luck," she said. "Your nephew happened to come into quite a lot of money after he went to America, and your redheaded stepchild is the last of his heirs. We've set up an account in a bank in Ålesund. Anna has chosen to leave quite a bit of it for you and to Sofi's family to use however you wish."

Dreu glanced over at Janet, whose face showed as much surprise as Kari Eikram's. The old women turned her head from one to the other, her milky eyes regained their shine. She seemed to need no further explanation.

"Father would be so pleased," Janet said with a laugh.

Tears were now streaming down the old woman's furrowed cheeks, and she reached out for Dreu's face. "You have all blessed an old woman in so many ways," she whispered. "And I know you all must leave. But there is something I want you to take with you. Something for the woman who sent you to me."

She lifted her hand from Sofi's and turned to her granddaughter.

"Would you get the little box from my dresser in the bedroom?"

When the box was in her lap, she reverently lifted the lid and sorted with her fingers through the items that filled the small wooden chest. Her smile changed as she touched each, remembering what treasured moment in her past each represented. When she found the one she was seeking, she held it longingly with the fingers of both hands for a long moment, then held it out to Dreu.

"This is what I have of my first great love," she said. "It needs to be with his last great love." Her hand held a set of silver wings embroidered onto a black background, centered by the letters *RAF* beneath a royal crown.

Dreu took the wings, held them up for Adam and Janet to see, then returned them to Kari's hand. "She would want them to stay here," she said. "They were from a part of his life he spent with you." The old woman clutched them in her hands and pressed them against her heart.

"We need to be going," Adam said from beside the door. "The woman in question has a plane waiting for us, and for the moment, the police seem to be through with Anna. We should get her out of the country while that's still the case." The two women rose, and Adam joined them in kissing Kari Eikram on both cheeks and pressing Sofi into a tight hug as she led them out into the cool afternoon of Giske Island.

At the end of the gravel path, the three turned to wave back at the young Norwegian woman who watched from the doorway. Beyond the cottage, the gray sea rolled silently against the rocky beach, and across the hedge fence, a pair of shaggy red cows chewed contentedly on coarse brown grass.

"A lonely place," Adam murmured. "I hope Sofi can get Kari away for a while."

"I think she'll want to go see the park when it's finished," Dreu said. "This little adventure has given her new life."

"I gather the information Josif left Chow gave you the bank-transfer information," Janet said quietly.

Dreu smiled. "Gavran was a careless data manager. His files also contained the account-access codes."

"What did you leave them?" Janet asked.

"Just over twenty million kroner. About two million dollars."

"And the transfer payment for the virus was . . ."

"The initial transfer was one hundred eighty million. The other third was to be transferred after delivery."

"Which means . . . ," Janet pressed.

Dreu gave a final wave to the woman in the doorway. "Let's just say the Unit now has a sizable slush fund."

Adam held the doors on the passenger side of the Nissan for the women to climb inside.

"We need to get you out of Norway," he said to Janet, "and get that identity changed. Are you still happy with Brittany?"

"I've decided to go with just Britt."

"Any thoughts about a last name?" Dreu asked.

Janet glanced back at the white cottage as the car pulled away.

"Kari Eikram deserves a namesake," she said. "I can't safely stay with Eikram, but when she knew Bud, she was a Haugen. As of today, I'm Britt Haugen."

Allen Kent

Author's Notes

Prior to beginning a second career as a writer, I spent my professional life as an educator. I still see it as part of my responsibility as an author to educate, to ensure that when readers finish one of my novels, they know more about the world than they did when they began. The challenge, of course, is that in the interweaving of fact and fiction, readers can confuse the two. So I add these postscripts in part to emphasize which parts of the book you can tuck into your treasures of truth and remember as fact, and which are my inventions.

In 1967, there was an outbreak of a disease very similar to Ebola in both Belgrade and the German city of Marburg. It has since been referred to as the Marburg virus. The disease appears to have been transported into the laboratories of a pharmaceutical company in Marburg in test monkeys imported from Uganda. These monkeys were then dispersed to two other company locations, including one in Belgrade, resulting in breakouts in each city. Like Ebola, the disease is highly deadly but is transmitted only through direct contact with someone who is in active stages of the illness. Its high-mortality rate has made it of interest to those trying to develop biological weapons. But the same characteristic makes it impractical to weaponize in its present form. It kills itself off too quickly.

As far as we know, unlike the Japanese, the Germans were not involved in the development of chemical or biological weapons during the Second World War. The lab in Ålesund and German efforts to develop the virus are completely fictitious and are creations of my imagination. Ålesund, however, is a very picturesque Norwegian fishing town that played a vital role in *Hjemmefronten* activities during the war. That is *not* fiction. The city burned almost completely in 1904 and, with substantial assistance from German Kaiser Wilhelm II, was entirely rebuilt over the next five years in the Art Nouveau style popular at the time. Its freshness and architectural uniqueness and uniformity make it one of the most interesting and visited cities along the Norwegian coast.

While all characters and character situations in the novel are fictional, I have tried to present geographic settings as accurately as possible. Gravediggers (Kavanagh's Pub beside Glasnevin Cemetery) is one of the more interesting old public houses in Dublin and dates to 1833, the year after the cemetery opened. Gravediggers claims to serve the best Guinness in the city, though I don't know how the locally brewed stout can differ that much from one Dublin pub to another. Kavanagh's does serve a very good Dublin cottle—a salty hot-pot stew made with sausage, bacon, onion, and potato.

I hope from reading this novel you could visit the charming village of Rothbury in northern England, make an informed dinner choice, and find your way to the Queen's Head, where I know you would receive a hearty English welcome. The story about the earlier manhunt in Rothbury is factual, and ironically, while I was working on this manuscript, an explosion rocked the village, caused by the detonation of a WWII bomb discovered in a nearby field. I had asked some English friends who have a summer place in Rothbury if they thought a detonation would be heard four miles south of the village at the Gate pub. This detonation allowed them to assure me that it could! (You can find photos of Kavanagh's, Glasnevin Cemetery, the Queen's Head, the Gate Pub, and the fortress in Belgrade on Allen Kent's Facebook page.)

I selected Mbandaka in the Democratic Republic of Congo as a test site for Gavran's virus because I needed a large but remote city in the Congo basin. Its isolation makes it a place where an experiment like Sava's could reasonably be carried out without destroying the rest of humankind. There are few ways in and out of the city, and it could easily and quickly be sealed off to prevent spread of an airborne virus. (For those of you who thrive on trivia, Mbandaka happens to be the site of Millard Fuller's first Habitat for Humanity house.) Gabon in West Africa remains a close ally of the United States. Our Eighty-Second Airborne annually carries out jungle-warfare and emergency-medical exercises with the country's military.

As I wrote this novel, I found the idea of mutation increasingly interesting. In addition to the changes that occur in the virus, Unit 1 evolves in this book to be quite different from the "single agent, working independently" model developed by the original Fisher. Janet, who struggles to get a handle on the consonant mutations in early Gaelic, finds that she also passes through at least four incarnations as context changes in her life. Though I haven't completely formulated an idea for the unit's next action, I think it will take us back to the Near East or Asia. I'm eager to see which members of the unit show up and what they become. Thanks for reading!

ACKNOWLEDGMENTS

I am most grateful to my great editing team: Richard and Anne Clement, Holly Farnsworth, Diane Andris, Marilyn Jenson and Paul Farnsworth. As always, their help has been invaluable, both in terms of shaping the story and in minimizing errors. My appreciation also to my friends and travel agents, Karol, Bart and Ken Mayer, who helped find a fun and creative way for me to get to Ireland and Rothbury, England, to research setting. Kevin and Christine McGreevy were kind enough to show us around Rothbury and the surrounding area and acquaint us with its local history. And thank you to Jillian Farnsworth for her creative and attractive cover. This book would not have been possible without you all.

COVER DESIGN: JILLIAN FARNSWORTH

Also by Allen Kent

<u>Unit 1 novels</u>

The Shield of Darius
The Weavers of Meanchey
The Wager
Straits of the Between

<u>The Whitlock Trilogy (Historical novels)</u>

River of Light and Shadow
Wild Whistling Blackbirds
Suzanna's Song

<u>Mystery/Thriller</u>

Backwater
Guardians of the Second Son

Made in the USA
Columbia, SC
21 July 2019